Books by David Lee Summers

The Solar Sea
The Astronomer's Crypt

The Space Pirates' Legacy Series
Firebrandt's Legacy
The Pirates of Sufiro
Children of the Old Stars
Heirs of the New Earth

The Clockwork Legion Series
Owl Dance
Lightning Wolves
The Brazen Shark
Owl Riders

The Scarlet Order Vampires Series
Dragon's Fall: Rise of the Scarlet Order Vampires
Vampires of the Scarlet Order

THE ASTRONOMER'S CRYPT

DAVID LEE SUMMERS

Hadrosaur Productions, Mesilla Park, NM

The Astronomer's Crypt
Hadrosaur Productions
Second Edition: June 2020

First date of publication: December 2016
Copyright © 2016 David Lee Summers
Cover Art Copyright © 2020 Laura Givens

Editor: Joanna D'Angelo
Copyeditors: Debra Glass and Kumie Wise

ISBN-10: 1-885093-91-8
ISBN-13: 978-1-885093-91-2

ACKNOWLEDGMENTS

It's impossible to thank everyone who deserves it for a novel based as strongly on life experience as this one is. Although I have not lived the literal nightmares of this novel, much of it is pulled from nearly thirty years of life experience and casual conversations during many nights working at observatories in California, Arizona, New Mexico, Massachusetts and Chile. I have had particularly memorable conversations that contributed to this novel with such people as Don Mendez, Krissy Reetz, Hal Halbedel, Jennifer Hedden, Kurt Loken, Brent Hansey, Doug Williams, George Will, Christian Soto and Charles Corson. I reserve special gratitude for Dr. Lori Allen, Director of Kitt Peak National Observatory, who has supported my writing career, even while expressing concern about titles like *The Astronomer's Crypt*.

In college, I took a course in the Paranormal and the Scientific Method taught by Dr. Steve Shore and the late Dr. Robert Cormack. It gave me a good grounding in the hauntings described in this novel.

I am grateful to the Mescalero Apache tribe for their helpful website: http://mescaleroapachetribe.com/

The non-profit Native Languages of America also has a very helpful site: http://www.native-languages.org/

Finally, the documentary Homeland Nation proved a valuable resource: http://www.homelandnation.com/

The Coyote story recounted in chapters 23 and 24 is based on a traditional White Mountain Apache story recorded by Grenville Goodwin in 1939 in *Myths and Tales of the White Mountain Apache*.

Many thanks go to my editor, Joanna D'Angelo who has been on board with this project and engaged in many fruitful discussions about it since I first started dreaming it up at the World Science Fiction Convention at San Antonio in 2013. Thanks to my copy editors Debra Glass and Kumie Wise who also had many wonderful suggestions that improved the novel. Thanks, as always, to my daughters, Autumn and Verity, for their support.

Thank you to my Patreon supporters who have helped make this new edition possible. If you're not already among my supporters, I hope you'll consider signing on so you can get an early look at my stories and insights into my creative process at http://www.patreon.com/davidleesummers

Finally, thanks to you, my readers, for daring to tread into this nightmare world of mine and I look forward to sharing more scares with you in the future.

This novel is dedicated to all my fellow telescope operators with the greatest respect and admiration. May you never experience any of the nightmare visions contained in these pages.

THE ASTRONOMER'S CRYPT

PROLOGUE

The storm rolled over the mountain.

Mike Teter gritted his teeth as he watched clouds billow across the observatory's all-sky camera, obscuring the stars. His heart pounded as he considered the benefit of maximizing telescope data against the risk of snow damaging precision instruments. "We better close up. That storm's coming in faster than the weather service predicted."

"That's a shame," said Ron Wallerstein, the red-haired, bespectacled astronomer, sitting across the room. "Can't we stay open just a few more minutes so I can finish this exposure?" He controlled an infrared camera mounted to the 2.5-meter telescope Teter operated.

"No can do." Mike's angular, bearded face hardened in resolve. "You know the rules. It's my call." As operator, Teter's job was to keep the telescope safe. If rain fell on the electronics and optics, literally millions of dollars of precision scientific instrumentation would be destroyed, costing many astronomers their opportunity to gather data, fulfill grants, and finish graduate theses.

Wallerstein sighed and gave a brief nod. "Shutting down the camera. You can close up."

Mike set to work at the computer, stowing the telescope in a safe position and closing the covers protecting the huge mirrors that captured light from stars and galaxies, billions of light years distant. As he did, he anxiously watched the humidity gauge climb. The moisture from ground-level clouds rolling across a mountaintop was just as dangerous as rain falling out of the sky. He breathed a sigh of relief when the first stowage operations completed and he could press the button that closed the shutter, shielding all the electronics inside the dome.

As the dome closed, Mike looked up at the view of the all-sky camera and saw nothing but clouds. Even if he had allowed Wallerstein to finish his exposure, it would have been for naught. No starlight would have reached the instrument, and he wouldn't have been able to observe anything anyway. Once he was sure the telescope was safe, Mike turned off the motors, stood, and stretched his tall, lanky frame. His easy smile returned. "I'm going to go outside and take a look."

"Sounds good," said Wallerstein. "I'll come with you."

The two men grabbed their coats, strode along a hallway lit by dim red bulbs, then down a flight of stairs. Mike struggled against the strong wind to push the door open. Finally he succeeded, only to be hit by numerous pinpricks from the icy rain and snow.

So much for getting up early and hiking down to see some of the caves below the summit during my off time.

Still, it meant he could get an early start on his weekend and spend more time with his fiancée Bethany, an astronomer he'd met at New Mexico State University while they were both studying there. Eager to get started on their plans for the future, Mike got a job straight out of school, while Bethany had continued her studies and was now working on her PhD. He grinned like an idiot as he thought about her. She was the furthest thing from a stereotypical astronomer. She was more Deanna Troi than Dr. Crusher with her long, dark hair, hazel eyes, and killer curves. He was gobsmacked from the first moment he laid eyes on her in their first-year physics class. Not to mention she was brilliant and probably had the biggest heart of anyone he'd ever met. He still couldn't believe she'd fallen in love with him, a quiet introvert with Buddy Holly glasses and a life-long devotion to *Star Trek* and Spiderman. She'd told him early on that she couldn't resist his smile. Many times he'd thanked the genetic gods and his mother for gifting him with dimples.

Carson Peak Observatory stood on a remote mountain in the Sacramento range of Southern New Mexico, so different from the urban landscape of Mike's youth. He'd fallen in love with the peace and quiet on his first visit. The area was ideal for an observatory. Except for the occasional mountain storm, the site was high and dry. Because it was near the tribal lands of the Mescalero Apache, there were no large cities nearby. In fact, the closest settlement was a virtual ghost town called Toledo that used to be a mining camp in the 1800s. Mike would have loved to live in the funky little town with its cute shops and cafes, where some of his fellow observatory staff members were based, as it was closer to work. The stories of the haunted mine tempted him even more, but Bethany's studies made it easier for them to live near the university in the larger city of Las Cruces.

Wallerstein harrumphed at the cloudy skies and the heavy snow. With no way to clean his glasses properly in the blizzard, he removed them, quickly gave them a shake, and tossed them in his jacket pocket. "Well, I guess we're not getting any more work done tonight." He shouted to be heard over the wind.

Mike envied Wallerstein his stronger eyesight. He'd be blind without his own glasses. He'd have to live with the water spots till he went back in. "No chance now that it's snowing. Besides, it's about an hour until twilight." No matter what, the brightening sky would bring an end to Mike's work night. He just wanted to curl up in the warm blankets of his dorm room.

A strong gust of wind whipped at their faces, chasing both Mike and Wallerstein back inside the building. In the dim light of the ground floor, they brushed snow from their jackets. Mike rubbed his hand through his short brown hair. Reaching into his pants pocket, he grabbed a rumpled cloth and cleaned the spots from his glasses. His vision cleared, Mike and Wallerstein hiked back to the telescope's control room. Wallerstein installed a flash drive in the computer he was using to copy the data he had managed to get for the night. Once finished, he set about packing up his laptop.

Mike turned on the lights in the dome, so he could inspect to make sure no snow had fallen on the telescope and take care of his last chores before he called it a night.

"Thanks for your help," said Wallerstein. He looked up and brightened slightly. "Actually, it wasn't a bad night, but I sure could have used an image of that last cluster." Mike knew Wallerstein referred to one of many balls of stars that orbited the Milky Way Galaxy. As a student, Mike had learned that globular clusters contained only older stars, but astronomers had recently discovered they encompassed a mix of old and young. What's more, they were evolving in unexpected ways. The more clusters they photographed, the more likely Wallerstein could understand the nature of these formations.

"I know. Better luck next time." With that, Mike and Wallerstein shook hands, and Mike opened a heavy door into the telescope dome. The sight of the telescope never ceased to give his stomach a slight flutter. The "2.5-meter" in the telescope's name referred to the diameter of the large mirror that collected light. In the early twenty-first century, there were much bigger telescopes, but few were more advanced. The 2.5-meter included a series of motors that pushed and pulled the wide, thin mirror into the best shape possible so it produced remarkable images no matter where it was pointed. A computer orchestrated the delicate dance of sixty motors adjusting the shape of a thin sheet of glass all night long. Mike harbored just a tinge of fear that one night the computer might drive a motor just a little too far. With luck that would never happen.

He turned his attention to the telescope itself—a large, boxy skeleton of pipes. At the bottom of the frame rested the primary mirror, perfectly safe. Suspended above the primary, a smaller mirror focused light to a third mirror and out to the side of the telescope where the cameras were mounted.

The 2.5-meter at Carson Peak employed advanced internal optics that attempted to correct for atmospheric distortion from wind and heat waves that plagued all telescopes. Mike was both thrilled and a little nervous to be responsible for helping astronomers get the best science they could from such a marvel of a telescope. Keeping it safe, so as many astronomers as possible could use it, was an enormous responsibility. One he took very seriously.

The wind wailed as it passed by the telescope's dome, a half-sphere a little like a cathedral—or more like a factory, thought Mike, with large cranes overhead and tools for servicing the motors and instruments. Observatories were a fascinating blend of bulky, industrial equipment, needed to move the huge mirrors around, and delicate precision instrumentation to view objects invisible to the naked eye.

Mike whistled to distract himself from the wind's howling while he circled the enclosure. Pleased to see no water drops on the equipment, he gathered heavy, insulated gloves to prevent frostbite and a fifteen-gallon container of liquid nitrogen. The nitrogen cooled the advanced digital camera mounted to the telescope.

Mike hooked the liquid nitrogen fill line from the bottle to the camera and spun the valve next to the safety vents. Too much pressure and the liquid nitrogen could explode. His thoughts drifted to the caves he'd hoped to explore. Mike's co-worker, Stan Jones, had told him about several caves with many ancient Apache artifacts. There were arrowheads, pots, and tools that could easily be sold to collectors for a little extra money. Mike wasn't interested in selling things to collectors, but he'd still enjoy seeing the ancient sites—and if he found something cool, he didn't think it would be a big deal if he snatched it for himself.

Just as that thought crossed his mind, a tremendous bang echoed through the cavernous dome. Whipping his head around, he wondered if something had hit the enclosure— perhaps a chunk of ice or maybe something as benign as a pinecone from a nearby tree.

He turned back again and his mouth fell open in shock.

On the dome floor, next to the telescope, stood a grotesque figure resembling an unholy merging of a predatory dinosaur and some kind of alien creature from a sci-fi movie. Its body crouched atop long talons that looked as though they could easily rip the tiles from the floor. The creature's nose consisted of two slits above a sharp, beak-like mouth. But it was the eyes that froze Mike in terror. Dark. Mesmerizing. They were like black holes in space. Mike had no idea where the creature had come from or how it managed to get into the dome. But he did know one thing for certain. It wanted to kill him.

The creature hunched low, its obsidian eyes probing into Mike, leaving him weak and nauseous. It seemed to swallow not only light and heat, but joy as well.

In a sudden flash of movement, it sprinted forward.

Mike stumbled backwards and fell hard, the wind knocked out of him. Wheezing and shaking with fear, he thrust his arms in front of his face in a feeble attempt to protect himself. The clacking of claws on the tile floor pounded in his ears as the creature launched itself at him.

Mike thought of Bethany, and closed his eyes, praying his death would be over fast . . .

And, then. Nothing.

Everything was quiet once more, except for the howling wind.

Mike slowly lowered his hands and opened his eyes. All he saw was the nitrogen tank connected to the camera, spewing liquid onto the floor. The camera was full.

"Jesus! What the fuck was that?" Mike burst into bewildered laughter. He'd really thought he was a goner—that some freaky creature had somehow found its way into the dome and was hell bent on devouring him for breakfast.

He must be over-tired, working too many long, winter nights. The unrelenting wind sparked his imagination to run wild, that's all. He scrambled to his feet, and brushed off his pants. That's when he realized that he had fallen over something.

The corpse of a mangy coyote lay on the floor at his feet. "How the hell did that get here?" The smell from the carcass was strong enough that Mike had to suppress his gag reflex. He eased around to the nitrogen tank and shut it off. As he disconnected it from the camera he thought the coyote must have sought shelter from the cold and somehow found its way into the telescope's enclosure. As he wheeled the nitrogen bottle to its storage place by the wall, he wondered how he was going to get rid of the carcass.

He turned back to the dead coyote and got his second shock of the morning.

The animal stood up and shook its shaggy coat, sending up a spray of rain and blood. Mike couldn't believe what he was seeing nor what happened next.

The coyote's mouth fell open, as though the tendons no longer held it shut. "Beware the caves," the coyote said in a deep, raspy voice. "They are the portals of mankind's doom . . ."

With that, the coyote turned and ran straight for the wall . . . and vanished.

Mike blinked and looked around. No water or blood anywhere. It was as though the coyote had never been there at all. He rubbed his bloodshot eyes and considered whether he was too sleep deprived to drive home right away. On the other hand, he wasn't sure he could get to sleep after the double dose he'd just experienced.

He left the dome and returned to the control room. Wallerstein had already left. Still feeling a bit shaky, Mike collected his laptop and the Stephen King book he'd been reading on his shift, and stuffed them into his backpack. *The Shining*. His favorite King book. He shook his head and chuckled. Maybe next time he'd grab one of Bethany's sci-fi romances instead.

He slung his pack over his shoulder and turned out the lights.

As he left the dome, snow was falling harder than before and the emerging twilight barely illuminated the landscape. Mike knew that if he went back to his dorm room to get some sleep, he would most likely be trapped at the observatory until the snowplow came through—possibly for days, if the storm lasted long enough.

Pursing his lips in resignation, Mike locked up, tossed his backpack in the back seat of his car, and drove down to the office and dorm building. Fresh tracks in the snow told him that Wallerstein had left ahead of him. Mike collected his dirty laundry from his room and returned to the car.

Turning on the radio, he caught the weather forecast as he left the observatory grounds. The snow was expected to continue on through the rest of the day and well into the night. Tired as he was, Mike felt he'd made the right decision to leave immediately. Within half an hour, he would reach the desert floor. After that, it'd be a straight shot home. If he needed to, he could pull off to the side of the road and get a short nap.

As he drove down the mountain road, a set of red taillights appeared before him. Mike slowed down, not wanting to push the car ahead too much. The snow fell hard enough that he didn't feel he could pass safely. They progressed slowly and steadily about two miles until they came to a bridge over a place called Nana's Ravine. Although it sounded like it was named for someone's grandmother, it was actually named for Geronimo's brother-in-law. Whenever moisture fell and the temperatures dropped near freezing, winds from the deep gorge froze the water into a thin sheet of treacherous ice.

Mike willed the car ahead to slow down. Instead, it sped up and hit a patch of ice, spinning out of control. He gasped as the car slammed into the guardrail just beyond the bridge and toppled over the side.

As he reached the bridge, the wheels of his own car started to skid. He geared the engine down low and eased his foot onto the brakes. The car fishtailed across, but he maintained control. Once on the other side, he pulled up to the broken guardrail. It was just beyond the ravine and the ground sloped away gently. The other car had rolled over onto a boulder, which kept it from sliding into the depths of the ravine itself.

He knew who it was.

Mike sprang from his car and scrambled down the hillside. Reaching the vehicle, he found the window on the passenger side smashed from the impact of the crash. Carefully reaching in, he unlocked the door and forced it open. As he worked, he didn't hold out much hope. The car's roof and driver's side had caved in. Looking inside, he saw Wallerstein's crushed body engulfed by a deployed airbag. His head hung by tendons as blood seeped out of the stump of his neck.

Despite oozing blood and ravaged flesh, Mike leaned in closer and saw the flash drive containing the night's data clutched in Wallerstein's hand—the one thing he couldn't bear to lose.

Mike scrambled away from the car, heart pounding in sheer panic. He threw up into a bush, lightly dusted with new fallen snow. He slumped onto his butt, heedless of the icy ground, and tried to calm his breathing.

A rush of questions tumbled through his brain: Why didn't he let him take just one more image? Why didn't he make him stay at the observatory and wait out the storm? Why couldn't they have stayed and waited? Waited?

Mike started shaking from head to toe as he thought what could have happened if he'd left before Wallerstein. Would he be dead now? Would Wallerstein be sitting here staring at his severed head?

A flash of brown fur brought him to his senses. Mountain lion? Coyote? That last made him shudder as he remembered the weird vision in the dome. He pulled his cell phone from his pocket. He tapped it, not surprised by the lack of signal. He climbed back up to the road, knowing he would have to drive a ways so he could call 911.

When he reached his car, he turned back and gazed at the wreck. A brilliant scientist had just died before his very eyes. Could he have prevented Wallerstein's death? He didn't know the answer to that. But what he did know was that the difference between life and death could be measured by just a few seconds . . .

PART 1

SACRED PORTALS

CHAPTER 1

Roscoe Perkins woke up with a raging headache.

He felt like he was on a merry-go-round even though he was lying in bed, covered in sweat-soaked sheets. Groaning, he cracked open his bleary eyes and gingerly lifted his head to peek at the alarm clock. 7:12 a.m. No way could he shave and shower in time to make his eight o'clock start time at Carson Peak Observatory. He must have slept past the alarm. Or, had he even remembered to set it?

Roscoe eased out of bed and padded to the bathroom, groaning more loudly this time. Once he relieved his bladder, he shuffled into the kitchen with four ibuprofen clutched in his palm. He popped the pills into his mouth, and swallowed them down with a few gulps from a half-empty fifth of Southern Comfort. *Hair of the dog*, he thought as he let out a loud belch. He grabbed onto the counter, and waited for the room to stop spinning.

Returning to the bathroom, he stripped out of his boxer shorts, and stepped into the shower. A few minutes later, the throbbing headache started to subside. The previous night's events came back to him in a haze. Slots. Blackjack. Endless rounds of shots at the Sacred Portals Casino, over on the Mescalero Apache Reservation. He was a big loser last night. In fact, he'd been on a losing streak for months now.

Feeling a little more human, he turned off the shower, toweled dry, and ran a comb through his thinning, salt-and-pepper hair. He looked at the gray stubble on his chin, but decided to light a cigarette instead of shaving. Astronomers didn't care what you looked like, as long as you kept their goddamned cameras and telescopes working.

Throwing on a pair of jeans and a flannel shirt—the only

clean one in his bedroom closet—he rolled up the sleeves and returned to the kitchen. He pulled a sausage croissant out of the freezer and microwaved it while he poured himself another shot of whiskey. He wasn't much of a cook. At least he didn't have to worry about getting fat. Drinking and smoking kept him trim. He snorted to himself. Plopping into a chair, Roscoe pulled on his socks and shoes. The microwave beeped and he reached in, grabbed the croissant, and went out the back door to his 1968 cherry-red Mustang convertible.

The car roared to life and he backed out of the driveway, drove down a couple of streets, turning onto the main highway that led from Toledo to the observatory. He ate his croissant as he drove along the quiet, winding road. Sunlight streamed through the treetops and the scent of pine perfumed the air, but Roscoe really didn't care. He just had to get through the next few hours of repairing more useless junk at the observatory, then he could go back to the casino where he could forget about pushy astronomers, his ex-wife's alimony payments, the mortgage on his dumpy house, and the fact that he was growing older every day with nothing to show for it. At least he still had his sweet car.

A blaring horn brought him out of his reverie. Just as he started across the bridge that spanned Nana's Ravine, he realized he had crossed into the lane of oncoming traffic and a truck bore down on him. He quickly swerved into his own lane, narrowly avoiding a collision. The driver threw him the finger and Roscoe shot back a string of curses.

He crossed the bridge and pulled off by the side of the road to pull himself together. He glanced over his shoulder at the guardrail. Two years ago. It was the biggest local news story for weeks. A tragedy, they said. The roads needed better maintenance . . . That telescope operator . . . What was his name . . . Dieter? Teter? He'd stopped and tried to help, but Wallerstein was already dead. The kid had taken it hard and quit. Roscoe didn't get why. Just another whiny astronomer and it was his own damned fault for going too fast across an icy bridge.

Roscoe scratched his stubbly, itchy chin. He spied a coyote trotting out from the woods, which wasn't strange, since coyotes were common in the area. The coyote stopped in front of Roscoe's car and gazed at him for a few moments, like it could see into his mind. Then it opened its mouth and spoke: "Enter the sacred portals and you will doom all mankind."

"Da'fuck?" Roscoe leaned forward and peered at the coyote. He sat back, shook his head and closed his eyes tight. When he opened them, the coyote had vanished. "Never had a goddamn hallucination talk to me before." He shook out a cigarette, lit it, and revved the car's engine. Taking a few drags, he pulled back onto the highway and continued his drive to work, wondering if his hangover had sparked the talking coyote show.

"Shake it off Roscoe. Shake it off."

Fifteen minutes later, Roscoe reached Carson Peak Observatory. He stepped out of the car and stretched, wishing he had the bottle of whiskey with him. Instead, he lit a fresh cigarette and smoked for a moment. The observatory consisted of two telescopes. The famous one was a 5-meter built on the north end of the observatory grounds. The twelve-story tower housing it loomed over the pine trees. Until the Apaches built the Sacred Portals Casino, it had been the tallest building in all of Southern New Mexico. At the southern end of the grounds was the 2.5-meter—half as big as its companion, but more powerful in that it delivered sharper images—and was a real pain in the ass as far as Roscoe was concerned. The smaller telescope was nothing but computers and electronics that constantly broke down. He could almost guarantee there would be work to do there today.

He crushed out the cigarette and shuffled through the door of the observatory's office building. He scurried by the site manager's office and quietly unlocked his own door. Sitting down, he brought up his email, scanning what jobs he had in store for the day.

Roscoe heard a man clear his throat. He looked up and knew he was in for it. A six-foot-tall Apache composed of pure muscle, his long, black hair tied back in a ponytail, leaned on the doorframe, his arms folded. Jerome Torres, site manager of Carson Peak, looked pissed.

"What the hell are you doing skulking in here at nine in the morning?" Torres barked. "They had problems with the active optics over at the 2.5-meter last night."

Roscoe snorted. "Again? I thought I got that working yesterday."

"And you thought you had it working the day before that." Torres took two steps forward and put his massive hands on Roscoe's desk. "Man, you look terrible."

"It was a late night." Roscoe shrugged.

Torres's nostrils flared. "Smells like it." The manager dropped into a chair and shook his head. "Roscoe, I can't have you coming to work drunk."

"I'm not drunk," said Roscoe. "Just a little hair of the dog, if you know what I mean."

"Smells like the whole goddamned pelt." Torres shook his head. "Man, I've warned you before. Late I can excuse. Drunk I can't. Pack up your stuff. You're outta here."

"What?" Roscoe rolled back in his chair as though he'd been slapped. "You can't be serious!"

"I've never been more serious. I need someone I can rely on. I'm going to call in Jones."

"Jones don't know a tenth of what I know," spat Roscoe.

"Yeah, he's a little slower fixing things than you are, but when he's finished, I know they'll work . . . and he doesn't show up drunk." Torres stood. "I want you outta here within the hour."

"You can't do this!" shouted Roscoe.

As Torres cracked his knuckles, Roscoe could see muscles ripple under his shirt.

"If you're sober enough," Torres said, "you can call human resources in Las Cruces and take it up with them when you get home."

Roscoe glared at Torres, then thought better of it. "Whatever," he grumbled. He looked around, dumped out a box that held a few spare parts and began collecting up his belongings. "I was gettin' tired of workin' here anyway."

"C'mon! Daddy needs a new entertainment system!" Roscoe

blew into the dice in his palm and tossed them wildly across the craps table.

"Loose Deuce!" called the stickman.

Roscoe pounded the edge of the table.

The stickman glared at him, and Roscoe picked up his tall, cool drink and took a gulp. "At least I still got you, love," he said to the glass. He stepped away from the craps table and took a moment to absorb the ambience of the Sacred Portals Casino. He loved the lights, sounds and smells. It was nothing like the observatory, where it was always dark, the air was always cold, and everyone talked like they were in a goddamned library. Here, his blood raced and he felt alive, just like he did when he roared along the road in his Mustang. What was it the coyote in his hallucination said? Stay away from the Sacred Portals? Hell no, this was the only place he felt at home.

He pulled out a cigarette from his side pocket and lit up, pleased that anti-smoking laws didn't apply to Native American casinos in New Mexico. He staggered over to the banker's window to collect some more chips.

The banker looked up with sympathetic eyes. "Luck not with you tonight, Roscoe?"

"Today has been one big suck-fest, my friend. Do you think you can see fit to run another thousand on my credit line?"

The banker checked his computer. "I think this is the last payout I can do for you," he said, as he counted out the chips.

"You're a real pal." Roscoe put the chips in his pocket, drained the last of his Long Island Iced Tea, and returned to the bar. This time he ordered a Jack and Coke. He downed half of it, wandered over to the blackjack table, and tossed three chips out. The dealer passed him a jack and a deuce. The dealer's face-up card was a five. "Hit me," said Roscoe.

The dealer passed him a ten. Roscoe shook his head and passed the cards and the chips to the dealer. He took another sip of the Jack and Coke, then stood, bumping into a young stud wearing a navy blue designer suit. The musclebound young man had a gorgeous blonde on his arm. She gasped, as she attempted to avoid Roscoe's drunken movements, protecting the front of her shimmery red dress with her sequined handbag.

Unfortunately, the stud wasn't so lucky. His drink splashed back, drenching Roscoe's shirt.

"Hey! Watch where yer goin'!"

"You're the one who bumped into me! Be more careful next time." The man started to walk away, pulling the blonde behind him.

"Think yer so smart, just like them astronomers at Carson Peak." Roscoe reached out and grabbed the stud by the collar of his designer shirt.

The musclebound stud wrenched himself from Roscoe's grip, spun on his heel and threw a punch into Roscoe's jaw, sending him into a group of people standing by the roulette table. A tall woman in the group, built like a female wrestler, growled, whirling around. She grabbed Roscoe by the shoulders and kneed him in the groin, dropping him to the floor.

A small crowd gathered around as Roscoe lay groaning. Finally, the pain began to subside and he brought himself to his knees. A middle-aged Native American man in a tailored forest green suit jacket with the Sacred Portals logo stitched into the breast pocket, pushed his way through the crowd. He waved around a stack of papers. "Free drink vouchers on us. Sorry for the disturbance." After passing out vouchers, he helped Roscoe to his feet and led him to a table in a relatively quiet part of the room.

"Mr. Perkins, I'm Wilson Enjady, manager of the casino. How are you doing?"

"I've had better nights." Roscoe grabbed a napkin from the dispenser in the center of the table and applied pressure to his split lip. "Still, a bad night at the casino is better than a good day at work, if you know what I mean."

"That's the problem, Mr. Perkins. You see, we just learned that you're no longer employed at Carson Peak Observatory."

"What's it matter to you?" Roscoe narrowed his gaze.

"The last few months, you've racked up a considerable debt to us," said Enjady with a pleasant smile. "We're just concerned about your ability to pay it off."

"Don'cha go worryin' about ol' Rossss-coe." His words came out slurred, both from the alcohol and the throbbing lip. "I'll find work soon enough and getcha paid right back."

"I'm also concerned about how much you've been drinking tonight." He reached out and grabbed Roscoe's arm. "I think it's time we got you a ride home."

Roscoe shrugged the manager's hand away from his arm. "I don't need no ride home. I can ge' home jussss fine all on my own . . . after I have 'nother drink."

Enjady lifted his chin. "No more drinks for you, Mr. Perkins, and no more gambling. I'm afraid the Sacred Portals Casino is closed as far as you're concerned."

"Whadda ya' mean closed?" Roscoe jumped to his feet, but before he could do anything more, two very large men grabbed onto his arms and escorted him toward the entrance. He tried to turn his head. "You'll hear from my lawyer!"

There was no response. The gamblers in the casino continued with their games. Laughter trilled from the dining room as the two bouncers pushed Roscoe through the doors. "Can we get you a ride home?" asked one of the bouncers.

Roscoe blinked at the polite question. He dabbed his split lip with the napkin again. "No, I'm fine to drive. I'll just get the valet to bring the car around. I probably have enough left for a tip."

The bouncer shook his head. "You don't have a car anymore, Mr. Perkins. Mr. Enjady ordered it to be impounded as partial payment of your debt."

"Fuck! You have got to be kidding me." Roscoe spit on the ground and stared at the mixture of blood and mucous in the moonlight. "All right, I suppose I better take you up on that ride after all." Roscoe snorted and remembered the coyote's warning. Maybe he'd pay more attention to his hallucinations next time.

CHAPTER 2

It gave up the ghost.

Mike Teter sat at the workbench in his garage, testing a computer's power supply with his voltmeter. As he suspected, it was dead. He searched the shelves above the workbench and found one compatible with the computer he was repairing. Fifteen minutes later, he swapped out the power supplies, turned on the computer, and it fired right up. Wiping sweat from his brow he decided a cold drink and a quick break were in order.

Opening the door to the main part of the house, a refreshing blast of cool air from the evaporative cooler hit him. He missed having his workshop in the spare bedroom, but he and his wife, Bethany, were in the process of converting it into a nursery. He reached into the fridge and pulled out a pitcher of iced tea. Filling a tall glass, he sat down at the kitchen table.

The house he shared with Bethany was a tidy, two-bedroom bungalow. The kind of place real estate agents called a "cozy starter home." Ideally, Mike and Bethany wanted to upgrade to a slightly bigger house because of the baby, but she'd only just begun her new job as an Assistant Professor at New Mexico State University and Mike hadn't been employed full time since he quit Carson Peak.

Mike shuddered as he remembered the gruesome sight of Ron Wallerstein's battered and virtually headless body. Despite being commended for his actions, he couldn't stay at the observatory. Nor could he excise those apparitions from his head. What were the 'portals of mankind's doom' anyway? Had those apparitions been some eerie portent of Wallerstein's death? Mike wasn't sure what he would do if he ever saw something like that again. So he'd quit, and started his own home business repairing personal computers and tutoring students at New Mexico State.

At first, business had been brisk. Personal computers were sufficiently expensive that people repaired them when they broke down. Over the course of two years, though, they'd begun to come down in price, making it easier for most people to just buy a new computer rather than get it repaired.

Plenty of students still called him for tutoring in physics and calculus, but tutoring didn't pay very much. What's more, Bethany wanted to take some time off to be with the baby. She hadn't earned enough time in her current position to take sabbatical leave. She could take a few months family leave, but no paycheck would come in during that time.

Mike jumped as he heard the key turn in the lock. He glanced at the door, as Bethany walked in. She was only four months pregnant and barely started showing yet, but her hazel eyes sparkled with anticipation and the rosy hue in her cheeks wasn't just from the hot New Mexico sun.

"You're home early," said Mike, looking up at the clock. "Can I get you something to drink?"

"The faculty meeting was canceled this afternoon. Too many people are out on vacation," she explained. "Is there still some lemonade?"

Mike checked the fridge, but didn't see any. "No, but I can make some now."

"That'd be great," she said, dropping her messenger bag on the table as she jogged to the bathroom. Bethany might not be showing yet, and fortunately she'd been spared the worst of morning sickness, but the pregnancy already had her bladder working overtime.

Bethany returned as he finished mixing the lemonade concentrate with water. She wrapped her arms around him from behind. He turned within her embrace and kissed her. "You've been eating garlic pasta again."

She grinned and poked his nose. "Hey, can't I be allowed my cravings when I'm pregnant?"

"You liked garlic pasta even before you were pregnant." He kissed her again, then stepped away to grab a glass. Throwing a few ice cubes in, he filled it with the sweetly tart drink and handed it to Bethany, who'd sat down at the table.

"Thanks hon." She took a few deep sips and sighed. "Oh there is nothing like cold lemonade on a hot day."

Mike grinned and refilled his own glass with iced tea. His wife might like cold drinks but she also liked them sweet. He, on the other hand, preferred his unsweetened iced tea.

She chewed her lower lip for a moment. "I got a call today."

Mike's brow furrowed at her tone. "Trouble?"

She shook her head. "No, nothing like that . . . at least not exactly. It turns out Jerome Torres had to fire Roscoe Perkins."

Mike rolled his eyes and sat down at the table next to Bethany. "Don't tell me. He showed up to work drunk again."

Bethany nodded.

"So, who are they going to get to replace him?"

"Jerome decided to promote Stan Jones. He's been considering that for a while," said Bethany. "He's a little weird, but he knows his way around a circuit board and an oscilloscope."

Mike frowned. "That means they'll be down a telescope operator." He sipped his lemonade. "That's going to be tough on the rest of the staff, not to mention the visiting astronomers." Mike knew that in order to meet the demand for telescope time, observatories did everything possible to work every clear night, even during most holidays. "What are they going to do about the open position?"

Bethany took a deep breath and let it out slowly. "Jerome was hoping you'd come back."

Mike's eyes widened. "You've got to be kidding me."

"You had a great record at the observatory. Jerome really liked you as did the rest of the staff. It was a real blow to them when you left," said Bethany.

Mike stood and looked out the window at their small back yard. "I'm not concerned about what they think of me. You know what kind of hours are involved in operating telescopes. I'd be on the mountain for a week and off again for a week." He turned around. "We have a new baby coming. It would be like missing half of his life."

Bethany stood and took Mike's hands. "How do you know it won't be a *her*?" she teased.

Mike snorted. "It doesn't matter. Plus, you know how dangerous that road can be during the winter."

"I know," said Bethany, softly. "And I know you've seen the danger firsthand." She squeezed his hands and kept her gaze fixed on them. "It's just that you haven't had much luck finding any other jobs and this one pays pretty well." She raised her eyes to his. "Maybe you could work there just a couple of years—long enough that we could afford a mortgage on a bigger house and get me past my time off at the university."

Mike cupped her cheek, kissing her tenderly on her lips. Despite his protests, he'd enjoyed working at the observatory. He felt it was important work—it was one of the most economical ways mankind could explore the universe. Not to mention, he helped students run the experiments that were vital to their studies. What's more, the observatory was located in such a breathtaking setting, he'd finally be able to explore those caves everyone talked about. On the other hand, the hours were long, the commute was brutal, and the time away from his wife and the coming baby would be tough . . . And the apparitions . . . Would they happen again? Or had they been a trick of bad weather and a tired mind? That's what he and Bethany decided at the time, but now that he faced the prospect of returning, new doubts emerged.

"Let me think about it some," he said, turning around and picking up his glass. As he took a long slow sip of tea, Bethany's hands began rubbing his shoulders. She had magic hands, his Bethany.

"I can't say I'm happy about the prospect of you on the mountain either, but I'm not sure I see many choices." She stopped her impromptu massage, much to his disappointment, and pulled her cell phone from her messenger bag. After tapping a couple of buttons, she wrote a number on a Post-It note and handed it to him. "Here's Jerome's number if you decide to give him a call."

Taking the note, he slipped it into his jeans pocket. "I promise to give it serious thought sweetheart. Just give me some time." He kissed Bethany once more, tucking a few strands of her lustrous, dark hair behind her ear, and went back to his workshop to finish working on the computer repair.

The next morning, Mike awoke to a ray of sunlight warming his face. He sat up in bed and rubbed his eyes. Bethany lay next to him, breathing softly. Sometime during the hot summer night, she'd kicked the sheets off. The early morning light bathed her nude body in a golden halo. She was the most beautiful woman he had ever seen. He reached out and laid his hand on her gently rounded belly. Their child. He loved them both more than anything in the world.

Bethany's eyes blinked open. "You're awake early," she said in a husky voice. "Are you okay?"

He shook his head. "Yeah, I'm fine. Just thinking."

With a Cheshire Cat grin, her palm skimmed down his chest, and over his stomach. Lower still, she curled her fingers around his penis, making him catch his breath. "I have a feeling I know what you're thinking about."

"You are everything to me." Mike's hand moved from her belly to her breast. Running his fingers over the sensitive nipple, he leaned in and captured her moan with a deep kiss. They made love as the sun continued its ascent. Afterwards, they lay with their limbs entwined. Mike caressed her soft skin. He'd miss her touch in the mornings during the weeks he'd be away.

A few minutes later, the clock radio kicked to life in the middle of a news story about a new wave of soldiers being deployed overseas from nearby Fort Bliss in El Paso. Suddenly Mike felt a little selfish about his comfortable life. Those soldiers would be away from their families for months at a time, not certain if they would come home after facing enemy soldiers or a roadside bomb. Taking the observatory job, he'd be home every other week. What was the worst thing he would face? An angry astronomer?

He needed to let go of the past. The visions and the memories. He'd been powerless to stop Wallerstein from crossing the bridge too fast. Powerless to stop his death.

He did his best to shake off his dark musings as he padded to the kitchen and started a pot of coffee. Entering the bathroom, he caught a glimpse of his face in the mirror, angular and tanned from regular exercise, the shaggy beard of two years ago now trimmed into a neat goatee. "Looking good dude," he said with a stupid grin to himself. He wondered if he could keep up his exercise regimen during the long nights operating telescopes.

After grabbing a quick shower he made breakfast while Bethany got ready for work. As he watched her eat the huevos rancheros he'd made, he knew he would do anything for her and the child she carried. At the very least, he could make a phone call and find out if Jerome Torres was serious about his offer. After all, he'd been away long enough that he'd most likely forgotten the myriad details of the job. Maybe the director wouldn't be so interested when he realized he'd need training just like a new operator.

Mike kissed Bethany good-bye and stood in the doorway, waving as she pulled out of the driveway.

The portals of mankind's doom.

Those words had haunted him over the past two years. The Apaches considered the area around Carson Peak sacred. The Sacramento Mountains were said to be the portal where mankind had entered the world. That's why the nearby casino was called Sacred Portals. But what did the apparition really mean? Was Wallerstein's death just a fluke? Or was there something else lurking in those mountains?

Stop it! You're being an idiot.

Mike sighed. Wasn't life really just a series of portals— transitions from one state to another?

He glanced at the clock on the microwave and saw it was a quarter past eight. Jerome Torres would be in his office by now. He blew out a breath, and dialed the number.

CHAPTER 3

Things were looking up.

"I'm glad you called," said Jerome as he chatted with Mike.

"Thanks man," said Mike. "Did Bethany mention she's expecting?"

"Yes, she did." Jerome Torres thought of his own young son. "There's nothing saying you couldn't move up to the mountains. Houses in Toledo aren't that expensive. My grandfather watches Derek during the day. I'm sure he'd be happy to help out."

"That sounds great . . ." Mike replied, sounding hesitant.

"I know," said Jerome, "the problem is that Bethany just got hired for a tenure track position down in Cruces. She doesn't want to leave town."

"That . . . and the winters up there."

Jerome frowned even though he knew this subject would come up. "We all know you did everything you could for Ron Wallerstein. That was a freak accident and the roads up here usually aren't all that bad, especially if you wait for the plows."

"I know all that—at least intellectually I know all that." Mike paused and Jerome sensed he held something back.

"If there's something bothering you—something personal—you can tell me. This is just between us."

Mike took a deep breath and then his words poured out in a torrent. "Before I left the mountain, I thought I saw something in the dome."

Jerome's brow furrowed. "What do you mean?"

"It was a blustery night—that storm was raging. I was tired and I think all the noises—the howling wind, tree branches hammering the building, you know, that kind of thing—were playing tricks on me." Mike stopped. Even over the phone

26

line, Jerome felt a palpable tension. "I thought I saw a monster of some kind—like a feathered dinosaur with big black eyes and sharp talons. After that, I saw a coyote and it spoke to me, warning me not to go near any of the caves."

Jerome picked up a pencil and began bouncing its eraser off the desktop, but didn't say anything.

"Are you still there?"

"Yeah," said Jerome slowly. "Did you explore the caves, or only think about it?"

"I never got a chance to," admitted Mike. "I'd heard about how cool they are and I'd wanted to check them out."

"I think it was a warning. The caves in Carson Peak aren't on reservation land, but they're still sacred to the Apaches."

Mike was silent for a moment. "If I remember right, you have a master's degree in engineering and one in physics. You're not telling me you take Apache tales seriously?"

"Man, I *am* an Apache," said Jerome. "My grandfather is a medicine man. I think science is important, and it's the way we progress, but I also think there are other forces that science doesn't always see. Legends like the Apache stories often have a basis in fact."

"In other words, I haven't convinced you I'm crazy." Mike laughed.

"Not at all. At the very worst, you were tired and your imagination ran away with you. It happens to the best of us." Jerome had a thought and debated whether sharing it would help Mike or not. Realizing how much Mike had trusted him, he continued. "Did you know that my grandfather blessed the 5-meter telescope when it was first opened?"

"I had heard it had been blessed, but not that it was your grandfather."

"When the university dedicated the 2.5-meter, there was a bad storm up here. Lots of wind and rain. It wasn't safe to go up to the telescope."

"Yeah, I remember," said Mike. "They set up a big pavilion so the governor and the president of the university could make speeches. It got torn to shreds."

"Yeah," laughed Jerome, "they had to cram into the little office building here. It was pretty funny. My grandfather insisted that he bless the 2.5-meter as soon as possible after it was built, but it proved a long, hard winter. That was the winter you left. He was finally able to bless the telescope in the spring."

"So, are you trying to tell me it's safe now?"

Jerome grunted. "The building feels better to me. I think it's quieter, and we haven't had any incidents in the past two years."

Mike seemed to ponder that for a minute. "Speaking of two years, it's been that long since I've even touched a telescope. I'm going to need some training."

"Not a problem," said Jerome. "In fact, I appreciate your honesty on that score, but I think it'll come back to you quickly if you decide to take the job. I'll spend less time and money training you than I would someone fresh out of college."

"I appreciate the vote of confidence," said Mike. "Okay, I still need to think about it, but what do I need to do if I decide to apply?"

"The university is running an ad in area newspapers tomorrow. Just send your résumé into the office with Bethany." Jerome stopped bouncing the pencil and leaned forward over his desk. "We'd be really grateful if you would come back. We could use your experience."

"Thanks," said Mike. "I'll think about it and let you know what I decide tomorrow."

"Sounds good. Thanks for calling. I hope we'll hear back from you." Jerome hung up and sat back in his chair. He hoped Mike wouldn't take too long to think it over. He could sure use him back at work. He'd allowed Roscoe to stay far too long. Jerome had turned a blind eye to Roscoe's alcoholism because he was a talented engineer, but that had been a mistake. Having him around could have been disastrous.

That afternoon, Jerome heard a door open at the end of the hall. Poking his head out of the office, his eyes lit up at the sight of his wife Kendra. The blond, blue-eyed woman showed off toned muscles as she hefted a suitcase out of the room she used when she was on duty, operating telescopes. Jerome strode down the hall and wrapped his arms around her. "Sleep well?"

"I've slept better. You really ought to replace these beds over here."

"As soon as the state . . ."

". . . gives you more money," she finished for him. "How are things going? Can you give me a ride home?"

Jerome nodded. "I think we're covered. Stan tells me the problem with the 5-meter's spectrograph is fixed. John is coming in to operate the telescope tonight and we have no one scheduled on the 2.5-meter. I just need to finish a couple of emails and we'll be good to go."

"Help me with the bags, then I'll grab something to eat while you finish up."

"You got a deal."

Kendra and Jerome gathered up her bags and carried them out to their pick-up. Back inside, Kendra put the kettle on and prepped her breakfast in the small kitchen that the astronomers used while on site and Jerome returned to his office to finish up some work. In addition to the telescope operations crew, Jerome oversaw the staff that maintained the buildings and facilities. When he emerged again, Kendra was eating oatmeal and sipping tea. Because optical observatories operated from sunset to sunrise, it wasn't unusual for Jerome to see his wife having breakfast in the early afternoon.

"I heard from Mike Teter today," he said.

"That's great," she said. "Is he going to come back?"

"He's thinking about it." Jerome sat down on a couch facing the kitchen area and wondered how much of his conversation he should reveal to his wife. "He's concerned that he's been away for a while."

"Well, some things have changed," she said as she finished her breakfast. She brought her dishes to the sink and washed them. "There are some new computers and a couple of new instruments. I don't think he can just walk in the door without a little training." Kendra set the dishes in the drying rack.

"Yeah, but he won't be like someone brand new."

"Of course not, coming back will be like riding a bicycle. He'll pick it up in no time."

"Would you mind overseeing his training? Make sure he's ready and comfortable?"

"Comfortable? You want me to brew him some tea? Fluff him a pillow?"

He snorted. "Nothing like that. You know Wallerstein's death was hard on him. Let's just say I want to make sure he's not being haunted by demons from his past."

She reached out and took her husband's hand. "Why me?"

"You're my most experienced operator," he said with a grin. "And my best." He leaned down and kissed her, savoring the taste of cinnamon and apples from the oatmeal on her full lips. He smiled thinking back to when they first started dating. They'd both been into weight training and often worked out at the same time in the 5-meter telescope's weight room. Of course, he'd thought she was hot from the moment he'd laid eyes on her, but he'd been respectful. Something his grandfather had taught him from a young age: *Respect women, children and nature, and your life will be as smooth as a pond at midnight.* As they got to know each other they'd become friends and quickly moved past any cultural barriers that might have separated them. Realizing they shared a mutual desire to start a family, as well as the same tastes in movies, music and books, had only brought them closer. Not to mention their ability to go toe-to-toe, dissecting every scene in the original *Star Wars*. Now, five years and one son later they were still happy both at work and at home. And he still had the hots for her.

Before leaving, Jerome locked his office door. Anyone else who had permission to use his office would have a key. Locking up was a precaution he exercised to keep nosy staffers and astronomers from poking around his files. He also kept petty cash on hand for emergencies. Since firing Roscoe, he wasn't taking any chances. He knew the guy was in debt up to his eyeballs from gambling at the casino. Word traveled fast in a small town. Jerome wasn't taking any chances in case Roscoe had a notion to "stop by" when he wasn't there.

As they left the building, Kendra glanced at him with a twinkle in her eye. "You sure you're not just giving me extra hours because you're sweet on me?" she said winking at him. "Better be careful, someone might think you're playing favorites."

Letting out a hearty laugh, he wrapped his burly arms around her slender frame. "Oh, baby, I'm beyond 'sweet on you.'" She pulled his head down for a deep kiss that made him wish they had time to make out in his truck. He'd file that one away for their next date night.

"You're on salary," he whispered in her ear. "I don't think we have anything to worry about."

She shivered and ran her hands up and down his back in that slow sexy way he always loved. He leaned down and kissed her again. Reluctantly, he stepped back and opened the door to the passenger side.

He sighed, gazing at her perky bottom as she stepped up into the truck.

Man, I can't wait for date night.

As they pulled out of the parking lot, he looked up at the twelve-story tall building that enclosed the 5-meter. Even after so many years working there, he was still filled with awe at its power and potential. He knew some of the Mescalero Apaches considered the building an abomination because it was built by white men for their purposes, but he was also a man of science and he was proud of the work they did in their quest to understand the mysteries of the universe. His grandfather had a different understanding of the universe, but just as important. Jerome had learned to balance both perspectives in his own life.

They made the fifteen-mile drive down the winding, twisty mountain road to the small town of Toledo. Kendra kept the window rolled down and Jerome enjoyed catching glimpses of her blond hair as it blew on the wind. His grandfather hadn't been entirely happy that he'd married an Anglo woman, but as the years went by, the old man had come to love her as part of the family.

Toledo, New Mexico was listed in many tour books as a ghost town, despite the fact that it was still inhabited. It had been founded in the early part of the eighteenth century as a Spanish mining camp. The mine had operated until the early twentieth century, but closed down just after World War II when the demand for coal diminished. Jerome liked the rustic wooden houses, each painted in its own bright color. He also liked his neighbors. It was a small community, and close knit. A good place to raise their son.

The town consisted of a few hundred houses perched along the walls of a canyon. Deep shadows kept the mountain canyon cool even during the height of the New Mexico summer. They drove past the Ore House Tavern and Museum built beside the entrance to the old mine. Jerome didn't buy the stories that it was haunted. Still, he had never liked going down the mine. Not even as a kid. Even though some of his childhood friends had, usually because of a dare. Nothing scared him more than the idea of getting caught behind a cave-in and slowly suffocating to death.

A little farther on, they came to an old rooming house that had been converted into a bed and breakfast called the Dogwood Inn. The old two-story building was mostly empty during the summer, but would fill up during the winter ski season. Their house was just across the street, but they kept driving until they came to a dirt road that took them off the main highway and doubled back behind the row of houses. Jerome parked in a driveway behind his house.

They collected Kendra's luggage and clomped down a set of wooden steps to the backdoor. Their five-year-old son, Derek, shouted as he ran from the living room. "They're home!" Jerome caught his son and spun him around, before handing him to Kendra who snuggled his neck.

Jerome's grandfather, Mateo, hobbled through the kitchen. "He has been anxious for you to come home all day."

"Grandfather, can I talk to you in private for a minute?"

"Certainly."

They stepped out the front door onto an enclosed porch. Jerome dropped down onto a padded folding chair, while his grandfather eased onto a glider. "Mike Teter is thinking about coming back to work at the observatory."

"That's good news," said Mateo. "He seemed like a decent young man."

"He told me a story about his last night at the observatory. You remember the night Wallerstein died."

His grandfather nodded solemnly.

"He saw an apparition." Jerome described the feathered entity that Mike had told him about.

The old man's face drained of blood and he chanted a few words in the Mescalero language.

"You know what he saw?" pressed Jerome.

"Do you remember the story of White Painted Woman and her two sons?"

"Yes," said Jerome. "Her sons were called Killer of Enemies and Child of the Water. Killer of Enemies had to fight monsters so people could settle the Earth."

Mateo smiled. "It's good to know you remember the old stories, even if you work for the university." The old man's smile faded. "The apparition you describe sounds very much like a creature called He Who Kills With His Eyes. He is one of the monsters from the very dawn of time and he's sometimes called Great Owl."

Jerome snorted a laugh. "Give a hoot, don't pollute." He quoted the slogan from the Woodsy Owl signs posted by the Forest Service.

"He is not like the white man's owl," chided Mateo. "To the Mescalero, the owl is a symbol of death and an unlucky omen. I'm glad I asked the gods to bless the site. I'm worried that it's close enough to one of the sacred portals that a monster so heinous has the power to manifest itself."

Jerome shuddered in spite of how warm it was out on the enclosed porch. "Do you think there's any danger now?"

Mateo shrugged. "There is always danger." He held up his hand when Jerome opened his mouth to speak. "The existence of danger does not mean that one will come to harm. If you hike in the woods, you're just as likely to pass near a mountain lion as a deer."

Jerome nodded and looked out at the street. "You've told me that humans can attract demonic forces, such as He Who Kills With His Eyes. What about entities that have already crossed over into other planes of existence . . . entities like Professor Burroughs?"

Mateo folded his hands in his lap and closed his eyes.

"Ah, the ghosts of white men. That's a very complex subject indeed . . ."

The two men continued their conversation for a while longer. Jerome hoped that all would be well, at least for now.

CHAPTER 4

A loud pounding jolted Roscoe awake.

The noise subsided and he started to drift off to sleep again. A moment later, it returned with renewed force. He glanced at the clock and saw it was just past noon. As the pounding subsided a second time, he realized it wasn't entirely in his head. Someone was at the front door.

He lay quiet for a moment, hoping whoever it was would decide he wasn't there and just go away. He didn't want to talk to anyone today. The knocking stopped and he let out a sigh of relief. After a couple of minutes, he threw back the blankets, eased his feet into slippers and grabbed his bathrobe. He shuffled into the bathroom and opened the medicine cabinet. His eyes roved over the contents at least three times before they finally settled on a bottle of ibuprofen.

Just as he shook two pills into his open hand, the knocking resumed and he dropped the pills into the sink. "Shit!" Whoever was at the door wasn't going away anytime soon. He scooped up the pills, which were now slimy from the moisture in the bottom of the sink, and tossed them in his mouth, then chased them down with a cup of water.

As the banging continued, he hoped it was an enthusiastic Jehovah's Witness so he could give them an earful. He'd come to the conclusion long ago that even if there were a God, He didn't give a shit about anyone. Roscoe threw open the door and was surprised to see Jesse Bowen, the local mailman.

"Jesse! What the fuck are you doin' poundin' on my door?"

"What the hell are you doing sleeping past noon, Roscoe?" asked the mailman. "I have a certified letter for you." He reached into his mailbag and retrieved a letter along with an electronic signature pad.

Roscoe took the letter. "How'd you know I was home? Seems kinda stupid for you to be standin' out here bangin' on the door like an idiot."

Bowen thrust the signature pad at Roscoe. "Heard you'd been fired from the observatory."

Roscoe frowned. "I coulda' been out lookin' for work." He signed for the letter and handed the pad back to the mailman.

The mailman shrugged. "Not much call for an electronics engineer up here, unless you work for the observatory or the casino." He cast a sidelong glance at the letter. "From what I hear, that doesn't seem too likely."

"What exactly you been hearin'?"

"Just that you ran up a big bill and they kicked you out. That, plus no job, spells a lot of trouble."

"Ya think?" Roscoe started to close the door, but the mailman thrust his foot in the crack.

"Look, I know how tough it can be. My brother's an alcoholic. There's an Alcoholics Anonymous group that meets at the church every week. You should think about it."

"Oh, sure, I'll be there after choir practice." Roscoe sneered. He slammed the door just as the mailman removed his foot. He turned the deadbolt, grumbling to himself. The one thing he hated about small towns was how everyone knew your business before you did.

He plodded into his kitchen and dropped into a chair. The return address on the envelope indicated some law firm in Las Cruces. He tore it open and read, his heart hammering in his chest. It was a notice that the Mescalero Apache tribe had started proceedings to acquire his house in partial payment of debts accumulated at the Sacred Portals Casino.

He crumpled the letter and hurled it into the corner. Slumping back in his chair he vigorously scratched his head. "Fuck!" He needed a drink.

Hauling himself to his feet, he went to the bathroom and showered. As the water poured over him, he took a mental inventory of his resources. First they'd taken his car, and now were about to seize his house. And that was just a drop in the bucket of what he owed. He had just enough in the bank to survive a couple of months without work. And then, what?

Bowen might be a small town jerk, but he was also right about one thing. The only work for an electrical engineer was at the observatory or the casino. He supposed he could apply to the local utility company—if they were hiring. He could always move to Las Cruces or Albuquerque, but that would be difficult with no car. Disappear into the woods? It could be done. He had his camping gear and his guns. Reappearing in a new town weeks down the road, he could set up a new identity and leave all this behind. The idea had appeal.

He turned off the tap when the water turned cold. Stepping out of the shower, he wiped the steam from the mirror. He contemplated the stubble on his face and decided not to bother shaving. Once he was dressed, he checked his wallet and saw he still had a couple of twenties—enough for a trip to the bar.

A light breeze cooled the summer air. Clouds formed over the mountain. It wouldn't be long before the summer monsoon season hit. Roscoe's idea of disappearing into the woods lost its appeal as he pictured soaking rains every afternoon. As he turned the corner and walked along the highway, he looked up and saw Jerome Torres's house. He felt a rush of rage. That Indian got him into this mess. The Indians at the casino waited till they had all his money, then took his car and now they threatened to take his house. Fuckin' Indians! They were probably working together. He had to do something and fast. He continued down the highway until he came to the Ore House.

The tavern had a small lunch menu and catered to weekend tourists from Las Cruces and El Paso. On a weekday in the early afternoon, the place was mostly empty, except for the gray-haired, potbellied Latino man named Jerry who sat on a stool behind the bar reading a newspaper.

Garish red and gold wallpaper covered the walls. The chairs were upholstered in red velvet and photos of "soiled doves" from the nineteenth century were lacquered to the tabletops. Behind the bar hung a painting of a nude woman, reclining on an old-fashioned couch. The tourists loved that the place reminded them of an old west brothel. Roscoe didn't care as long as they served alcohol.

He dropped down on a barstool and Jerry looked over the top of his newspaper. "What can I get you?"

"Shot of tequila and a beer."

Jerry cast a glance at the row of beer taps. "What type?"

Roscoe scowled as he considered the choices. "Guinness," he said. At least the heavy ale would quiet his grumbling stomach.

Jerry took his time folding up the newspaper. Once done, he dropped a shot glass in front of Roscoe and added a splash of tequila. Roscoe downed it as Jerry filled a pint glass with dark beer. "What else can I get you?" asked the bartender.

Roscoe shrugged. "You know anyone looking to hire an engineer?"

Jerry smiled and shook his head. "Can't help you there, bro." He returned to his stool.

"Damned Apaches wrote me a letter. Said they're gonna take my house. They already took my car."

"That sucks," said Jerry. "Whatcha gonna do?"

"I dunno." Roscoe sipped his beer. "I suppose I should talk to a lawyer, see if there's anything I can do to stop them. If they're goin' ta take the house, maybe I can get my car back at least. After all, it's hard to get a job around here without one."

Jerry shrugged as he picked up the newspaper. "Maybe if you had a job, they'd agree to a wage garnishment instead of taking the house."

"Exactly." Roscoe slammed the bar, with the palm of his hand.

"Speaking of money, you do have that drink covered, don't you?"

Roscoe frowned and stood. He removed a twenty from his wallet and slapped it on the counter. Jerry made no move to collect it, but nodded approval. He started reading another article. As Roscoe continued to drink, he stared up wistfully at the nude in the painting, wondering who she was. *Damn sight better looking than my ex-wife.* Roscoe's mouth ticked up in a grin.

After a moment, Jerry looked over the top of the newspaper again. "Say . . . there's someone new in town who might be able to help you out."

Roscoe's eyes remained on the painting. "You're not gonna recommend Alcoholics Anonymous are you?"

Jerry snorted a laugh. "And get rid of one of my best customers? No way!"

"Then what? Debt counseling?"

"Nothing like that." Jerry shook his head. "How well do you know that mountain you worked on?"

"Carson Peak?" Roscoe shrugged. "I've been hunting around there a few times. I know the trails pretty well."

"Ever been in the caves?"

"A few." Roscoe eyed the bartender warily, wondering where this was going.

Jerry folded up the newspaper again. He pulled out a small, cardboard box filled with business cards, took one off the top and handed it to Roscoe. The name on it was Solomon Vassago.

Roscoe narrowed his gaze. "Who the hell is this?"

"He's a lawyer from back East," said Jerry. "He just bought a house here in town."

"If he's from back East, how does that help me? Is he licensed to practice law in New Mexico?"

Jerry shrugged. "He moved here because he collects Native American artifacts. He was looking for someone who could bring him new and unique things."

Roscoe looked over his shoulder to make sure there was no one else in the bar listening. He lowered his voice. "You know the tribe frowns on pilfering native artifacts."

"That's why he's interested in Carson Peak. It's not tribal land."

Roscoe shook his head. "This guy sounds like trouble."

"More trouble than you're already in?"

Roscoe didn't have an answer to that. He lifted the glass and drained his beer while Jerry took the twenty to the cash register. "Set you up for another?" asked the bartender.

Roscoe shook his head. "I'll take my change."

Jerry handed over a few small bills. Roscoe took the business card and reluctantly left a tip. He stepped out of the bar and read the address on the card. His brow creased and he looked up the hill, across from the tavern. A winding road led up to a two-story Victorian house—the biggest house in Toledo and, at one time, the most beautiful. The owner had died two years ago and the house had been on the market ever since. People said the house was haunted by a Civil War era colonel. Roscoe had heard stories of people looking up and seeing someone staring down at them from the windowed garret.

He dismissed it as an excuse. No one in Toledo could afford such a large house. There were people with money in Las Cruces and El Paso, but they didn't want to buy in such a remote location. Drug lords were rumored to have checked it out, but it stood exposed on a hill. There was nothing to stop a rival gang from attacking the place. Roscoe might not believe in ghosts but the idea of rival gangs shooting it out sent a shudder up his spine.

His stomach rumbled as he hiked back home. He wished he had taken the time to order breakfast. Sighing, he poured a bowl of cereal. He grabbed a carton of milk from the fridge, looked at the date, and decided to leave well enough alone.

Turning on his computer, he did a search on Solomon Vassago, while munching on the dry cereal. A moment later, he stared at the website for the law firm of Marbas and Vassago in New York. As far as he could tell, they specialized in trusts, estates and property. Maybe this Vassago could help him after all.

The business card had a local phone number. Roscoe set the cereal aside and went in search of his cell phone.

CHAPTER 5

He couldn't believe he was actually doing this.

With a hollow feeling in his stomach, Mike tossed a duffle bag filled with clothes into his car's trunk. The observatory was a little over three hours from his home in Las Cruces. Even working short summer nights, it would be a tough commute to make every day. In winter it would be impossible. Even staff members who lived in the small town of Toledo opted to stay in the dorms for the duration of their shifts.

Satisfied he had everything he needed, Mike closed the trunk. Bethany stood in the doorway watching him. He forced a brave smile, walked over to her, and wrapped his arms around her. They kissed—sweetly at first, then more passionately. After a moment, Bethany gave his chest a gentle push. "You better get going or you'll never get to work on time."

"Are you sure this is the right decision?" asked Mike.

"I think we need the income and you're good at this. We can revisit the decision once our baby is here."

Mike nodded, a lump in his throat, then with one final, brief kiss, he turned and climbed behind the wheel. The long drive carried him over the San Augustin Pass and into the stark, empty Tularosa Basin, which held the Army's White Sands Missile Range. Across the basin was the Holloman Air Force Base, along with the White Sands National Monument, and the small town of Alamogordo. As the road wound into the basin, he gazed at the austere beauty of the Sacramento Mountains rising from the desert floor. A feeling of optimism floated through him.

This is going to be a fresh start.

He turned on the radio, opened the window, and pushed the accelerator downward. The wind whipping by the car eased his mind. With a job, there were no worries about providing for his child while Bethany took time off work. He had to admit it felt good to get away from the house for a time, doing work that was challenging and paid well, instead of worrying about when the next computer repair job would come in.

The music played while the wind tousled his hair. The illusion of freedom was spoiled when a commercial for the Sacred Portals Casino came on. He reached down and searched for another radio station, but the only other one he could pick up was National Public Radio talking about a terrorist bombing somewhere in the world. He turned off the radio and settled for the sound of the wind whistling through the window, thankful that operating telescopes was not usually a perilous occupation. An hour later, a looming traffic signal brought him out of his reverie. He'd entered Alamogordo.

It occurred to Mike that Alamogordo might provide an alternative to living in either Toledo or Las Cruces. It had a municipal park and a small zoo, which would be great for family outings. The problem was, it would only put him an hour closer to work while taking Bethany an hour farther away. If he wanted to spend his life commuting, he could move back to Los Angeles where he'd grown up. He'd left all that behind when he went to college. Three hours once a week through desert and mountain scenery still beat an hour-and-a-half daily commute on congested freeways.

Partway through town, he turned onto the highway that led up into the Sacramento Mountains. The rolling desert terrain soon gave way to a highway shaded by pine trees. He passed the occasional cabin and roadside business. Deer crossing signs warned him of more abundant wildlife than lived in the basin. Despite the idyllic surroundings, Mike's muscles began to knot as he guided the car along the winding mountain road.

Eventually, Mike came to an intersection and turned right toward Carson Peak. Most other cars continued on to the Sacred Portals Casino or turned left toward Toledo.

The thickening pine trees cast deep shadows on the road ahead and seemed to absorb the sound of his car's engine. Mike swallowed and forged ahead, disoriented by the scattered sunlight filtering through the branches in sparse patches. It was like entering a portal to another world.

The portals of mankind's doom . . .

A little farther on, the trees thinned out and the land transitioned from dark soil to rock. There it was. The bridge spanning Nana's Ravine. His heart began to thud and he eased down on the accelerator as he approached the spot where Ron Wallerstein had gone off the road.

Not slowing down . . . Not going to look . . .

He looked anyway, and glimpsed a flash of movement at the edge of the road, on the far end of the bridge. His heart kicked up faster and sweat beaded on his brow. He forced his eyes forward and sped up a little more.

As he reached the other side of the bridge, something hit the left bumper with a sickening *wump* and a shock reverberated through the car. He screeched to a stop, his heart pounding in his ears.

"What the hell?" Had he hit a rock? He pulled off to the side of the road, flicked on the hazards and got out of the car. He turned around and his stomach lurched as an icy dread shot through him, freezing him to the spot.

In the middle of the road lay a mangy coyote.

Dead.

Beware the caves. They are the portals of mankind's doom.

The apparition from two years ago flashed through his mind again. Another dead coyote. Only that one had suddenly come back to life and gave him the ominous warning, before vanishing. Looking down the road, he could see the rocks where Ron Wallerstein's car had crashed.

He began to shake. His heart hammering in his chest. His breathing, fast and shallow. He stood there for what seemed like hours, but was only a few minutes.

He expected the coyote to stand, its mouth to fall open, and another dire warning to escape.

But it just lay there.

Mike took several deep breaths to calm himself.

"It's just a dead coyote . . . Just a dead coyote . . . Just a dead coyote . . ."

He kept repeating the words like a mantra as he slowly

approached the fallen beast.

He tentatively reached out, intending to pull it off the road and then—its ear twitched.

"Holy shit!" He jumped, stumbled, and almost fell backward.

At that point, he noticed a ragged rise and fall of the animal's chest. A moment later, the coyote lay completely still.

This is not what I want to be doing on my first day back to work . . . Fuck it!

He approached again. The coyote's glassy eye was open, staring at him in silent accusation. He took a deep breath, grabbed the animal's forelimbs and dragged it off the side of the road. He ran back to the car, got in, and opened the glove compartment. There he found some anti-bacterial wipes. He frantically cleaned his hands and dropped the wipes to the car's floor. Grabbing the steering wheel, he leaned his forehead on his hands.

"I can't do this. It's happening all over again."

He looked up the road and wondered what he should do. He picked up the cell phone, and groaned. *Great. No fucking signal.* He turned off the phone to save the battery. Looking in the rearview mirror, he saw no cars. He glanced out the window.

The coyote had disappeared.

He swallowed hard and scrubbed his jaw with his left hand, his right hand clutching the steering wheel.

Perhaps he'd just dragged it farther off the road than he'd thought. It had still been breathing a moment after he hit it. Maybe it was just stunned? Not dead.

"It's not dead . . . Not dead . . ."

It just got up and trotted away . . . That's it.

He started the car. With a deliberate force of will, he put it into drive and continued forward.

He turned on the radio. The signal faded in and out, more static than music. Turning it off, he drove for a few minutes until the silence in the car grew palpable. He turned on the radio again and kept it low, preferring the white noise of the static to the oppressive dead air. Eventually, the road climbed high enough that he could see the two observatory domes reflecting the sunlight. He sighed with relief. Why did he feel like he'd just run a gauntlet?

The 5-meter telescope's enclosure, capped by its distinctive rounded dome, towered above the mountaintop. Many people likened it to a wizard's ivory tower in the wilderness. A comforting thought. He hoped he would feel that sense of comfort he used to feel before the apparitions. Before Wallerstein. Before the dead coyote.

Across the ridge, was a silver enclosure, much lower to the ground. Instead of a rounded dome, this one was octagonal. The doors that allowed the telescope to peer at the sky opened sideways on a pair of rails. With the dome closed, the rails stood out on the side, like the horns of a steer. Mike had always thought the building looked like some gigantic robot cow.

His heart began thudding again when he reached the observatory gate, this time nervous about his return. He stopped the car. A big sign posted beside the gate read, "Carson Peak Observatory." Another, smaller sign declared, "No Hunting. No Hiking."

After passing through, he followed the road up to a brown, one-story building that resembled a large cabin. The sign on the door read, "Administration." Below, another sign read, "Authorized Personnel Only." Mike parked and grabbed his duffle bag from the trunk.

The front door opened into a spacious common area with a kitchen and a TV. Immediately to Mike's right, was Jerome Torres's office. Kendra Torres sat on the couch, watching the news. She turned around at the sound of the door. "Ah, there you are. I was getting worried you'd lost your way."

Mike smiled. "Good to see you, Kendra." He dropped the duffle bag and shook her hand. "I hit a coyote on the way up. I stopped and pulled him off to the side of the road."

She frowned and surreptitiously rubbed her hands on her jeans. "Good thinking. The highway department doesn't get out here very often."

"I remember." He looked over his shoulder at the office. "Is Jerome in?"

"He left early. He had to take Derek to a doctor's appointment in Alamogordo. You probably passed him on the way up."

Mike nodded. Although there hadn't been any cars on the road to the observatory, there'd been plenty before that.

"Anyway," continued Kendra. "Jerome left me a set of keys for you." She pulled them from her pocket and tossed them to Mike. He caught them neatly in one hand. "You're going to be in room two." She pointed down the hallway that led away from the kitchen area.

"Not room ten? That was my old room." He referred to the room at the end of the hall, favored because it was farthest away from the common area.

"That's mine now. Seniority has its perks." She winked at him. "And don't make any mistakes coming down the hall. You know Jerome is the jealous type."

Mike blushed and shuffled his foot, not certain how seriously to take Kendra's flirtatious teasing.

She let him off the hook. "We'll start our training over at the 5-meter tonight." She looked at her watch. "The observers will arrive in about an hour. Why don't you go settle in and we'll meet out here in an hour, have dinner, then I'll take you over and show you around."

"Sounds perfect," said Mike.

"It's good to have you back." Kendra gave him a sincere smile.

"It's good to be back." Mike wasn't sure if he believed his own words.

CHAPTER 6

A man stood at the garret window, watching him.

Roscoe Perkins trudged up the long, winding drive of Solomon Vassago's house. A shiver went up his arms as he recalled the ghost stories. "Hmmph," he grumbled, shoving the thought aside. "Guess he likes to observe his visitors before he meets them."

The two-story Victorian manor house was built from the surrounding yellow and gray rock. A person in the garret atop the house could view the entire valley. Although the house stood on high ground, out of the canyon's shadow, it looked a little dull and dingy. The only plants nearby were native scrub. The desiccated skeletons of vines, maintained a death grip on the side of the house. Roscoe couldn't tell whether they were dead from neglect or the altitude. The door and the windowsills had once been painted white, but they were streaked in shades of gray, with fissures where the sun had split the wood. The wooden porch creaked as it took his weight and he was half afraid the ancient timbers would give way.

He grabbed a rusty knocker and banged on the door. It barely registered a thump, so he knocked with his hand. A moment later, the door opened, framing a tall, gaunt man who wore a pair of jeans, a plaid Western shirt and a bolo tie as though it were a uniform. Roscoe suspected he'd be more comfortable in a dark suit.

He must have sprinted down the stairs from the garret. Weird. He doesn't look out of breath.

"Mr. Vassago?" he asked aloud.

"Yes, I'm Solomon Vassago."

He shook Roscoe's hand. The strength of the attorney's grip startled him.

"Please come in." Vassago stood aside, allowing Roscoe to enter the parlor. Imported marble covered the floor and a sturdy, like-new staircase led upstairs. Vassago closed the door and ushered Roscoe into a comfortable sitting room. From the outside, Roscoe had expected dust, cobwebs and worn velvet. Instead, the sitting room was comfortable and modern. A display case containing Native American pots and baskets sat against one wall. Framed displays with Native American tools and arrowheads hung around the room. In one frame, Roscoe recognized a Folsom point. In another was an even older Clovis point. He whistled in appreciation.

"Would you care for a drink?" asked Vassago, stepping over to a liquor cabinet.

"Do you have whiskey?"

"Scotch, Irish or bourbon?"

"Whatever you have." Roscoe usually drank bourbon, but he liked them all and normally couldn't afford good scotch.

"I have a 25-year-old Glendronach." The attorney held out a half-empty bottle of amber liquid.

Roscoe licked his lips in anticipation. "Sounds perfect."

Vassago grabbed two glasses. "This costs about $200.00 per bottle. It's about as close to perfection as any scotch can come." He poured and then handed one glass to Roscoe.

Roscoe inhaled the fumes from the alcohol. He took an uncharacteristically slow sip. The liquid went down smooth, heating his gullet. As it settled in his stomach he closed his eyes, savoring the heat. *Perfect.* He realized at that moment that Solomon Vassago was a man who knew what he wanted and could pay for it.

"On the phone, you said you knew Carson Peak and the surrounding area." Vassago took the briefest of sips. With a contented sigh, he set the glass aside.

"I worked at the observatory for a decade. I hiked and hunted in that area on my days off. Sometimes I explored the caves, or took shelter in them during hail storms."

Vassago smiled. His teeth were unnaturally white and sharp. "Are you familiar with the Native American legends concerning this area?"

"You mean that the gods first created man in these mountains, right?"

Vassago's mouth broke into a mirthless smile. *"Woman,* actually and she gave birth to two sons." He waved his hand. "The details don't matter. What matters is that the Apaches have been in the area for centuries. They used to trade with the Anasazi to the North and the Aztecs to the South. They bartered in gold and precious stones, and I believe that many of those are in the caves of Sierra Blanca, Guadalupe, Three Sisters, and Oscura Mountain." He referred to the four sacred mountains of the Mescalero Apaches.

"But all of those are either on tribal or government land. You can't take artifacts from there." Roscoe took another sip of the fine scotch. Although he drank more than his share of alcohol, this was strong stuff. It was already going to his head.

Vassago retrieved a map from his desk that showed the locations of the mountains he named. He pointed to a spot in the center—a place neither on National Forest nor reservation land. It was neither the tallest nor most prominent peak, just tall enough to serve the needs of the astronomers who used the land. "Right here in the center is Carson Peak. I believe the Apaches have left some of their most important artifacts on that mountain."

"I'd certainly be happy to go searching for you," said Roscoe. "For a finder's fee."

"You come right to the point, don't you?"

Roscoe opened his mouth to protest, but Vassago cut him off, saying, "That's fine. I'm not really interested in gold and jewels per se. I'm looking for one particular artifact. If you can find it, I would be willing to pay a great deal of money."

Roscoe took a gulp of whisky, then leaned forward. "Tell me more."

Vassago folded the map so neatly it looked as if it could go back on the rack at a gas station. He then picked up a leather-bound sketchbook. He flipped through a couple of pages. When he found what he sought, he turned it around and showed Roscoe a sketch of a round disk. On its face was a creature. Roscoe couldn't decide if it was a deformed raptor, a strange dinosaur, or an alien from another world. Its eyes were large and pitch back. Roscoe felt as though he were falling into them, even though they were only drawings in a notebook.

"The eyes are captivating, are they not?" It seemed as though Vassago could read Roscoe's mind. "It's believed they're obsidian. The talisman itself is pure gold."

"How big would it be?" asked Roscoe.

Vassago curled his fingers into a circle a little bigger than an Eisenhower silver dollar. "Based on other similar talismans that have been discovered, I'd say an inch and a half or so in diameter."

Roscoe downed another gulp. "You think this thing's on Carson Peak?"

"I'm certain it is."

"If you're so sure," asked Roscoe, "why bring in a guy like me at all? Why not go search for this treasure yourself."

Vassago closed the book and set it down on the desk. "No doubt you can tell I'm not a local. I don't know the caves, but *you* do."

"If I find this thing, what's to keep me from taking it for myself and selling it to the highest bidder?"

Vassago smiled. "You really are a man after my own heart." He folded his arms. "The problem is that you'd run the risk of attracting the Apaches' attention. The artifact might not be on their land, but it wouldn't stop them from laying claim. I'm offering money up front. No one has to know you're involved. This transaction would be our little secret."

"How much are you offering for this little venture?"

"Enough that you could pay off your debts to the Mescalero Apache tribe and start anew, someplace far away," Vassago replied.

"How do you know about my debts?" Roscoe asked, his eyes riveted on the attorney.

"It's a small town." Vassago shrugged nonchalantly. "Word gets around."

Roscoe scowled, knowing the truth of that statement. He sat back and lifted his tumbler for another sip but realized it was empty. Vassago smoothly took his glass, refilled it and handed it back to a surprised Roscoe.

"All right then. What happens if I search around and don't

find this thing? I don't have a lot of time before the Apaches are gonna take my home away. What if someone already has it and hasn't told anyone? What if conquistadors took it five hundred years ago and buried it somewhere else?"

Vassago snorted. "If they had, I'd know. Trust me." He leaned forward. "I'll make it worth your while. I'll give you some money to hold you over for a week or two as you get started. If you fail, I'll set you up with an attorney here in New Mexico that will fight like a shark to help you keep your house."

"Why would you do that?" Roscoe narrowed his gaze in suspicion.

"Consider it an investment of sorts. If you fail to find it, there are other possibilities . . ." Vassago spoke in a measured tone. After a moment, he broke into a predatory grin. "But I don't expect you to fail."

Roscoe rubbed his stubbly chin, the scratching sound echoing throughout the room. "What sort of possibilities?"

"I'm not prepared to discuss them at this point. Suffice it to say, I have every confidence in your ability to locate this artifact . . . and deliver it to me."

Roscoe stared at Vassago for a few moments. "You seem to be an observant man. I saw you watching me from the garret room."

Vassago arched an eyebrow. "I think your imagination is running away with you. The contractors still need to finish that room. The floor is not safe." He shrugged. "I was here in my study when you knocked. I trust you will be more observant in your quest for me."

Roscoe shuddered. "It must have been a trick of the light."

"No doubt." Vassago inclined his head and his pleasant demeanor returned.

Roscoe downed his whisky in one big gulp and placed the empty glass on the small table next to his chair. "All right. I'll take the job." He announced, slapping his hands on his thighs.

Vassago nodded as though he'd known all along that Roscoe would agree. He withdrew a checkbook from the drawer of a stately mahogany desk. He filled out one of the checks and passed it over to Roscoe. "That should be enough to get you started."

Roscoe's eyes widened as he looked at the amount. "What's to keep me from running out on you?"

"You have no car, Mr. Perkins. If you're foolish enough to hike down to Alamogordo to buy a bus ticket, I'll know." He smiled again.

Roscoe was beginning to dread that smile.

"That should be enough for you to stock up on camping gear, maps, and ammunition. Everything you need for several days out in the wilderness. I'll expect a report two weeks from today. If you have the artifact, wonderful. If not, I'll introduce you to my attorney friend and we'll proceed from there."

Roscoe stood up, a little unsteadily on his feet. "You have yourself a deal, Mr. Vassago." He reached out and shook the man's hand. As he did, he could have sworn he saw a light flash in the man's eyes.

On the other side of the highway, at the far end of the canyon, Mateo Torres sat in a recliner sipping his coffee while his grandson, Derek, played with his Lego set. The boy was intent on building an exact replica of Carson Peak Observatory. Mateo smiled indulgently at the look of determination in Derek's eyes. Just like his father. The phone in the kitchen started ringing and Mateo pushed the lever that lowered the recliner's footrest. As he got up, his head began to spin and he fell to his knees. The cup thudded on the carpet splashing coffee onto the rug and leaving a dark stain. Derek looked up. "Grandpa, Grandpa!" He ran over to the old man.

Mateo wasn't aware of his worried grandson. He wasn't aware of anything except what he saw in his mind's eye. A vision that would haunt him for the rest of his life. Giant creatures tall as houses. Arms and legs covered in scales. Still others in feathers. But it was their eyes that were the most terrifying. Black like obsidian. In one swipe, a monster scooped up a child, no older than Derek, and swallowed him whole. Another uprooted great pine trees with gnarled, misshapen antlers, and flung them onto the cluster of man-made lodgings, crushing the people inside. A third giant swooped down from the skies and shot lightning bolts from his eyes, setting the surrounding forest ablaze. These were the monsters bent on exterminating humanity at the beginning of time. But they were eventually subdued by man . . .

Mateo blinked, once more aware of his surroundings. His grandson's eyes were wide, glistening with unshed tears. Mateo scooped him up and hugged him. "Everything's all right." He set Derek down. "Would you like a snack while I clean up this mess?"

Derek sniffed and nodded. Mateo led him into the kitchen, took two chocolate chip cookies from the tin on the counter and poured his grandson a glass of milk. He returned to the living room with a rag and some carpet cleaner. Fortunately there hadn't been much coffee left in the mug and he quickly cleaned up the stain.

Stepping outside, he took a deep breath and inhaled the invigorating fragrance of the surrounding pines. He looked up at the vibrant blue sky. His son and daughter-in-law worked to understand the universe, but he wondered whether they would comprehend the evil he'd just envisioned. He chanted a prayer and asked for guidance and strength. Gazing out at the rugged beauty of the surrounding mountains, he knew one thing for certain . . . There was evil out there. He saw it in his vision. Bad things were going to happen. Terrible things . . . and he didn't know if this evil could be stopped.

CHAPTER 7

It felt like a crypt.

A faint musty odor wafted out, as though the room had been sealed for a long time. Mike flicked on the light switch of his home for the next week. Beige paint covered the cinderblock walls in the windowless room. None of the dorm rooms had windows so the telescope operators could sleep during the daytime. Unfortunately, it also gave a distinctly crypt-like feeling to the space. A double bed occupied most of the floor, obscuring the lime green carpet. A small, wooden desk, dresser, and a closet with a teakwood door helped relieve the room of its desolate character. A few posters, photos, and personal items would improve it further.

Mike tossed his duffle bag and backpack onto the bed, closed the door, and stepped into the small bathroom. Flicking the light switch, he remembered, there was no space for a tub, just a shower and toilet. The sink was just outside the closet in the main part of the room. He sighed as he realized that the morning after his shift would be the first time he wouldn't be sharing a bed with Bethany since they'd gotten married. Quirking a smile, he thought of one positive in all of this. Since getting pregnant, Bethany had begun to snore, so he'd get better sleep at least.

He unpacked his clothes and laid his toiletries out on the sink. Once everything was squared away, he grabbed his backpack, turned off the light, and opened the door. The hallway was completely dark. The lone, weak light bulb overhead must have gone out. What's more, someone had shut the door at the end of the hall. Too late, Mike remembered that one of the observatory rules was to carry a flashlight at all times. There were many walkways and small spaces one could get trapped in without light. Over the last two years, he'd fallen out of the habit of carrying a flashlight in his pocket. He turned around and felt for the door to his room, but it had locked behind him and it was so dark he couldn't easily tell which of his keys was which.

With a sigh, he decided to edge his way along the hallway to the exit rather than blindly try keys in the lock. As he started forward, he heard one of the doors creak open, but the only illumination was a faint green light, reminiscent of the glow sticks kids carried around on Halloween.

He kept walking, wondering where the green light came from. But what he saw next made his heart stop.

A glowing skull floated in the middle of the hallway. Mike's skin crawled with unseen goosebumps, but he was too shocked to scream or call out.

Wallerstein?

The skull loomed closer and Mike stumbled back a few steps. Sweat beaded on his brow. There was no escape. As the skull advanced, Mike's eyes adjusted and he realized the head wasn't floating at all. It was attached to a cloaked figure. His hand ventured forward until he felt rough cloth under his fingertips. The skull's cheekbones rose and fell as it drew in ragged breaths of air—glow-in-the-dark latex.

Just then, the door at the end of the hall opened and Kendra switched on the light. "What the hell's going on here? Who closed this door?"

Mike jerked the skull mask from the cloaked figure.

Stan Jones.

Mike recognized the freckled-faced, red-haired telescope operator who'd started a few weeks before he left.

"Stan! What do you think you're doing?" asked Kendra, crossing her arms over her chest.

"Just having a little fun." He grinned as he turned to Mike. "You should have seen the look on your face!" He stood back and eyed Mike's crotch. "Wet your pants?"

The tension released, Mike barked out a laugh. "Fuck you, Stan."

"Stan, don't be a jerk, okay?" Kendra said in a stern tone.

"I was just welcoming Mike back."

"Gee thanks, Stan. I feel right at home." Sarcasm dripped from Mike's words.

Stan reached out and shook Mike's hand. "Sorry dude. It's good to have you back."

"No worries, man. So what are you doing here?" asked Mike. "Besides scaring the crap out of returning employees? I thought Jerome said he promoted you into Roscoe's old job."

"He did," said Stan. "But we're shorthanded until you're back up to speed. I'm operating the 2.5-meter tonight while you learn the 5-meter."

On the way to the kitchen, Stan tossed the latex mask and cloak in his room.

Mike noticed how much Stan had changed. He used to be slim, but now his stomach protruded over his belt buckle. The hazards of shift work. He'd have to be careful and make sure he kept up with his bike rides on his days off. "So, what's the deal with the costume?"

Stan shrugged. "Ah, you know how uptight astronomers can be. I just like to break the tension. Besides, there's a rumor that you saw some ghosts on your last shift up here. I wanted to make sure you weren't going to bolt the first time you saw something strange in the dark."

"Stan!" Kendra planted her hands on her hips. "That's uncalled for."

Mike rubbed the back of his neck, uncomfortable that Stan brought up the subject of ghosts. He diverted the conversation back to the costume. "It's okay. It was pretty funny . . . once I figured out what was going on."

"Dude, you were terrified." Stan laughed. "I saw it in your eyes." He punched Mike in the arm.

"Sure, you had me going there for a bit."

"More than a bit, I think." He winked.

The door to the office building opened and two women entered. One woman with dark hair, streaked with gray, wore a tailored blue pantsuit. The other with a mop of mouse-brown hair was dressed casually in jeans and a T-shirt. They looked around as though trying to get their bearings.

Stan continued. "Of course, you wouldn't be the first person around here to think they saw a ghost. Doesn't help that they buried ol' Professor Burroughs in the telescope's pier."

"Really?" asked the woman in the suit. "I'd heard that, but was never sure if it was true. Could we see the crypt?" The woman shook hands with Kendra. "I'm Amelia Mitchell from Harvard." Mike remembered her name from the telescope schedule. He'd heard a little about her research from Bethany. Harvard was one of the universities that ran Carson Peak and they received several weeks of observing time on the telescope each year. Dr. Mitchell put her hand on her companion's shoulder. "This is my student, Dorothy Pendergast."

"I'll get you! You and your little dog, too!" Stan cackled.

Dorothy rolled her eyes, clearly having heard the joke one too many times. Mike and Kendra introduced themselves and shook Dorothy's hand.

Kendra jerked her thumb at Stan. "This joker is Stan Jones. He'll be operating the 2.5-meter tonight. Well away from us."

The tension rolled off Mike as the banter continued. One of the things he liked about working at the observatory was the easy way most of the academics from prestigious universities got along with the technical staff. It made for a relaxed working environment. Sure, some professors could be demanding, but most were great people to work with.

As Kendra helped the two new arrivals settle into their rooms, Mike went out to his car and retrieved an ice chest containing his food for the week. He came back in as Kendra returned to the common area. She showed him where he could put his food. Stan was nowhere to be seen.

Once Mike unpacked, he carried the ice chest back to the car, and then went back inside to make supper. The women soon joined him.

Once they each had their meals, they sat down around the table and discussed the observing plans for the evening. It was an easy program that required only a few telescope pointings through the night—perfect for Mike to reacquaint himself with the job.

As supper drew to a close, Amelia leaned forward. "So, no one ever answered my question. Can we see Dr. Burroughs's crypt?"

"If you want," said Kendra. "We go right by the crypt when we do our walk-around of the building."

"I heard a story about how Professor Burroughs died. He was observing one night and just keeled over," said Dorothy with a thrill of fear in her voice. "Is that true?"

Kendra nodded. "It was back in 1972, not long after the telescope opened, before digital cameras, when they still used a camera with glass plates. Dr. Burroughs used to ride around in the prime focus cage at the top of the telescope. He'd go up for a couple of hours at a time, talking to the telescope operator on the intercom. One night when they'd been at work for a few hours, the operator called him but didn't get an answer, so he brought the telescope down to the loading platform where people could climb in and out of the prime focus. When he opened it up, he found Burroughs dead."

Mike continued the story. "The doctor who came in from Toledo figured he'd had a heart attack. It seems like that would be a hard way to go. All alone and cold, in the dark, in a space smaller than one of those capsules they sent into orbit."

Amelia's eyes took on a faraway look. "Then again, he was doing what he loved. I'd rather die that way than with my mind gone to mush in some nursing home."

The four nodded solemnly. Kendra cleared her throat and stood up. "Better get going." They cleaned up and retreated to their rooms to gather what they needed to take to the telescope. In Mike's experience, observing nights could be a lot of boredom punctuated by brief, almost frantic periods of activity. People took laptops, books and other work to occupy themselves during the quiet spells. Although the control room was heated, they all wore sweaters to guard against the chill, mountain air.

Ready for work, they walked out to the parking lot. It was a quarter mile to the telescope, not a bad hike for a pleasant summer evening, but daunting at the end of a long night, especially in the colder months. Mike and Kendra took an observatory truck while Amelia and Dorothy drove their rental car. On the way, Kendra stopped at the generator house. She showed Mike how to check the fuel supply and what to do if utility power went out, which could happen during strong storms.

They continued the rest of the way to the telescope enclosure. Once there, Mike noticed a third vehicle already parked at the telescope's base. He shrugged. Perhaps someone had left it there, or maybe Stan had gone in for supplies. He turned around and looked at the building that rose twelve stories above the mountaintop. Large round girders crisscrossed the outside of the building, supporting the enormous weight of the dome up above. It seemed both functional and spare, more like an enormous silo, or a monolith towering over the countryside.

The sun hovered a little over the horizon, casting rays of orange light through the clouds. The 5-meter enclosure cast a long shadow that already reached two of the adjoining peaks. Mike took a deep breath. He hadn't realized how much he missed the sight.

Kendra patted him on the shoulder. "Glad you came back?"

He pondered the question as he gazed at the telescope. "Yes, I am." He hoped that would prove true.

CHAPTER 8

Everything was the same but different.

The first room in the 5-meter enclosure was a bare bones handling area for loading and unloading telescope instrumentation. As they entered the room, Mike noticed the pipes running up the walls that carried water to the upper levels. Several doors led to maintenance areas that included electrical junction boxes, which supplied power to the telescope, as well as the specialized instruments used in the various rooms scattered throughout the skyscraper-like facility. Next to the entrance was a garage door for loading and unloading large equipment. At one end of the room were bottles of nitrogen gas, used to prevent water from condensing on the camera lenses. Kendra reminded Mike to check the nitrogen levels and promised to show him how to swap out the bottles later in the week.

They walked the circumference of the building into a machine shop, which housed a lathe, drill press, mill, and power saw. Cabinets contained everything from tools to cleaning supplies. Mike spied a pile of aluminum shavings on the floor. Someone had recently been busy on a project. He was curious as to what it was. Almost certainly it would be a part to repair a telescope or the camera mounted to it. Observatories had lots of "one-of-a-kind" parts. If something broke, you couldn't order it out of a catalog. You had to make it on site. He loved doing that—it made him feel like MacGyver.

They moved into a handling area even larger than the first. It also had a large, garage door, this one two stories tall. At one end of the room stood an enormous blue tank, almost as large as an efficiency apartment. The top was a bell-shaped dome and the bottom was a flat, pie-plate shaped cart that rolled on train-like wheels.

"What's that?" asked Dorothy.

"That's our aluminizing chamber," explained Kendra. "Telescope mirrors are coated in a fine, even coat of aluminum to make them reflective." Kendra glanced at Mike. "Want to explain the rest?" she asked with a smile.

The women looked at him expectantly.

Mike cleared his throat. "It's actually a vacuum chamber. When it's closed, all the air is sucked out." He walked over and pointed to a series of coils inside. "Aluminum is superheated and it condenses on the surface of the glass in a very even coating." Kendra gave him a quick nod of approval.

Just like riding a bicycle, he thought. He'd done some reading in advance to bone up on the mechanics, but he was relieved that it was all coming back to him.

"How often do you have to coat the mirrors?" asked Amelia.

"About every two years," said Kendra. "We try to keep water and condensation off the telescopes, but perfection's impossible when you expose them to the elements. Eventually, the aluminum oxidizes."

Mike pointed to a door in the room's inner, rounded wall. "This is the telescope pier. We'll find Dr. Burroughs in here." He opened the door and turned on the light. They entered a large cylindrical space. A round, Greek temple-like structure dominated the space. They faced a locked iron door with the single word "Burroughs" inscribed above it. Pillars stood around the crypt's perimeter, supporting a roof reminiscent of an observatory dome. Five stories above the crypt was the base where the telescope was mounted.

Dorothy stepped close to the structure and looked at a brass plaque mounted on the door. "Robert Burroughs," she read. "Born 1885. Died 1972." She turned around. "You said he was observing when he died. The man was like eighty-seven years old. That's devotion to your work!"

"Absolutely," said Amelia. "From what I've read, nothing made him prouder than seeing this observatory built on Carson Peak."

"Imagine being born in the nineteenth century and witnessing all those changes and advancements in science.

How remarkable it must have been to him," Kendra added in a reverent tone.

The four of them stood silent for a moment, each lost in his or her own thoughts, until Mike opened the door behind them and they filed out. They took the elevator to the second floor. Stepping into the warehouse-like room, Mike remembered it was filled with old supplies, including teletype machines and the reel-to-reel tape decks that used to stand beside the old computers. A set of shelves contained now-ancient computer monitors. Obsolete instrumentation occupied another shelf.

"It's like a museum of antique computer equipment," commented Dorothy.

"They hold onto it because every now and then they find something useful they can cannibalize," Kendra said as she ushered them into the elevator to the next level.

The door opened onto an orange-carpeted hallway illuminated by fluorescent lights. Kendra's brow furrowed and she turned to the visiting astronomers. "Why don't you go on up to the control room and get settled in. Mike and I just need to finish making our rounds." She pointed to the elevator controls. "The console floor is at the top, labeled 'C.' Send the elevator back to us here on the third floor."

"Sounds great," said Amelia. "See you in a few minutes."

Mike and Kendra stepped off the elevator and continued their rounds. Mike remembered that this level contained the original living quarters for the observatory but it was used for storage now. He couldn't help feeling like he'd stepped into an abandoned missile silo after some apocalypse. They came to a kitchen that clearly hadn't been used for years. Beyond that, they found a recreation room with an old console television, a Ping-Pong table, and a pool table with worn felt. Mike remembered that this dormitory space had been abandoned in the 1980s because the engineers realized the heat from the rooms prevented the telescope from getting the best possible images.

He'd also heard stories of people seeing things on this level. Old Sam Baylor, a technician who'd retired the year he started, told him about the time he saw a shadowy figure standing at the end of the hall. He called out to the figure but it didn't respond. It just stood there. But as he began walking toward the shadow, it backed into a darkened doorway before he got close enough to see who or what it was. When he reached the doorway and turned on the lights, nobody was there. What was even weirder, he'd told Mike, were the sudden cold chills he felt when he reached the spot where the figure had been standing.

At the time, Mike thought it was just Sam's imagination. Too many years cooped up in the observatory could lead to some wild notions. Mike had prided himself on his rational, scientific training. He wasn't given to belief in the paranormal, but then he'd started seeing shadows and hearing strange squeaks and thumps too. Even though he kept telling himself that ghosts don't exist, he couldn't help wondering if there was *something* there. The night he saw the apparitions of the dinosaur creature and the coyote confirmed it in his mind. *Just because you can't rationalize it, doesn't mean it doesn't exist.*

Mike wondered why the lights were on as he followed Kendra into a corridor where a set of doors lined the right-hand wall. These were the old dorm rooms. A sliver of light shone under a door at the end of the hall.

He and Kendra approached quietly. From within, they heard a strange animal-like grunting. They both turned to each other. Mike couldn't help but think about the coyote. Kendra rocked on her feet as though deciding whether or not to press on.

After a moment, she reached down and turned the handle. The door creaked open.

Stan Jones sat at a desk similar to the one in Mike's room, his hands in his lap, his back to the door. His pants were down around his ankles and he was staring at a magazine. Even from the doorway, Mike could see a photo of a busty, naked woman, her legs spread wide.

Kendra cleared her throat. Stan jolted, and then was suddenly still.

"Aren't you supposed to be at the 2.5-meter tonight?" she barked.

"Uh . . . yeah . . . but it's an engineering night. There's no hurry." Stan's voice was hoarse. Doing his best to be nonchalant, he reached down and tried to pull his pants up. He stood slightly, revealing his bare, hairy ass for a moment before he brought the pants up to his waist. Finally, he turned around, his face as red as a tomato.

"You know, no one's supposed be in here during observing hours," said Kendra.

Stan swallowed hard. "S-sorry about that. I didn't think you'd check this floor on your walk-around. I never do."

"Be that as it may," said Kendra, clearing her throat. "I think you better get back to work."

Stan nodded, his head bobbing like an apple in a water barrel. He took a step toward the door. Almost as an afterthought, he scooped up his magazine and brushed past Mike and Kendra.

"I'm bringing my camera on rounds next time. If I catch you again, Jerome will get pictures," Kendra called after him.

"Hey, don't forget to send the elevator back up," called Mike. He and Kendra shared a laugh as the door at the end of the hall banged shut.

"What is it about this place that attracts people like Stan and Roscoe?" Kendra asked, shaking her head. "I'm glad Roscoe's gone . . . At least Stan isn't dangerous." She cast a glance down the hall after him. "I don't think."

Mike sighed. An observatory like Carson Peak hired the best and the brightest, but all too often, brilliance and eccentricity went hand-in-hand. Roscoe would have been tolerated if he were merely a curmudgeon. The problem was his alcoholism. Mike hoped Jerome could intervene with Stan's impulse control issues before they became something darker.

They made their way down the hallway, shutting off lights as they went. They reached the elevator just as the doors opened again.

The next level they came to held the telescope drive's oil pumps, plus breakers for most of the telescope's systems. Mike pointed to a set of air cylinders he didn't remember seeing before. "Oh yeah," said Kendra. "This is part of the new primary mirror air support system they installed a year ago. We get much better image quality than we did before."

Convinced everything was in order, they continued upward, past three more levels, stopping and making sure the lights were out. "Big as this building is, I'm actually kind of surprised we caught Stan down on the third floor," commented Mike as they reached the console floor.

"Yeah, if he hadn't turned on the lights like an idiot, we wouldn't have even known he was there," said Kendra.

"You know, this isn't the first time it's occurred to me that someone could hide in this building for a very long time without anyone knowing."

Kendra nodded and the two entered the console room. There were two computers. The astronomers used one with two screens to control the instrument mounted on the telescope. The operators used the one with four screens to steer the telescope around the sky.

"Are we just about ready to go?" asked Amelia.

"Almost, we just need to fill the instrument with liquid nitrogen and open up," said Kendra, facing the bank of telescope control buttons. She turned off the lights out in the telescope enclosure, then activated another control that started the dome opening.

"Mind if we come out to watch while you open up?" asked Dorothy.

"Of course," Kendra replied. With that, they stepped out onto the darkened telescope floor. The dome motor, on time delay, rumbled to life and began rolling the shutter open like an enormous multi-story garage door. Soft twilight spilled in, illuminating the 5-meter telescope. The entire structure was six stories tall from the base, two floors below them, to the top. The opening dome, which was one story beyond the top of the telescope, made a rhythmic clunking as it rolled open. The enclosure was a huge open space, like a sports stadium. Kendra walked over to a set of controls mounted on the far side of the dome. She opened a set of louvers that allowed air to flow in during the night, regulating the temperature. Seeing how it was done, Mike went to the opposite side and opened a second set. A fringe benefit of the louvers was that they provided a great view of the mountaintop.

Mike's breath caught as he saw the deepening red of the western horizon. He'd never get bored of seeing that spectacular view. Maybe Amelia had been right about Burroughs. He'd died doing something he loved, photographing the stars.

There are worse ways to go.

The image of Wallerstein's bloodied corpse flashed before his eyes. He swallowed hard. It had taken him a while to get over the astronomer's death. But now that he was back, those images felt fresh and raw. He'd have to deal with it, or it would haunt him the rest of his days.

He climbed down a small staircase mounted to the telescope's side that led to a cage just below the primary mirror. There Kendra filled the spectrograph camera with liquid nitrogen, reminding Mike to be careful around the liquid that could freeze skin on contact. The spectrograph allowed astronomers to study the chemistry of distant objects by breaking light up into its component parts. Once they finished servicing the instrument, the group returned to the control room.

"Do you remember the safety talk?" asked Kendra.

"Most of it," said Mike.

She printed out a sheet with information. Mike grabbed it and read off several bullet points to Amelia and Dorothy, indicating which areas were off limits, and stressing that they needed to carry a flashlight at all times.

Dorothy rolled her eyes. "What do they think we are, idiots?"

"No, but smart people forget themselves sometimes," said Mike. "Did you ever hear about Jim Murray?"

Dorothy shook her head. "I don't know that name."

"He was one of Dr. Burroughs's grad students when this place opened up," said Mike. "One night while he and two other students were working with Dr. Burroughs, he left without telling anyone where he was going . . . and never returned.

"What happened to him?" Dorothy's eyes widened.

"They found him the next day, two floors below. He'd wandered into a restricted area where the dome trucks are located . . ." Mike hesitated for a moment, recalling the first time he'd heard the story when he was in training. He would never want anyone on his watch getting caught in there.

"Dome trucks are the huge train-like wheels that allow this whole enormous dome to turn," Kendra stepped in to explain.

"Well, don't leave us in suspense," Amelia piped in.

"Murray got trapped in there," Mike continued. "The dome rolled right over him—50,000 tons of solid metal—"

"Sliced him right in half," interjected Kendra. "Blood all over. I've been down there. Still smells a little like a charnel house forty years later, although that could be my imagination."

Dorothy and Amelia gasped at the same time.

"They say Dr. Burroughs never forgave himself for letting his student investigate on his own," said Mike. "Always tell your operator where you're going." He pointed a flashlight at them. "Always carry one of these, and never go into an area that's off limits."

The women nodded and Mike felt reassured that they understood the danger. Exploration was tempting, but it could also get you killed.

CHAPTER 9

A man could get lost in these woods.

The thought flashed through Roscoe Perkins's mind as he hiked along an old Forest Service road he'd discovered years ago. The road had not seen use in some time. Stubby grass, fed only by spring runoff, grew between the tire ruts. Nevertheless, it provided a good view of the landscape as it sloped upwards toward the summit. He paused frequently and peered up into the trees and scrub for signs of caves.

Throughout the morning, he'd scrambled up the hillside looking for cave entrances, only to discover it was just two or three boulders that had fallen together making an archway of sorts. If he'd been hunting, he would have prized these finds. They would have left him obscured in shadow while he watched for prey, but they were useless to him on his current quest.

By the time the sun had climbed halfway to its zenith, sweat sheened Roscoe's forehead. Wiping his brow with a handkerchief, he smiled triumphantly when he spotted a hole in the mountainside. He climbed up and found timbers lying around the outside. Flicking on his flashlight, he gazed into the darkness. The hole ran at least a few yards in. He gulped some water from his canteen and pressed forward. Ten yards in, timbers shored up the roof. The walls revealed scrapes and scratches from pickaxes. At twenty yards, he came to a rock wall peppered with drill holes, most likely for sticks of dynamite. But whoever had dug this mine had eventually abandoned it, possibly running out of funds, or finding a more lucrative strike elsewhere.

Roscoe peered into the dark corners with his flashlight, but found nothing of interest. The cave was clearly manmade and too recent to contain any valuable Apache artifacts. He returned to the road and continued hiking.

An hour later, he stopped at a rock and dropped his backpack to the ground. Sweat drenched the front of his shirt. He pulled out a hip flask and took a swig of bourbon. With a contented sigh, he retrieved a sandwich from his pack and ate as he studied the area, searching for something, anything that looked even a little odd . . . And then, he saw it. A tree clinging to an outcropping at a precarious angle. Tall grass obscured the view and the tree's roots reached out into empty space. He shoved the last bit of his sandwich into his mouth and slung the pack over his shoulders as he scrambled up the hillside.

Let's see if I hit the jackpot.

As he pushed through the grass, he stumbled into the roots, breaking some of them off. He rubbed his head and realized that he'd found what he was looking for. He clicked on his flashlight and stepped inside the dry cave carved in dark, volcanic rock. As he shone his light around, the beam fell on various light-colored drawings. Some were abstract shapes, like spirals and jagged lines. Others looked like depictions of hunting parties with stick-figure people chasing animals.

The petroglyphs struck Roscoe as eerie. The animals were huge compared to the people, almost monstrous. Was the artist exaggerating—to show the prowess of the hunters? Was it truth or legend?

He followed the cave back farther into the mountainside. As he did, he realized the pictures always showed two hunters. Never any more, never any less. Watching, as though from a safe distance, was a lone female figure. Roscoe wondered whether the pictures showed a competition for the woman's attention.

A dozen yards more, the drawings stopped. He scanned the walls with his flashlight beam. Instead of hitting a back wall, the light seemed to be absorbed somehow, only penetrating the gloom a short distance. It wasn't dust or mist. If so, he would have seen the light beam.

The beam just vanished.

He took a few cautious steps toward the gloom. The flashlight began to flicker, and the light went from bright white to rusty brown, as though it were dying. He removed his pack and fished around for fresh batteries. When he turned the light on again, it remained weak, barely penetrating the darkness.

He took a few steps back and the light was strong again—stronger, because of the fresh batteries. He approached the gloom once more and the light dimmed. On a hunch, he opened up a side pocket of his backpack. There he carried an old-fashioned carbide lantern like the miners from Toledo used in the old days. He'd bought the thing from an antique store, figuring it might come in handy if he ran low on batteries.

He poured a small amount of carbide fuel into the base and added some water from his canteen. After screwing it back together, he applied a match to the gas outlet. It threw out a bright beam of light. He attached the lantern to a band on his hat. With a quick swig from his flask for courage, he took a few steps toward the void. The light didn't flicker like the electrical light, though the thick atmosphere still absorbed it. He licked his chapped lips and swallowed.

If he kept walking, it could either lead him to the end of his life or the end of his quest. Either way, he'd get out of debt. He chortled to himself.

After hooking the canteen to his belt, he pulled on the pack and stepped into his future . . .

Walking a short distance in the dense atmosphere, he paused to get his bearings. His head was swimming and he had to reach out to the wall to keep his balance. A faint thrumming noise sounded in the distance . . . Drums?

"What the hell . . . ?"

The drums grew louder, the farther he ventured. He shook his head, wondering if the fatigue mixed with those ancient Apache stories were getting to him. He stopped for a moment to wipe his brow and take another sip from his flask. He took three more steps—and nearly toppled over a drop-off.

"Fuck!" He fell back and started shaking. "Fuck! Fuck! Fuck!" No amount of money was worth this shit. He took off his hat and scratched his scalp. The payday would mean he wouldn't have to worry about a job or his mortgage for a long time. Hell, he could pay back his entire debt and make a fresh start. No. He had to keep going.

He shrugged off his pack, got down on his belly, and peeked over the side. He couldn't see how far down the cavern went, but he did see finger- and toeholds in the side of the cliff face. He pocketed his flask along with a bottle of water, and stashed his pack behind a rock.

Better take it easy if I want to make it out of this alive.

After a few minutes of careful descent, he gingerly put his feet down on the next level. Looking back up the cavern wall, he figured he'd gone down about eighteen feet. He realized he could have hung off the edge and dropped down with no problems, but he was glad for the divots in the rock, otherwise, he'd never be able to get back up.

He tried to get his bearings and suddenly the vertigo returned with a chaser of nausea. The drumming started up again, this time accompanied by a flute. He took a sip of water instead of bourbon, and slowly scanned his surroundings. He was in a small chamber. Pots and baskets containing pungent herbs sat atop an altar-like rock. A depression in the wall held a disk, about the size of his palm. His light beam reflected back to him, bouncing off the polished gold medallion—except for two black stones set in the golden disk. Those black eyes.

It had been one thing to see a drawing of the creature in Vassago's book. It was another thing to see the talisman in person. He could feel the evil emanating from it. It made him physically ill. Hot bile rose in the back of Roscoe's throat. For a moment, he thought he would vomit the sandwich he'd eaten earlier. Everything about the disk and its raptor-like image repulsed him, made him want to turn around, climb out of the chamber, and get the hell out of Dodge.

But what about his debts? The Apaches had taken his car and threatened to take his house. He was up shit creek thanks to those Indians. Not to mention Jerome Torres, who'd fired him and forced him, literally, between a rock and a hard place. If that damned Indian had been there, Roscoe would have punched him.

With a force of will, Roscoe swallowed the hot bile and stepped toward the talisman. He reached out, to grab hold of it. Strangely, the air around the amulet was as thick as mud, and he had to force his hand through the ooze to get to the artifact. As soon as he touched it, a searing heat burned his hand. Steam rose around the talisman as he jerked his hand back, blowing on it to cool it off. He was determined though, and reached out again, but this time a sharp pain pierced his stomach. Howling in agony, he fell to his knees, holding his head as he tried to calm down. The pain was unbearable and he vomited violently. The throbbing in his head matched the drumming. *Thump. Thump. Thump.* The flute echoed around the chamber, screeching like a murder of crows. All he could see were flashing lights as the world spun out of control.

And then there was only darkness.

The room was pitch-black.

The only light came from the soft glowing numbers on the clock radio. In a burst of sound, it kicked on, mid-song. Something about a broken-hearted cowboy wanting just one more dance with a blue-eyed gal.

With a groan, Mike stretched and switched it off. "Sorry, cowboy. You're never gonna get that dance." High in the remote wilderness, it seemed the only radio choices were country music, conservative pundits, and the higher-power stations across the border in Juarez playing Mariachi music.

He blinked, just registering that it was one in the afternoon—a little earlier than he would have liked to get up, but Jerome wanted to meet with him before his shift.

Mike clicked on the bedside lamp, crawled out of bed, and made his way to the shower. After toweling off a few minutes later, he picked up the phone and called Bethany. She answered with a sunny hello. He missed being physically close to her vibrant spirit.

"Doctor's appointment went well," she said. "The baby's healthy and growing as expected."

He felt a twinge of guilt that he'd forgotten today was the day of the appointment—the first he'd missed—no doubt there would be others. He forced himself to sound cheerful. "That's great."

"How's the job going?"

"Getting the hang of things again. It's strange being back, but also familiar." He would never tell her about hitting the coyote on the drive up. Nor, that it seemed to vanish into thin air. He didn't want to worry her. Hell, he just wanted to forget it ever happened.

They discussed plans for the coming break. Bethany went through their to-do list with enthusiasm. He'd never known anyone who loved to-do lists as much as Bethany.

"Oh, I've been pricing cribs too. I'll email you the list."

"Okay, hon. I'm looking forward to putting it together, once we get the nursery done. He was just as excited as she was about the baby's room. They were planning a Milky Way Galaxy mural. It was only fitting, since they were both astronomy geeks.

"It's going to be a beautiful room . . ." Bethany seemed to hesitate for a moment. "Mike, are you really doing okay?"

"Yeah, I'm fine." It was sort of a lie and sort of the truth. What happened to Wallerstein was just an unfortunate and tragic accident. And had nothing to do with his vision or the apparition. Two separate events. He had a job to do and a wife and baby to care for.

"Everything is fine, hon," he repeated. "I promise." Was he trying to reassure her or himself? He didn't know the answer to that but the only way for him to get over his shaky feelings about that day was to just move forward and get on with things. Life was going to be full of ups and downs. Tragedies and happy times. And he had a lot of happy times to look forward to.

CHAPTER 10

"Is it all coming back to you?"

"I'm remembering more than I thought I would."

Jerome raised his eyebrows at Mike's flat tone. "You sound like that's a bad thing."

"Not at all." Mike cracked a self-conscious grin as he got up and put his empty cereal bowl in the sink. "I suppose I've gotten used to working at home on my own schedule. Waking up with sunshine streaming in through the window . . . Making a batch of blueberry pancakes . . . Going to work in my boxers . . ."

The corner of Jerome's mouth twitched. "TMI, buddy."

Mike laughed. "Sorry, Boss." He opened the cupboard and grabbed a travel mug. "Seriously, it's strange being away from Bethany, especially now that she's expecting." He reached for the pot of fresh coffee.

Jerome nodded thoughtfully. "I remember how it was when Kendra was pregnant with Derek."

Mike read the understanding in Jerome's eyes. Jerome got it. That feeling of needing to protect the woman you love and your unborn child. To be physically close, not hundreds of miles away.

They left the kitchen and stopped at the electronics and instrument lab. Mike looked around at the circuit boards stacked on wooden shelves. A workbench with a swivel light held precision tools, a voltmeter and an oscilloscope.

"As you know, this used to be Roscoe's office. This is where you'll find Stan most of the time once you're trained up."

Mike noticed a poster with a bikini-clad model leaning against a Corvette. He suppressed a snort—definitely Stan's office.

Jerome arched an eyebrow, but didn't say anything. Instead, he led the way to a storage room that housed the first aid supplies, including an Automated Electronic Defibrillator, oxygen, and other items for emergency care in a remote wilderness. "How well do you remember your first aid training?" asked Jerome.

"I could use a refresher," admitted Mike. He didn't want to be caught off guard if something should happen on a shift.

"We'll get that scheduled as soon as possible." With that, Jerome led Mike outside. The sky was a deep blue and a light breeze whistled through the branches of the tall pines. Mike breathed in the fresh air, enjoying the birds chirping and small animals rustling through the undergrowth. He'd forgotten how peaceful it was. One of the reasons why he'd loved working here was because of the setting. Mother Nature certainly flourished here. It was good to remember that.

As they strolled to the 2.5-meter, Mike noticed the paint had faded and peeled over the last two years. They stepped into the instrument handling facility area on the lower level.

Jerome led the way upstairs and down the hall into the control room. It struck Mike how little the room had changed since he last operated the telescope. There were new computers and monitors, but the arrangement was nearly identical, including some of the books that lined the shelves on the wall.

As they made their way to the door that led into the telescope enclosure, Mike hesitated.

Jerome stood in the doorway and winked. "It's broad daylight. I don't think we'll see any ghosts."

"Yeah, I know, man." Mike chuckled, clasping his hands behind his head. "Sorry, last time I was here . . . " Those deep black eyes that absorbed all light, mesmerizing him, as though they were trying to pull the very soul from his body. He took a step backwards.

"Listen Mike, I want to tell you something that I think will help."

Mike nodded, waiting for Jerome to continue.

"My grandfather found your vision fascinating. You see, the Apache elders believe whenever ground is broken around here, it weakens the portals to other realms. When you worked here, the elders had not yet blessed the building." Jerome let the door close and dropped into one of the control room chairs.

Mike took a seat as well. "How exactly would a blessing have kept me from seeing those things?"

"Blessing might not be the right word, or maybe it's just not strong enough for what goes on in our culture." Jerome leaned back in his chair and crossed his right leg over his left. "Have you heard the Apache creation story?"

Mike shook his head.

Jerome pressed on. "According to this ancient story, White Painted Woman came to this world through a portal with her sons, Child of the Water and Killer of Enemies. When they arrived, they discovered evil monsters. There were several, but one of the worst was *Bindáayee'ighání*, Great Owl. In some versions of the legends, Child of the Water and Killer of Enemies slay the owl creature. In other versions, they simply trap him on the other side of a mystical portal. The elders say the final confrontation with Great Owl happened right here on Carson Peak."

Mike laughed. "I've always thought of owls as wise and peaceful," he paused for a moment, not wanting to offend Jerome's heritage. "Whatever it was I saw, was no owl. It was more like a demon from Hell."

Jerome was unfazed by Mike's words. "*Bindáayee'ighání* literally means 'He Who Kills With His Eyes.' I don't really know why my people call him 'Great Owl.' Maybe he shares a few features, and owls have always been ill omens for my people, but according to the stories, I think 'demon from Hell' is a much more apt description."

"So, how is any of this supposed to make me feel better about working in this building?" asked Mike. "Presuming, of course, I believe your creation story more than anyone else's."

"As I said, anytime people dig into the earth around here, the portals are weakened. The blessing of the medicine man re-seals the portals and assures that whatever is trapped on the other side stays there."

Mike sipped his coffee and considered Jerome's words for a moment. "So you believe all this stuff?"

"I've heard these stories my whole life and it's hard for me to deny that there's a certain mystical quality in these mountains."

Jerome leaned forward. "I don't know if these stories are literal truth, but I believe there is *some* kind of truth behind them."

"I'm sure there is," said Mike, nodding. "Your ancestors came into these woods and found mountain lions, bears, and who knows what else—maybe some big-ass, wicked owl. They had to kill some of these creatures to survive . . . but I have a hard time believing there's more to it than that."

"Look, the energy in this building feels different since the blessing—and that's something I do know."

Mike closed his eyes and blew out a breath. "Maybe."

Jerome stood and went to the door. "Mostly, I want you to know that I don't think you're crazy. Whether or not you saw something doesn't matter. What does matter is that you tried to help Ron Wallerstein when he ran off the road. That shows a caring and conscientious person and I'm glad to have someone like you up here on the mountain."

"Thanks man, I appreciate that."

"Over the years, I've come to learn that being a technical wizard isn't the only thing that makes you a good fit here. If you don't care about people, you shouldn't be operating these telescopes." With that he stepped into the enclosure.

Mike stood, and was about to follow Jerome when something flashed in his peripheral vision. In the next moment, a shadow of a beak swooped at him. He gasped and stepped back, lifting his arm to protect his head. And then he saw what it was . . . a moth flitting in a beam of light.

"Get a grip, man." Taking a deep breath, he followed Jerome into the next room. The 2.5-meter was spindlier than its larger cousin on the other side of the observatory grounds. Although the telescope itself seemed much more advanced, Mike couldn't help but look at all the broken tiles on the enclosure's floor. He knew they were broken from years of handling heavy instruments plus being subjected to extreme cold during the winter months. In his mind's eye, he saw the talons of a great beast tearing up the tiles. He gave himself another mental shake and focused on Jerome as he pointed out the changes around the telescope, including various new instruments.

Later, as they walked along the path to the office building, Mike regained his sense of calm. He came to the conclusion that the only demons he'd witnessed were his own. The sun was shining, the birds were chirping. It was a beautiful day. "You know, I think the site does seem more peaceful," he said.

"Huh, what?" Jerome blinked, and looked around as though distracted from a thought.

"I was just saying, I think you're right that the site does seem more peaceful."

Jerome's brow creased, as though worried, but he smiled reassuringly and patted Mike on the shoulder. "Glad to hear it. I figured all you needed was a little time to get your bearings."

The words sounded like an afterthought to Mike. Strange, given the time Jerome had just spent giving him a pep talk. Was there something else to all of this that Jerome hadn't told him?

As they stepped into the kitchen they found Kendra waiting for them. "Oh good, I was just about to call around for you," she said.

"Why, what's up?" asked Jerome, concerned.

"I just got a call from your grandfather. He's not feeling well. Sounds like he should go see a doctor."

Jerome placed his hands on his hips. "Anything serious?"

Kendra shook her head. "I don't think so, but would you mind taking off early to watch Derek? You may need to find a babysitter for tomorrow as well."

"Sure," said Jerome. "Let me just check a couple of things and I'll take off." He shook Mike's hand. "I'm glad you're back."

"Me too," said Mike, believing it this time.

Jerome disappeared into his office, while Kendra sat back down, and wrote something in her notepad. Mike lifted the coffee pot from the warmer to refill his travel mug. "He seems pretty worried. He's really close to his grandfather, isn't he?"

Kendra nodded. "He is, and so is Derek, but it's more than that, I think."

"Oh, how so?"

She flipped her notebook closed and slipped her pen through the spiral, clipping it to the wire. "Mateo's one of the few elders left in this area. When he's gone, there won't be too many folks left who remember the old language and all the old stories," said Kendra.

"How old is Mateo?"

Kendra laughed and shrugged. "You know, I'm not really sure. I don't even know if Jerome knows."

A few moments later, Jerome emerged from his office and gave Kendra a quick kiss.

"Give me a call when you get home, let me know how your grandfather's doing."

"Will do," said Jerome, already heading out the door.

The acrid smell of vomit woke him up.

Roscoe's eyes cracked open . . . How long had he been out? Minutes, hours, or days? His carbide lantern had not gone out, so he guessed it couldn't have been long. He struggled to his hands and knees and crawled away from the altar rock, wincing as his red and throbbing hand scraped the gravel through his glove. If he touched the talisman again, he'd get walloped by whatever voodoo magic was protecting it. He needed something to grab it. Unfortunately, his backpack was on the upper level of the cavern. Taking a deep breath he reached up the back wall and with a grunt, pulled himself up. Scraping his feet into the lower crevices he reached up and grasped the toeholds above him. At the top, he realized the same non-reflective atmosphere that obscured the back of the cave also kept him from seeing the exit. All he saw was a bright light from the cave's mouth and the shadows of moving figures. Someone else had discovered the cave. Roscoe doused the lantern, hoping no one had seen him.

He heard words in Spanish, followed by the *thwack* of skin on skin. One of the shadow figures dropped. A piteous wailing arose—a man begging for his life. Two shots sounded in quick succession followed by a thud.

"Let's get the fuck out of here!" Were the words Spanish or English? Roscoe blinked, uncertain. It didn't matter. He understood them clearly. Shoes scraped sand and sent rocks clattering. Twigs snapped and car doors slammed. A moment later, an engine roared to life. Gravel sprayed and a vehicle zoomed away.

He wasn't sure how long he waited. His arms burned, hanging onto the rock wall, and his right hand screamed in pain. No shadows moved in front of the cave's mouth. All was quiet. Roscoe finally pulled himself up and over the edge. He passed his pack, and moved out of the strange gloom toward the opening of the cave. Cautiously, he reached into his pocket and pulled out his flashlight. He turned it on, casting eerie shadows on the walls.

The first thing his light fell on was a pyramid of white bricks. A moment later, Roscoe realized they weren't bricks at all, but plastic bags filled with white powder—cocaine!

"Holy shit!" he shouted before clapping his burned hand over his mouth. A shock of pain traveled up his arm and he yelped. Sweeping his light around, his beam landed on a man's body, slumped over. His open eyes stared up at Roscoe in silent accusation. Two neat holes, like a second set of eyes were drilled side by side in the man's forehead. Rivulets of blood streamed out, trickling like twin streams. Execution style murder, a mountain of drugs—these were no small-time dealers. This was the work of a cartel.

Roscoe turned his light back toward the pyramid of cocaine. Vassago had offered him a small fortune for the amulet down below. He looked at his red and blistered hand. An even bigger fortune lay before him—one that wouldn't scorch him or make him puke his guts out.

He eased his way to the cave's entrance. The knee-high grass between the wheel ruts had been flattened. By climbing up to the cave, breaking off roots, and flattening grass, Roscoe must have made the cave's entrance visible from the road. How else would members of a drug cartel have found this place? He took a deep breath as another wave of nausea roiled through him. Damn! If he'd been hiking on the road when those killers had come along, he might have ended up like the stiff behind him.

Carson Peak was only two hours from the Mexican border and U.S. Border Patrol agents frequently scoured the roads looking for people illegally transporting drugs. Someone must have found the abandoned Forest Service road on a map and decided to look for a place to hide the coke until a pick-up could be arranged. He wondered what the dead guy had done to get whacked. Well, he wasn't about to find out.

He knew they'd come back for it. But how much time did he have? That was the question.

That's when Roscoe noticed the sun's position. It sat just above the eastern horizon and light poured directly into the cave. He'd discovered the cave just before noon. The sun should have been high overhead, or behind the mountain. How long had he been in the cave? A day? More? If that were the case, the carbide fuel of his lantern should have been exhausted. He took his cell phone out of the thigh pocket of his cargo pants and tapped it. It was dead.

He stepped out of the cave and looked up the road. He could just see the white dome of the 5-meter enclosure above the treetops—a virtually empty skyscraper in the middle of nowhere. A person could hide in there for days or weeks without being seen. He quickly weighed his options: Vassago could get Roscoe out of debt, allowing him to find a job someplace else, but his life wouldn't be much improved. On the other hand, if Roscoe could find a buyer for that pyramid of cocaine—even a few kilos—he could move to the Caymans, and lounge at some beach bar for the rest of his life surrounded by hot babes in bikinis. Plus, he wouldn't have to climb back down and face whatever evil juju was protecting that amulet.

Roscoe cracked a grin and rubbed his stubble-roughened jaw with his good hand. Damn! That fucking amulet may have brought him some good luck after all.

CHAPTER 11

"Die, fucker!"

Carlos Fuentes thumbed the controller, sending a hail of digital bullets at a shambling zombie. Blood and gore splattered and the creature fell to the ground.

"You got the zombie, but the queen is mine!" Carlos's brother, Ricardo, sent his character, who he called Little Ricky, up a staircase, and kicked open a door. As Ricky raised his weapons, a zombie dropped from above and impaled him through the heart. Ricardo groaned and dropped the controller to the floor.

Carlos laughed at his brother's demise. His brother was two years younger, tall and slim. Carlos, on the other hand, was shorter but big and beefy. He'd tried making it as a boxer but he always forgot to take a dive when his uncle told him to, and other times he would take the dive when his uncle told him not to. It was confusing. But it didn't matter in the end. In one brutal match, his opponent smashed his face in, and he couldn't remember if he was supposed to dive or not. His uncle decided he'd be better off working directly for him, and he could bring Ricky along, too. After all, they were the only sons of his beloved sister Maria Guadalupe, now gone from this world the last four years, God rest her soul. Carlos sent his character—named Montoya after a bad-ass vampire slayer from one of his favorite movies—up the stairs and through the door, firing a hail of bullets.

Several loud bangs resounded at the front door of the brothers' house in Alamogordo.

"Think we oughta get that?" asked Ricardo.

"Nah, I'm just about to win this." Montoya rounded a corner to face ten more zombies. The queen sat on a throne behind them. She stood and hurled fireballs at him.

Again, the banging sounded from the door. "Open up! Police!"

"Jesus, Carlos! It's the cops."

"Relax," said Carlos. "There ain't nothin' here and I want to get the queen."

Another round of banging sounded. There was a pause as Carlos continued to blast zombies to bits while evading the queen's fireballs. He aimed at the queen and was just about to fire when something heavy crashed into the door.

"Fuck!" yelled Carlos as the queen got Montoya with a fireball.

Just then, the police smashed through with a handheld battering ram. Three uniformed officers rushed in, aiming pistols at the brothers. Carlos and Ricardo stood, their hands in the air. "Hey! You got no right to bust in here!" shouted Carlos.

Two of the officers strode forward, whirled Carlos and Ricardo around, grabbed their arms and cuffed them. A *pendejo* in a suit stepped forward and pulled a piece of paper from his pocket and held it under Carlos's nose.

"This gives me all the right I need."

It was a warrant from the District Court in Las Cruces, granting the U.S. Drug Enforcement Agency the right to search the house in coordination with the Alamogordo Police Department. He dropped it on the mahogany table between the recliners where Carlos and Ricardo had been sitting. The warrant identified the *pendejo* as Agent William McCarty.

The cops fanned out, opening and overturning drawers. Finding nothing in the living room, they moved on through the rest of the house. If a door was closed, they kicked it open. Porcelain rattled and clanked as someone looked in the toilet tank. Meanwhile the zombie queen on the television cackled uncontrollably in her victory over poor Montoya.

The DEA Agent looked at the large curve-screened TV and grinned. "'Zombie Massacre' on the latest X-Station console. That's pretty high-end gear for a coupla guys without jobs livin' in a hole in the wall in Alamogordo, New Mexico." He rubbed his hand along the television as though stroking a lover. "I can't even afford one of these for my kids. Care to tell me where you got this one?"

"Eat shit," barked Carlos.

"It was a gift," sneered Ricardo.

"What? Rich uncle down in Juarez?" mocked the *pendejo*. He dropped into one of the leather recliners and propped his feet up. He looked around, ticking off items. "Blu-ray player, awesome sound system and sub woofers." He sprung from the chair and strolled over to a bar against one wall. He lifted a bottle of top-shelf tequila. "I got to taste some of this once down in Juarez. Would have set me back two months' pay to buy a bottle."

"What's it to you?" asked Ricardo.

"Justice Department might be interested to know about your uncle, especially if he got rich working for the Equis." Agent McCarty referred to one of the large drug cartels in Mexico.

A uniformed officer stepped up to McCarty and pulled the agent aside. Carlos strained to hear what he was saying.

"Place is clean," whispered the officer. "Not so much as an ounce of pot."

McCarty heaved a deep sigh and strolled over to the brothers. His face mere inches from theirs, he whispered, "Looks like today is your lucky day, amigos." McCarty pinned the brothers with his gaze as the other officer unsnapped their handcuffs.

"Hope to see you again soon." McCarty stepped back and motioned for the men to follow him out.

"Hey," called Carlos. "Who's gonna clean up this mess?"

Agent McCarty held his hands out to the side while walking backward. "Not my problem." He paused to slip on his sunglasses and flash a wicked grin. "Since you have no jobs, it'll give you something to do."

"You can bet your ass I'm gonna report you," said Ricardo.

"You go ahead and do that, son." Agent McCarty climbed into the squad car and rolled down the window. "I look forward to having a good laugh about it with my supervisor." With that, the officers drove off.

Carlos whirled around and kicked the leather recliner. The zombie queen's cackle resounded on the video loop. In a fit of temper, Carlos picked up the remote and threw it at the television.

"Careful, bro, you'll break our sweet new TV." Ricardo steadied the front door back on its hinges.

"What's the big deal, Ricky? Our uncle will just buy us a new one." Carlos switched the TV off, leaving them in silence. He felt around the back where Agent McCarty had run his hand. He didn't feel anything unusual at first, so he pushed the TV away from the wall to get a better look, trying not to let it tip and fall over. He saw the usual set of silver cable ports. He didn't even know what most of them did. What he did know was all but one had labels. He yanked at an unlabeled port and found it came off in his hand—a small, silver wireless microphone. He dropped it to the floor and smashed it under his boot. "I hope whoever was listening just got a real bad headache."

"Think we should check the rest of the house?" asked Ricardo.

Carlos rolled his eyes, wondering why his brother would ask such a dumb-ass question.

He put his finger up to his lips, gesturing for his brother to keep quiet and help him search.

Ricardo nodded in understanding and the two brothers made their way through the small house, picking up drawers and putting them back into their dressers. They didn't bother folding the few clothes they had, just chucked them in, after checking for microphones. They didn't have a landline telephone, just the cell phones they each carried in their pockets and those couldn't be tapped, their uncle made sure of that, by sending new phones every week.

In the bathroom, Carlos checked the toilet tank and found a microphone there. "Really?" He pulled it from the toilet and dropped it in the bowl. "Man I think those burritos really got the best of me." With that he released an explosive fart and flushed the microphone. "Assholes."

He returned to the living room and dropped onto the black leather recliner. "Find anything?" he whispered.

Ricardo shook his head. "I was just about to finish up in the kitchen." He disappeared around the corner. There was some clattering as he picked up a drawer and dropped the few pieces of cutlery they owned into it. The refrigerator door opened and closed again. A moment later, he appeared with two cans of beer. He tossed one to his brother, who caught it easily. Carlos popped the top and sucked the foam off.

Ricardo pulled another wireless mike from his pocket, dropped it to the ground and crunched it under his boot.

"Where'd you find that one?"

"In the fridge. Think we got them all?" asked Ricardo.

"In here at least," said Carlos. "I didn't see them touch anything but the TV. We probably got them, but we'll need to get Uncle's guys to come and do a clean sweep."

"So, how did the cops even get a warrant to search this place?" asked Ricardo. "You think it was that guy with the camera?"

Two days before, Carlos and Ricardo had smuggled a load of cocaine across the border from Juarez. They drove across the desert in their SUV to avoid the border agents and stashed the cocaine in a hidden cave up in the Sacramento Mountains. Their driver was a new falcon named Diego.

Falcons were the lowest ranked members of the cartel. Both Carlos and Ricardo were also "falcons," but had done their jobs well enough that if they saw this mission through, their uncle promised to promote them to hitman status. Then they'd only be one rung below the lieutenants, who had mansions in Juarez. While hiding the load of cocaine in the mountains, the new guy had brought out his cell phone.

When Carlos had confronted him, Diego had made some excuse about his girlfriend texting nude photos of herself. Carlos couldn't believe Diego had been able to get a signal and Ricardo had snatched the phone. That's when he'd noticed Diego had been snapping photos.

When Diego had rushed for the car to get away, Carlos leapt after him and shoved him to the ground. All the while, Ricardo had continued to page through the photos on the phone. Diego had recorded their faces, pictures of them holding kilos of coke, and photos of the location.

There was no doubt, Diego had been an informant and he had to die. They tied him up and put two bullets in his head. They left his body in the cave, knowing it would probably rot before anyone found him. They would return at a later date to retrieve the cocaine, when they got the all-clear from their uncle. Ricardo shuddered after the killing, but Carlos patted him on the shoulder and reassured him they were well on their way to being made men.

Carlos dreamed of sitting by a pool, served by a gorgeous woman as he took a big gulp of the beer and then wiped his mouth. "That guy was an informant and when he never called in, the cops got nervous and got a warrant to search our place."

"Do you think he sent out any of those photos he took?" asked Ricardo. "That could be bad for us if he did."

Carlos shook his head. "No signal up there. Besides, if he had, they would've already picked up the coke and arrested us."

Ricardo dropped into the identical recliner next to his brother's. He chugged his beer. Wiping his mouth, he looked around the room. "Do you think Tío Nesto set us up with a narc on purpose?"

Carlos narrowed his gaze. "What do you mean?"

"Nesto didn't get where he is by being dumb. Why would he send a new falcon with us? He would have sent someone more experienced with us. Ricardo took another swallow of beer. "Maybe Tío knew Diego was a narc and wanted to make sure we figured it out on our own and took care of him. Maybe this was like the big test before we're promoted." Ricardo set the beer down on the small end table next to him and put his hands behind his head, while pondering the thought.

"You know, there is one other possibility," said Carlos. "That guy may have been from a rival cartel like Los Niños or the Chávez Family. He could have been getting information to double cross us."

Ricardo's brow furrowed. "It's possible . . . but then how did the cops know to search here?"

"Well, if there's a rival cartel trying to get in on the action, they may have reported us to get us out of the way. Then when we're out of commission, they swoop in and steal the cocaine."

"You think so?" Ricardo shook his head.

"I dunno." Carlos shrugged and sipped his beer. "Either way, I think we should get that coke out of the cave before much longer. The cops think we have drugs somewhere, but they don't know where. We have to be careful, lay low for a coupla weeks, cuz the cops will have guys watching us, and the other cartel may also be looking for the stash. If that cocaine doesn't make it to Tío Nesto's buyer, we'll be dead for sure. Either the rival cartel will silence us, or our dear uncle will put us in our graves because we fucked up."

Ricardo shuddered and finished his beer in one gulp.

Carlos stared thoughtfully down at the tattoo on his forearm. It depicted a skeleton wearing a dress and headscarf, reminiscent of a horror movie incarnation of the Virgin Mary. It was Santa Muerte, Our Lady of the Holy Death. He looked up at the TV and the X-Station console, then snorted. At least the cops had left those items alone. They'd only ransacked the trashy stuff around the house. Like all good *Americanos*, they knew that wealth was precious and holy, just like Santa Muerte. Carlos held up his beer can. "To Lady Death, better to live well and die young than live long and die poor."

CHAPTER 12

Everything was going to be fine.

Mike hummed to himself as he puttered around the observatory kitchen, preparing breakfast on his sixth afternoon of work. His co-workers were good people, and the work was far more challenging than fixing a frozen keyboard. He was making a difference, helping researchers and students in their quest to understand the universe. Being back on the job reminded him of that. Aside from hitting the coyote on the way to work his first day back, there had been no strange encounters, no creepy noises he couldn't explain. He enjoyed the work, and though he missed Bethany, and missed being close to their unborn child, he felt more productive than he had in a long time.

Kendra emerged from the dormitory hallway just as Mike poured a cup of coffee and sat at the table. She scrambled two eggs and made toast in silence. Mike noticed she was pale, her features drawn.

"You doing okay?" he asked.

"I'm fine." She dumped the eggs on a plate and joined him at the table. "I'm just a little worried about Jerome's grandfather. He's been having these sudden, sharp headaches. Jerome finally talked him into going over to the medical center in Mescalero for an MRI."

"Yikes, that sounds pretty serious," said Mike. "Is he insured?"

Kendra nodded. "Yes, but there've been some big changes lately. That's why they're going over to Mescalero even though Alamogordo's closer. Mescalero's on tribal land, and the office staff is better equipped to deal with his insurance."

"Mescalero's a pretty small town, I'm guessing they don't have the best facilities," mused Mike.

"They have a lot of hand-me-downs from other hospitals, but he gets along better with the staff there." Kendra scooped up some of her eggs with the toast and took a bite. "Really, the hard part was getting him to agree to the MRI in the first place."

Mike's brow creased. "Why's that?"

"He didn't want to go. Kept insisting there was nothing wrong." Kendra shrugged. She lowered her voice, as though afraid someone would overhear. "At least he kept insisting nothing was wrong *physically*. He keeps going on about premonitions of danger . . ." She stopped short.

Mike wondered why she would feel the need to hide the details, and tried to lighten the mood. "What? You mean premonitions like Obi Wan Kenobi had when Alderaan was destroyed in *Star Wars?*"

"Something like that," muttered Kendra. She looked up at the clock. "Jerome should be back home within the hour. He'll call and let me know what he found out." After taking a few more bites, she leaned across the table. "Thing is, I'm not sure if I'm more worried about the possibility of a stroke or something like Alzheimer's." She shook her head. "It's hard enough with both of us working to make sure someone's available to watch Derek. If we have to take care of Mateo as well . . ."

"I see what you mean." As he finished his oatmeal, he wondered what he'd do in a similar situation. His own father had passed away when he was young. His mother lived with his older brother in California. He hoped Mateo was going to be okay. Not only for the old man's sake, but for Kendra and Jerome as well. He knew how challenging it was to get by on one pay check in this day and age, especially when you had a kid. Not to mention, if Kendra had to quit, it would mean longer work shifts until they found a replacement. A new supervisor would mean someone who didn't know or necessarily care about Mike's past with the observatory.

Mike got up from the table and brought his dishes to the sink. The kitchen phone trilled as he was washing up. Since he was closer to the phone, he answered it. "It's Jerome." He held out the receiver to Kendra. As she stood, he whispered, "Take your time. I'll go on up to the telescope and get everything ready for observing."

She mouthed *thanks* and took the receiver.

Mike went to his room and gathered up a few things he wanted at the telescope that night, before stepping outside. The wind was blowing harder than it had all week and a few clouds lingered around the mountaintop. They'd have to be mindful of the weather as the night progressed. Mike climbed into the observatory truck and drove up to the 5-meter enclosure. Once inside the building, he did his usual routine walk-around. He poked his head into the pier, and made sure the lights were out. "Good night, Professor Burroughs. Sleep tight," he said to the silent crypt.

He stepped into the elevator and switched the lights from white to red, casting an eerie glow around him. The dim, red lights helped observers adjust their eyes, when they stepped outside during the night to check on the weather. The elevator opened onto the next floor. Cold, black darkness greeted him. This was his nightly ritual. Making sure that all the lights were off on his slow climb up.

When Mike arrived at the control room, everything was quiet, as it should be. He turned up the lights, but the windowless chamber was as claustrophobic as a cave. Mike pushed the button that started the dome's enormous shutter rolling open—a process that would take five minutes—before he stepped out into the telescope enclosure.

A sliver of afternoon light entered through the opening dome and grew brighter as the shutter rolled back. The wind caused the building to rattle and creak more than it had earlier in the week. As the wind caught at the closed louvers, it sounded like an unearthly moan. The control room was near the telescope's primary mirror, but the mount extended two floors below. Mike went down the two flights of stairs to make sure oil and coolant both flowed properly.

As he reached the lower level, the hairs on the back of Mike's neck stood on end. He turned his head slightly, his peripheral vision making out a shadowy figure in the alcove behind him. The alcove where Dr. Burroughs's grad student, Jim Murray, had gone through the wrong door, only to be sliced in half by the dome trucks. He turned fully around, facing the alcove.

No one was there.

"Kendra?" His heart hammered in his ears. "Is that you?" The wind hit the louvers and moaned.

He shook his head, thinking his imagination must be playing tricks on him. He continued on to the gauges he'd planned to inspect. Everything was as it should be.

When he returned to the control room he got his second fright. Spying a shadowy form in the operator's chair, he cautiously made his way closer. The chair swiveled around and he saw who it was.

"You okay?"

"Yeah, great." Mike chuckled self-consciously. "Just didn't expect you here so soon."

Kendra raised her eyebrows at that.

Mike hesitated and then asked, "Were you out on the dome floor just a couple of minutes ago?"

"No, I just got here."

Mike nodded, trying to shake off that eerie feeling again. "How's Jerome's grandfather doing?"

"Apparently the MRI didn't turn up anything." Kendra chewed her lower lip.

"You still seem worried." Mike folded his arms.

Kendra shrugged. "Doctors can make mistakes even in the best of circumstances. Out in a small clinic like the one in Mescalero . . . Let's just say I'm not as reassured as I could be."

"Well, maybe a second opinion will help," he suggested as he started a pot of coffee, Amelia and Dorothy arrived for the final night of their observing run. The good weather meant they had obtained useful data. Kendra told them about the weather conditions and warned them the viewing might not be as good with the clouds and wind, but the visiting astronomers were unconcerned as they turned their attention to their flight home the next day.

Once the sun dropped below the horizon, Mike pointed the telescope to the first field of the night. It was a so-called planetary nebula—a ring of gas and dust that remained after a star's core collapsed. At the center was a white dwarf star, which faintly illuminated the star's discarded atmosphere. Amelia and Dorothy were conducting a series of stellar post-mortems, figuring out what happened to stars after they died.

Mike sipped coffee and thought it was fitting, especially given the ghost-like nature of the planetary nebulae.

"It's a little chilling to think that one day our star will end up like one of these planetary nebulae," mused Dorothy.

Goosebumps rose on Mike's arm. "Do you suppose this star had planets? Could there have been people living on them?"

Amelia released a wistful sigh. "I'd like to think if there were people, they were advanced enough to escape the star's final fate."

"But what if they didn't? How many billions of ghosts would be in that cloud, slowly drifting into space? What would happen to them?"

"Don't tell me you believe in ghosts," said Amelia.

"Some days, I'm not so sure." Mike flashed a nervous smile before returning to his work.

An hour into the night, Mike's coffee habit caught up with him and he excused himself to go to the restroom. Amelia and Dorothy were in the midst of a sequence of long exposures and Kendra had reclined on a couch at the back of the control room, reading a book.

The closest restroom to the 5-meter control room was down two flights of stairs, at the end of a long, dark hallway. Most observers preferred to ride the elevator to the restroom, but Mike appreciated the opportunity to stretch his legs.

The howling winds continued their assault on the building. As he returned from his errand, walking along the dark hall, a cold chill skittered up his spine. Footsteps, rounded the corner up ahead. Was Stan playing yet another prank? He continued forward, holding his flashlight out to see if he could discern someone lurking around the corner. As he got closer, his pulse quickened at the rasp of heavy breathing. If Stan was hiding around the corner, he'd beat the shit out of him. He reached the corner. The breathing grew louder and more menacing. Or was that just his nerves? He took a deep breath, stepped around the corner and flashed his light.

"Who's there?"

No one.

What the fuck?

Something whooshed past him. It wasn't the wind, there

were no windows there, and it wasn't a touch, just the delicate sensation of passing within a couple of inches of a person, which would be difficult in the narrow corridor. Mike took two more steps and his flashlight flickered and went out. "Damn." Standing in the pitch-black corridor he switched the flashlight on and off a couple of times, but it was dead.

Glancing up, he caught a faint glow. Had someone left a light on that should have been turned off? Mike cautiously approached the glow. What he saw was hard to define. It looked like dust motes swirling in a sunbeam on a lazy afternoon, except there was no clear light source. Just then, the motes swirled into an oval, as though someone had run their hand in a circle.

The oval grew more distinct, manifesting two hollows, like a pair of eyes, and a gash like a mouth. It opened as if to speak, but just at that same moment, the wind blew against the dome once more, unleashing another moan. A whoosh of air passed by as though someone had opened a door. And in the next moment, the ghostly face was gone.

Mike blinked. Nothing. Pitch black. It must have been some unseen light source and the strange airflow through the building. He quickened his pace back to the control room. Once there, he found that Amelia and Dorothy were ready to move on to their next target.

Relieved to perform a routine task, he pointed the telescope and found a guide star to assure precise telescope tracking. With an hour to kill, he opened a web browser and found a page about Carson Peak Observatory's history. Halfway down the page, he saw a familiar photo of Robert Burroughs with his distinctly egg-shaped, bald head, and an old-fashioned handlebar mustache. Nothing new there.

He then searched for ghost sightings at observatories, which led him to a video link. Two investigators had posted a series of videos of their ghost hunting. This particular haunting was at the old director's cottage of an observatory outside San Francisco.

Mike plugged in his headphones and started the video.

The investigators stalked through a darkened house with an infrared camera. Shadows loomed ahead.

"Are you here?" asked one of the investigators.

"Did you hear that?" the other asked.

The two men whirled. And right there, caught on camera, was a glowing swirl . . . like dust.

"Sweet Jesus!" called one of the investigators.

Mike leaned forward.

"Whatcha watching?" Mike jumped when a hand settled on his shoulder.

He looked up and saw Kendra.

"Since things are going well here, I think I might call it an early night if that's all right with you. That way I can get home and check on my boys."

"Yeah, that sounds fine," said Mike, trying to relax after his scare. He needed to calm down or he wouldn't be able to function. He had to stop thinking there was a ghost around every corner. It was an old building full of creaks and groans. And he shouldn't be looking for trouble online. There was all kinds of crap out there, with plenty of crazy stories about hauntings and demons, that had nothing to do with him doing a good job.

That's what he needed to focus on, his job, and saving money for his family and future. "We'll be fine." He hoped his smile was convincing. With all the things Kendra had to worry about, his wild imagination shouldn't be one of them.

CHAPTER 13

If Perkins were dead, Solomon Vassago would know.

The attorney drove a sleek black Cadillac down the narrow road from his Victorian manor house in Toledo. Half a mile along the main highway, he turned onto one of the town's few side streets and pulled up in front of Roscoe Perkins's house. The mailbox was full, and turn-off notices were hooked over the door handle. Several copies of the *Alamogordo Daily News* were strewn about the lawn. As he suspected, Perkins had gone on his errand and vanished. Five days ago, he'd sensed one of the portals had been unlocked, but afterwards, nothing, as though it hadn't been fully opened.

Vassago drove to the end of the short street, executed a smooth three-point turn, and returned to the highway. He passed the road leading to his house and continued to the Ore House Tavern. There, he stepped from the car and strode through the doors. It was early afternoon, after the lunch rush, so there were only a few patrons there. It was one of the few restaurants in Toledo, so it did fairly good business, and because of that, it was a good place to observe and gather information. Vassago slid into a corner booth at the back of the restaurant.

A few minutes later, a buxom waitress in a tight pink blouse dropped a menu on the table. "Can I get you something to drink?" She winked at him, flashing a come-hither smile. Vassago had seen that expression many times. A common tactic used by waitresses the world over to ensure a good tip.

"Coffee. Black," said Vassago, without lifting the menu.

"Would you like to order something to eat?" she asked.

Vassago folded his hands in front of him. "I'll think about it."

As she returned to the kitchen, Vassago eased back into

the shadows. He looked around the room. A family of out-of-state tourists chatted about their adventures over plates of hamburgers and fries. The mother appeared partly incensed and partly titillated by the restaurant's decor inspired by nineteenth century brothels.

Two local shop owners lingered over their chicken-fried steak specials, clearly not expecting much business on this weekday. A man with blood-shot eyes and a hungry, desperate look like Roscoe's came in and strode directly to the bar where he ordered a Jack and Coke. Vassago sensed the man had been up since early in the morning, working on a highway crew. The man liked his liquor, but he wasn't the type to go into debt over it.

Vassago's coffee arrived. "Can I bring you anything else?" asked the waitress.

"Not just now." Vassago pulled the cup closer. "Check back with me in half an hour if I'm still here."

"Sure thing." The waitress gave him a polite smile. Vassago sensed she preferred the tips from customers who ordered more. Well, he would leave her a generous tip. It always paid to be kind, especially when he might require information or assistance down the road.

Vassago sipped his coffee and continued to scan the room. Eventually, a pair of police officers entered the tavern. The waitress stepped up and took their drink order. A few minutes later, she placed glasses of soda in front of them. They scanned the menu. The waitress returned to Vassago's table. "Did you decide on anything, hun?"

"I'll have a piece of . . . apple pie and a coffee refill, please," said Vassago.

She disappeared into the kitchen and Vassago focused his attention on the officers.

"Alamogordo cops been calling again, today," said the tall, hefty officer in a low voice. "They been askin' me if I seen any SUVs up here. I tell 'em, we're in the mountains. Almost everyone has an SUV." They both laughed at that.

The officers ceased their conversation when the waitress passed them. She placed a thick slice of pie in front of Vassago and refilled his coffee cup. Vassago sat back and watched as she sauntered over to the cops. Her hand on her curvy hip, she leaned down between the two men, her blouse at the point of mutiny if not for the tiny silver button laboring to keep those ample breasts in their polyester prison. She earned herself a wink from the heavyset officer. They were clearly well acquainted. She took their orders and made her way back to the kitchen, swaying her bottom as she went, and holding the undivided attention of the two officers. When she was out of sight, the slim cop asked, "So, what exactly are those guys in Alamogordo after?"

"Apparently they got a tip about some . . . *snow* up in the mountains." The hefty officer cast a suspicious glance around to see who might be listening. Vassago took a bite of his pie, and leisurely scrolled through his iPhone. He knew they weren't talking about the kind of stuff that required a corn-cob pipe and a button nose.

"Sounds like their informant went AWOL."

The thin officer shook his head and rolled his eyes. "Don't those city boys know there's more than three thousand square miles of mountain terrain here? Short of having a lucky horseshoe stuck up our asses, how are we gonna find a missing narc and some powder?"

Vassago smiled at the notion of the police from a town with a population of 30,000 being referred to as "city boys," but they were when compared to Toledo's population of about 250.

"Yeah," said the first cop. "It sounds like they've been bugging the BLM rangers and the tribal police, too. They want us to keep on the lookout."

Vassago considered the odds of Roscoe Perkins encountering men trafficking cocaine. By pure random chance, it would be unlikely. However, men intent on doing evil could be drawn to one of the portals. If they happened to be there about the same time as Roscoe Perkins . . . well, that was just one more temptation for a money-hungry, booze-soaked desperado wandering the wilderness alone. If Perkins had somehow shifted his sights to drug trafficking, Vassago would have to deal with him. At least the attorney could now sense the portal's approximate location.

He savored the last morsel of pie, and took one final sip

of coffee. Pocketing his phone, he got up and slipped out as unobtrusively as he'd arrived.

The waitress's mouth dropped when she came to collect his dirty dishes. Tucked under the plate was a crisp, hundred-dollar bill.

"I'm going out." Mateo Torres grabbed his denim jacket from the closet.

"You had a busy day, yesterday, Grandfather," argued Jerome. "Why don't you stay in?"

Mateo shook his head and sighed. "I may be old, but I'm not fragile. I have things I need to do and people I'd like to see."

"Is this about the visions?" Jerome raised an eyebrow.

Mateo remained silent while he buttoned his jacket. "I need to find out if something is going on," he said at last.

"Grandfather?"

"Yes, my grandson?"

"We love having you here . . .You know that don't you?"

Mateo hesitated—Apaches tended to show respect rather than affection. After a moment, he reached out and patted Jerome on the back. "I know."

"Good." Jerome accompanied his grandfather to the front door. "But promise me you'll come back for dinner. Kendra's worried about you, too."

Mateo nodded, resigned. "All right. I'll be back, soon. I promise I'll be good." He hobbled down the steps to his old Chevy pickup and climbed in. The first time he turned the ignition, it belched out a black cloud of smoke. The second time, it kicked over, and he grinned as he pulled out of the driveway.

"My friend, we may be ancient but we are strong."

He followed the dirt road to the main highway. He didn't need a doctor telling him what was wrong with him. The sharp headaches he'd been having were no mystery. No illness or tumor. Someone was tampering with the portals where the monsters from the beginning of time were sealed. Those ancient stories were only partly true. As tribal elder, he knew the whole truth. The monsters weren't dead. They could never be killed. Only contained.

His grandson knew the old ways, but he didn't truly believe them. He sighed as he pulled into the Toledo Community Center. That was the problem with the younger generation. They thought too much about the future, and rarely about the past. Because of that, the past was doomed to repeat itself.

He enjoyed spending time with Jerome and Kendra, and young Derek was a joy. But as an elder in his community, he had a responsibility to others who needed guidance.

He parked his truck and eased his way out, chuckling to himself as he recalled how fast he could move as a young man. *We trade swiftness for wisdom.*

He waved at a youth named Santana Chino, a good kid whose family had fallen on difficult times. Santana had turned to drugs to escape a seemingly hopeless situation. Mateo had helped him to see that drugs were a poison to his warrior spirit. His heritage could help him reclaim the strength of his ancestors. Tattoos decorated Santana's arms and he wore his hair in a buzz cut. "How's it going?" called Mateo.

Santana grinned and waved back. "*Hola*, Chief. They say you've been seeing visions." Santana always called him Chief. "You sure you haven't been getting into that stuff I used to be on?"

Mateo shook his head at the young man. He enjoyed his quick wit and ready smile. A sign of a strong and nimble mind. "This ain't bad drugs." He hobbled over to the bench and sat down beside Santana. "Don't get me wrong, something bad *is* happening. I just haven't figured out what it is. All I can tell you is nothing's wrong with my brain."

"That's good to hear," said Santana.

"How are you doing?" asked Mateo. "Any new job prospects since we last talked?"

"I heard there's a developer putting in condos up by Ruidoso." Santana shrugged. "I was going to drive up there tomorrow and see if I could get a job."

"Good, good." Mateo nodded. "Have you put any more thought into applying to the university?"

"Man, I didn't even graduate from high school. How am I gonna get into college?"

"You got your GED," said Mateo. "All we have to do is boost your test scores and you'd be ready to apply. The tribe needs leaders and college can help you do that."

"I don't get it," said Santana, "I thought you were all about 'the old ways' and shit, why do you keep encouraging me to go to college?"

Mateo nodded thoughtfully. "Remembering the old ways and learning all you can are not mutually exclusive. You can do both. The challenge is figuring out how to blend the old wisdom with the action we need today. With your background in the old ways and a college education, you'd have the makings of a tribal leader."

"Get out of here!" Santana shook his head.

"Really, I believe in you." Mateo spoke with conviction. "You have the warrior spirit."

Santana blushed but broke into a grin, his pride overtaking any embarrassment.

Mateo smiled as he looked off toward the mountains, his eyes misting at the beauty of his home. He would do what was necessary to protect it. "I sense evil in the wind . . ." He sighed. "Have you seen or heard anything?"

Santana shrugged. "I don't have your super mojo or whatever, but . . ." He hesitated. "I saw a couple of guys I used to buy from driving around up here a few days ago—Carlos and Ricardo Fuentes. They're brothers who live in Alamogordo. They used to sell me pot before they moved on to heavier things. They disappeared a few months ago, but I just saw them the other day. I kept a low profile, but then again, they didn't look like they were trying to get anyone's attention. They looked like men on a mission."

"A mission?" asked Mateo. "What kind of mission?"

"Hell if I know," said Santana. "All I can tell you is whatever they were up to, it wasn't good. They used to tell me one of their uncles was a big shot in the Equis cartel."

Mateo ground his teeth. "Where were they going?"

"They drove out of town on the road to Nana's Ravine and Carson Peak."

Mateo didn't need to hear any more. He knew some of the sacred caves were in that area. Bad men connected with a cartel could easily cause a spiritual upheaval. He just hoped they'd done nothing more than stumble into one of the caves. Taking anything from the caves could prove disastrous.

Despite his worry, Mateo knew Santana would appreciate his reassurance and patted him on the back. "Good luck talking to the developer in Ruidoso. No matter how that turns out, please come talk to Jerome and me. We'll find a way to get you into the university down in Las Cruces."

"I will. Thanks, Chief . . . for everything." Santana reached out and shook the old man's hand. He made his way to his 1989 red Dodge Ram, got in and waved at Mateo as he turned onto the main road.

That boy will be fine. Look at how he takes care of that old truck.

Santana had saved up doing handyman jobs for the locals to buy the truck from a friend of Jerome's. Mateo smiled, feeling hope swell in his chest for the young man.

He turned his gaze toward Carson Peak, his smile fading as he thought about what Santana had told him. The clouds shifted, hiding the sun from view, and a gust of wind blew toward him. He heard its whisper.

Following the sound, he turned and looked up at the old Victorian house on the hill. Some said it once belonged to a white colonel who'd fought Apaches in these mountains.

Mateo sensed a greater evil inhabited it now.

CHAPTER 14

Home. Sweet. Home.

Mike pulled into his driveway in Las Cruces just as the sun settled on the horizon. Between sleeping after his last night on shift and the long drive, he felt as if he'd burned his first day off just getting home. Fortunately, he still had seven more days before he had to return to work.

Bethany met Mike at the door. He dropped the bag he'd collected from the trunk and wrapped his arms around her. He kissed her long and slow. He loved to kiss her, loved to inhale her scent, loved to feel her soft skin.

When they pulled apart, Bethany eyed him with a coy smile. "We should send you away more often."

He grinned. "I suppose we'll be doing that just about every other week for the foreseeable future."

"True," she agreed. "But I have a surprise for you."

"Oh?" His eyes widened, curiosity piqued. "What is it?"

"I thought I'd take you out to dinner and tell you."

Mike blinked. "Out? We can't afford that."

"We can now that you have a regular full-time job again," she smiled. "Sure, not every night, but once in a while is fine, and this is pretty exciting news." She clasped her hands around his neck and kissed him once more.

"Oooh, my Spidey senses are tingling . . . along with a few other things," he said with a wink, catching her enthusiasm. "Where do you want to go?" he asked as they stepped inside and made their way to the bedroom.

"How about La Posta?"

Mike unzipped his duffel. "Isn't Mexican food a little spicy for our little one?"

"If she's going to grow up in New Mexico, she needs to get

used to chile peppers," she said with a smile as she rubbed her belly. "Besides, this early in the pregnancy, it all gets filtered out before it gets to her anyway."

Mike arched an eyebrow, but didn't say anything this time. They didn't know the sex of the child yet. He changed into a pair of fresh khakis and a fitted black T-shirt. "I suppose you're right, we want our kids to be chile-pepper-fearless." He took his dirty clothes to the laundry room where he dumped them in the hamper for washing later.

"So, your car or mine?" asked Bethany.

"How about yours? I've been driving for the last three hours. I could use the break."

With that, Mike and Bethany went out to her car and drove through Las Cruces into the adjoining village of Mesilla. The streets connected the two towns almost seamlessly. Historically, Las Cruces and Mesilla straddled the border between the United States and Mexico, but that had changed nearly 160 years ago with the Gadsden Purchase, which moved the border farther south, allowing the railroad easy access across Southern New Mexico and Arizona. It also meant a thriving tourist center with plenty of restaurants and quaint shops that Mike and Bethany enjoyed exploring.

They soon pulled into a dirt parking lot that was already filling up in the early evening. La Posta sat kitty-corner across from the parking lot. In the 1800s, the building had been known as the Corn Exchange Hotel and was once a stop on the Butterfield Stage Line. Back in those days, it played host to such diverse people as General John J. Pershing, Pancho Villa, Billy the Kid, and even Colonel Kit Carson, for whom Carson Peak was named. Mike loved the colorful history of the area. It was one of the things that attracted him to move there in the first place.

The lobby was an enclosed courtyard, lush with trees growing up through the floor. A cage surrounding the trees held an assortment of chattering parrots, cockatoos and toucans. Children were always hovering around the cage, calling to the birds. He couldn't wait for his kids to do the same.

Despite the number of cars in the lot, there were plenty of seats in the sprawling restaurant. The waitress seated them and brought them an order of chips and salsa, which they dug into immediately, while figuring out what to order. Mike decided on the chicken flautas with guacamole and Bethany chose the flat enchiladas, Christmas style—with both red and green chile sauce. After the waitress brought their drinks and took their order, Mike reached across the table and took Bethany's hands. "So, what's this big surprise for me? Pregnant again?" he teased.

"Nothing dramatic," she said. "Just that there was a cancellation next week on the observatory schedule. They checked around the department to see if anyone could use the time. I needed a little extra on that galactic survey I've been doing . . . so . . . I'll get to go up and spend the week with you. Isn't that wonderful news?"

Mike sat back, his smile dimming slightly. He reached for his beer and took a few sips while he considered her announcement. He would love to have her with him all week, but so many things were troubling him. What about her condition? How would she manage at the higher altitude? And then there were the strange feelings he'd been having. The "encounters."

Trained as a scientist, Mike didn't readily believe in ghosts or demons, but last night was the second time he'd seen a strange manifestation on the mountain. Admittedly, he'd been tired, and the apparition was nothing like the ones from two years ago, but it made him uneasy about his next shift. He couldn't be with Bethany every second of the time she was there. How could he protect her if something happened?

Bethany's smile turned into a worried frown. "It *is* good news, isn't it?"

"Oh, absolutely," Mike sputtered. "It would be great for you to be there." Something about that sentence came out wrong.

"You sure don't sound convincing." Bethany narrowed her gaze. "Are you having a fling with Kendra Torres?"

"What?" Mike blinked back his surprise before he recognized the glint of humor in her eyes. "Yeah, under the watchful eye of her husband, who just happens to be built like The Rock."

"I'm sure." Bethany winked and leaned forward. "But there's something bothering you, isn't there?"

Mike sighed, uncertain where to begin. He decided to start with the most rational worry. "I guess I'm just a little concerned about you spending time at altitude. Will that be a problem?"

Bethany shrugged. "I don't see why it should be. I won't be doing any heavy lifting. Pregnant women fly all the time. And I'm in good physical health, I work out regularly at the university gym."

Mike gazed down at the foamy beer in his mug. "So, what telescope will you be on?"

"It'll be the 2.5-meter. That's the best one for the work I'm doing."

Mike frowned and set the beer aside. "You know that's the one I was working on when I saw the raptor thing—whatever it was."

"I promise I won't take any mind altering drugs when I'm at the telescope."

Those last words stung. "You know I was just tired," he said sharply, he lowered his voice to avoid drawing attention.

"Well you're being overly protective," she shot back. "I get plenty of sleep. Trust me a little bit with our child." She laced her fingers together on the table and leaned forward as though she was about to say something else at the same time as the waitress appeared with their dinners.

Mike and Bethany glared at each other across the table, but sat back, allowing the server to deposit the plates. "I'll return later to check on you," she said with a nervous smile. Another customer hailed her and she hurried off to the other table.

Silence is golden. Was that the old proverb? *Yeah right.* At this point it was more like a lead balloon.

Mike barely even tasted his meal even though he knew it was delicious. He felt as if he'd screwed up and hurt Bethany, but she'd hurt him in return by making light of his experience two years ago.

Halfway through his meal, he looked up. "Honey, I'm sorry I was such a jerk."

Her lips trembled and her eyes grew teary. "I know you're concerned for my well-being. I'm sorry, too. I shouldn't have over-reacted like that."

He stood and went to her, knelt by her chair, and put his arm around her. "This project will give you data that you can work on for a while. I know it's important to you. I'm just letting unfounded worries get the best of me."

She pulled out a tissue from her pocket and blew her nose. "It's okay, the pregnancy hormones are kinda messing with me, too."

He gave her a tender kiss, then returned to his seat. As he did, the waitress approached, relief visible on her features. "Did you save room for dessert?"

Mike looked at his plate and wondered whether he would have room to finish what he already had, much less anything more.

Bethany pushed her cleaned plate away. "We'll have an order of sopapillas with honey."

Mike raised an eyebrow and she grinned. "I'm eating for two."

"Yeah, but one of you is the size of a peanut," he teased.

She chucked a wadded-up straw wrapper at him.

He held up his finger. "Is that any way to behave in front of our son?"

"I need to teach our *daughter* how to stand up for herself."

They laughed and he finished his meal. Mike surprised himself by finding room for one of the delicious puffy fried pastries. Afterwards, they went home and watched a movie before climbing into bed. Bethany rolled over to face him. She rubbed her hands through the hair on his chest and nibbled on his earlobe. "Did you miss me?" she asked in a throaty whisper.

"Apparently so," said Mike. He took her hand and brought it down to his throbbing erection. He reached out and fondled her breast. After a leisurely moment, his hand wandered lower while he suckled her, enjoying her sighs of pleasure. "I hope you won't deny me this once our son is born."

"You'll have to take a number," she giggled.

With that, she straddled him. He climaxed far too quickly— he hadn't been with her in more than a week after all—but she continued to ride him while he remained hard inside her until she gained a measure of satisfaction.

Finally, she leaned down and kissed him. "I love you."

"I love you, too."

She eased off of him and they pulled the blankets up, snuggling together for a time. Soon, Bethany was sound asleep, but Mike found himself wide-awake. Despite the stereotypes about men, Mike never fell asleep easily after sex. That, combined with being on a night schedule for the past week meant it would be a while before he nodded off.

He slipped free of Bethany's arms, pulled on a pair of boxer shorts and went out to the garage. Even though he'd started the new job, he still had a few projects to finish. He lifted a computer off the shelf and his thoughts turned to his conversations with Jerome about the creatures from the beginning of time. He thought about the strange, dust-mote apparition.

Mike unscrewed the computer's cover, trying to figure out a logical explanation for a bunch of floating dust particles that looked like a face. Of course, for years, people had suggested there might be residual energy of people that remained in the place where they died. Both Professor Burroughs and his student had died in the building. Could one of them be the reason behind all the "unexplained" noises and shadows that Mike had seen his first week back at work? Either one could be a spirit with unresolved issues. What's more, Burroughs founded the observatory, so he might feel protective. But what might he be protecting it from?

He reached over and turned on an oscilloscope. If digging into the mountain had caused a weakening of the portals between worlds, just how well were those portals sealed? Could someone digging a hole down the road release something? Foxes and rabbits dug holes all the time. Normally, he'd dismiss such idle speculation, but his brain wouldn't let it go, especially knowing that Bethany would be on the mountain during his next shift.

He positioned the malfunctioning video card and the light, and picked up the test probes, trying to focus on the work at hand. However, when he tried to place the probes, he found he couldn't. His hands trembled too much.

He put everything away and went back to the bedroom. Sitting in the overstuffed chair in the corner he watched his wife as she slept. Their unborn child safe in her womb.

PART 2

HE WHO KILLS
WITH HIS EYES

CHAPTER 15

"All clear."

Carlos and Ricardo sighed with relief. Their uncle's man, who everyone called El Gordo, had completed his sweep and found two more bugs, one in the basement, and the other over the back door. He was nicknamed El Gordo or EG for short because he was skinny as a rail even though he ate like a pig. Carlos thought it was a stupid name.

EG reached into his pocket and took out a movie-theatre sized box of malted milk balls. Without offering any to the brothers, he opened the box and tipped it into his mouth.

"Hey," he said around a mouthful of chocolate. "Weren't there three of you?"

Carlos and Ricardo exchanged a quick look.

"What happened to the new guy . . . Diego?" EG emptied the box in his mouth and crushed it in his hand, dropping it in the ashtray on the table between the two recliners.

"*Pendejo* was a narc, man," said Carlos. "We had to deal with him."

EG grunted and told them to expect a call from Uncle Nesto. "Be sure to answer it. He gets angry if he has to play phone tag." With that, EG left and roared away in his black Lexus SUV.

All the made guys drove Lexuses. Carlos wanted one too.

He locked the door and began pacing the living room. Ricardo sat in his recliner, playing on his tablet.

The brothers jumped when Carlos's cell phone rang. He swallowed hard when he saw the caller ID.

"The videos are ready for release. I trust everything is in order." Tío Nesto's cover business for smuggling cocaine was manufacturing DVDs and Blu-ray discs.

"We just need to pick up the goods," Carlos said.

"*Excelente*," Nesto switched to Spanish.

Carlos swallowed hard. "Only problem is, Billy the Kid's been riding our asses. Don't know if we can get to the merchandise without trouble." Billy the Kid was their code word for Agent William McCarty.

"Don't worry about him. EG will want to talk to you at a new number in an hour," said Nesto. "You know how important this is. I've put a lot of faith in you and your brother. Don't let me down. Check with me tomorrow when everything's ready and we'll work out the details."

"Yes, Uncle," said Carlos.

The line clicked off. Carlos knew that his uncle wouldn't reveal anything that could give them away to the cops. Nesto didn't get where he was by being careless. Even though their uncle sent them new phones every week, he made sure only to refer to the cover business and avoided any direct reference to cocaine, people or places.

Carlos pulled down one of the blinds and peeked outside. The coast was clear. He left the house, got into his Ford Explorer, and headed to the store. Checking the rearview mirror, he saw a police car following at a discreet distance. Typical cops. At the store, he bought some bananas, milk, and cereal; the fun kind that Ricardo liked, and granola for himself. He also bought a disposable cell phone, paying cash. Afterwards, he returned home, went out to the back yard and made a brief phone call.

"Billy the Kid's been called away to a meeting in Albuquerque." EG's voice was muffled, as though he spoke around a mouthful of food. "He'll be back in a coupla days."

Carlos might not understand complex instructions, but he recognized a window of opportunity. He hung up the phone and went inside. "We leave before sunrise."

Ricardo nodded, then went to the bedroom and peered out through the Venetian blinds. Carlos followed him in. "Any sign of the cops?"

Ricardo shook his head. Alamogordo had a small police department and the DEA agent would have been riding them hard to keep an eye on the Fuentes Brothers. The cops were no doubt on their guard, especially after all the wireless microphones had been destroyed, but even cops get tired and bored. The brothers made sure to give them nothing to get excited about. Even around the house, the brothers talked mostly about girls and video games, which wasn't much of a stretch. With McCarty gone, they'd likely relax their watch just a little, and a little was all Carlos and Ricardo needed.

"We can't afford to fuck this up, man," Carlos whispered to his brother at the window.

"If we do, what do you think Tío Nesto will do to us?" Ricardo whispered back.

Carlos ran his finger under his chin. "You never go against the family, Ricky," he said in his best Al Pacino.

Ricardo gulped. "If this job gets blown, it's because of that traitor. We took care of him. Nesto understands that . . . doesn't he?"

Carlos smiled at his little brother in reassurance. "Don't worry, Ricky . . . We're gonna be champs, man. Once the client gets his delivery, everything's gonna change."

Carlos and Ricardo left while it was still dark. They took back roads out of their neighborhood, watching for cops as they drove. Alamogordo was sufficiently small that there were few patrols after midnight. Sure enough, they seemed to avoid detection and no one followed them as they turned onto the highway that led into the Sacramento Mountains.

As they passed a roadside gift shop, a highway patrol officer pulled out behind them. Carlos began sweating and drove very carefully, making sure he didn't give the cop any reason to pull them over. Had the Alamogordo cops called them? He breathed a sigh of relief when they reached the turnoff to Carson Peak and the cop turned toward Toledo instead of following them.

The sun had not yet risen. They drove along the darkened road, between tall pine trees that loomed up on either side of them, casting shadows across their path.

Carlos was a good driver, but he didn't see it coming until it was almost too late.

He slammed on the brakes, jostling them both as they stared, wide-eyed through the windshield.

"Shit, man! What the fuck is that?" asked Ricardo.

A huge, monstrous creature loomed before them.

Carlos's heart thudded in his chest, but after a few moments he realized it was just an elk. He honked his horn and the animal lumbered off the road.

"Fucking nature, man," said Carlos with a snort. "When we get made, we're heading to Vegas to celebrate."

"Yeah, baby. We're gonna be high rollers all the way!" Ricardo grinned and high-fived his brother.

When they reached the bridge over Nana's Ravine, they knew they were getting close. Once they found the road, they followed it a short distance and stopped. Carlos killed the engine and the brothers napped while waiting for the sun to rise. The cave entrance would be impossible to spot in the dark. They were lucky they'd found it the first time they explored the road, a little over a week ago.

When the sun peeked up over the mountaintops warming the interior of the SUV, they set out along the twisty, bumpy dirt road. Carlos had taken careful note of the odometer readings when they left the cave after stashing their expensive cargo. When they reached the correct place on the odometer, Carlos rolled down the window and looked around, waving aside a cloud of dust stirred up by their vehicle. Try as he could, the landscape didn't look familiar.

"We could have driven past it," suggested Ricardo.

Carlos wanted to argue with his brother, but he knew Ricardo was right. He realized he hadn't started counting miles until they turned off the road and went around the corner. He turned the SUV around on the narrow dirt road and eased back the way they came.

"I think that's it," said Ricardo. He pointed up the slope to his right.

Carlos studied the grassy slope that ended in a few boulders. A tree grew out near the top. It was similar to what he remembered, but not exactly. Still, he admitted, he wasn't used to the wilderness. Things didn't always stay the same and one rugged path could look like another. He shut off the engine.

Ricardo grabbed a flashlight and a pistol from the glove compartment. He handed another flashlight and pistol to his brother. The two hiked up the gentle slope. Carlos found an occasional faint footprint within the grass, giving him some reassurance they were on the right path. He wondered how those cowboys and Indians of old were able to track through the wilderness so easily. Maybe, once they got made, he'd hire some old *vaquero* or chief to teach him.

Ricardo found the cave's mouth behind some clumps of scrub brush. Carlos frowned. It was windy a few nights ago, but was it enough to hide the entrance? The two brothers shone their flashlights into the cave.

Carlos recognized the channel through the ground and the structure of rocks. This was the place, after all. As his eyes adjusted to the gloom, he knew something was wrong.

"Where's the fucking cocaine, man?"

"Where's the fucking homeboy we plugged?" Ricardo waved his flashlight around wildly. "Are we in the wrong cave?"

"No this is the right place," said Carlos. "I'm sure of it." He illuminated the petroglyphs on the wall. "I remember those drawings."

Ricardo walked up beside him and the two brothers scanned the ground farther into the cave. Deep brown stains covered a rock. A few feet away were two shell casings. Carlos picked them up and slipped them in his pocket. He continued on and dug his toe around some indentations in the sand. "Here's where the cocaine was stashed. We're in the right place."

Carlos felt drawn to the back of the cave. He turned his light that direction. The wall, such as it was, seemed unusually smooth. Curious, he discovered that it wasn't actually a wall, but some kind of thick, soupy air—air that absorbed his flashlight beam.

He waved his hand through it, trying to clear it. He froze as a high-pitched, inhuman shriek called out. It sounded a little like the cry of an angry horse, but sharper, punctuated by some kind of clacking. The hairs on his arms stood on end. He'd seen Stephen King's *The Mist* and the sounds reminded him of creatures that could cut people in two with lobster-like pincers.

Wide-eyed, Carlos took a few steps back. "I think there's something alive back there."

Ricardo's head bobbed in agreement, and without another word the brothers backed out of the cave.

Once in the sunlight, they felt safer somehow. "You think some animal got the homeboy?" asked Ricardo.

Carlos shrugged. "There's all kinda mountain lions and coyotes up here. It's always possible."

"If it was the police, they would have taken the shell casings for evidence, wouldn't they?" Ricardo pocketed his pistol.

Carlos dug the spent shell casings out of his pocket that he'd found on the floor. "I would think so, but what about the cocaine. An animal wouldn't take the blow would they?"

Ricardo slapped his forehead. "Hey, I saw a show once on that animal TV channel. Maybe a couple of packrats used it for nesting material. They steal all kindsa shit."

"Nesting material?" said Carlos, incredulous. "If we don't find that cocaine, our uncle is gonna make us into nesting material or worse!"

Ricardo took a deep breath and let it out slowly. "Maybe someone stole it. What if someone from another cartel found it?"

Carlos considered that for a moment. "I don't think so. If it was another cartel, they wouldn't hesitate selling it. If Tío Nesto got word of that much blow hitting the streets on this side of the border, he'd get suspicious. I don't think we'd still be here to argue about it."

Ricardo frowned. "Yeah, I guess you're right. But if it wasn't animals or another cartel, what then?"

"Let me think." Carlos hiked back down to the truck. Maybe some animal *had* made off with the cocaine. If so, it might have been whatever made that god-awful screeching from far back in the cave. The pistol made him brave, and he would face it if he could see it, but he wasn't stupid. Going through that strange fog, whatever it was, would give the creature an advantage. It didn't matter whether it was some monster from Stephen King's imagination or a raccoon. It could still fuck them up pretty bad if it saw them before they saw it.

They did have some road flares. They could throw one of those in and see if it gave them a better view. Then again, that might just piss off whatever was back there. They might be better off waiting around a few hours and see if it came out of the cave to hunt, but they couldn't wait too long. Tío Nesto was expecting a phone call from them.

Ricardo knelt down on the road, looking at some tracks. He looked at the tires on the SUV, then he looked at the bottom of his shoes. "Hey bro, let me see the bottom of your shoes."

"What for?" Carlos narrowed his gaze.

"Just humor me."

Carlos held up his foot.

Ricardo nodded. "You wear these same shoes when we came here before?"

Carlos shrugged. "Hell if I know, but I think so. I only got a coupla pair and this is the scruffy one."

"There's a set of footprints that go up the road. The tracks aren't the same as either of our shoes." Ricardo pointed to the ground. "Looks like they came from the cave as well."

"Good job, Tonto," said Carlos with a grin, pleased they had an alternative to going deeper into the cave. "Someone did steal from us and they left on foot. Where the hell does this road go, anyway?"

Ricardo pointed up at a white dome at the top of the mountain. Thick clouds billowed up behind it. It was mid-summer. There would probably be a storm in the evening. "This leads to Carson Peak Observatory. Whoever took the blow went that way."

"You think some scientist geek took the cocaine?" Carlos shook his head.

"Being a scientist don't mean someone won't think they could get rich quick." Ricardo held his hands out to the side. "For that matter, someone coulda thought they were being a goody-two-shoes and taking it to turn it into the cops. Either way, I bet we'll find out what happened to the cocaine by following this road to the top."

"All right, we'll check it out." He held out the disposable cell phone. "Since you're so smart, you call Tío Nesto and tell him what's going on. He's expecting a report."

Ricardo took the cell phone and turned it on. "He may be expecting us to call, but we ain't gonna. There's no signal, bro."

Carlos swore under his breath. "All right. I'm guessing we've got about forty-eight hours to figure out what's going on before our beloved uncle sends hit men after us." They climbed back in the truck and started up the road toward Carson Peak Observatory.

CHAPTER 16

It was a perfect day.

Sunlight danced through the trees as Mike and Bethany drove along the mountain road to Carson Peak. As they passed an overlook, they caught fleeting glimpses of the observatory domes rising over the treetops.

At one point, the Forest Service had recommended the observatory paint the domes dark green, to blend in. The problem was the dark color would make the enclosures absorb heat during the day, which would create shimmering images at night. Mike couldn't help but chuckle. Whether they were green—red, white, or blue—they would still stand out.

"What's so funny?" Bethany smiled at his chuckling.

"I was just thinking about the irony of all of this."

Bethany quirked her brow. "How so?"

"Well, here we are heading to Carson Peak to study the universe so we can better understand ourselves and yet our very presence alters that understanding."

Her brow furrowed in thought.

"We've built these huge structures in our quest to comprehend something that is beyond us because we've changed it in our quest to understand it."

"Ah, well, that's the crux of everything isn't it? In fact, it's what Heisenberg's uncertainty principal is all about. You can't observe something without changing it."

Mike glanced at his wife with a grin. "But I do understand one thing for sure."

"And what's that?" She grinned back at him as if she couldn't help herself.

"That I love you now and forever."

She caressed his dimpled cheek. "I love you, too."

They spent the rest of the drive in companionable silence, but the closer they got to Carson Peak, the more restless Mike became. He couldn't help but worry about the upcoming week. Would he see another ghost? Would Bethany be okay? Would he be able to watch out for her? Why couldn't he shake these feelings? He would have to, otherwise he'd make himself crazy.

When they arrived at the observatory gate, Bethany hopped out of the car, unlatched the gate, and pushed it open before Mike could stop her. He frowned at her when she climbed back in. "You should have let me do that."

"Why?" She blinked at him. "It's not like the gate weighs much."

Mike let it go. He didn't want to start a fight. He wanted to stay calm and in control. As they passed the gate, he stopped and Bethany closed it behind them. They drove up the dirt road to the observatory office building. Mike looked from one telescope enclosure to the other. He had to admit it was good to have Bethany on the same mountaintop, but the distance between the buildings meant they'd only see each other when they weren't actually working. The bigger problem was that it meant he couldn't be with her in case something happened.

Nothing is going to happen. Stop it with these thoughts.

He could just imagine how he'd be once the baby was born. He had to get over this irrational concern he had over Bethany.

Although most of the sky was still blue, a few clouds had appeared. Bethany stepped up beside Mike. "Think we might get a rain shower this evening?"

Mike shook his head. "I doubt it, this early in the season. These are pretty small clouds and there wasn't anything in the forecast." He grabbed his duffel bag and Bethany's suitcase from the trunk and they went inside.

Jerome called out from his office. "Mike, is that you?"

Mike dropped their bags to the floor and peeked around Jerome's door. "What's up, Boss?"

"Kendra is taking the next three nights off to give my granddad a break from watching Derek," said Jerome. "She's satisfied you remember what you're doing and she doesn't really need to look over your shoulder. You can call her at home if you have any questions, though. Also, Stan is operating for Bethany at the 2.5-meter."

Mike fought to keep a neutral expression. He wasn't sure how he felt about a guy he caught whacking off at work, operating a telescope for his wife. Then again, if Stan had been doing it in the privacy of his own room, he and Kendra never would have known and it wouldn't have bothered him. He wondered if Kendra had told Jerome about the incident.

"You okay with the plans?" asked Jerome.

Mike realized he was still standing in his boss's doorway. "Everything sounds great. Thanks." With that, he carried the bags back to his dorm room. Bethany followed and unpacked while Mike returned to the car to retrieve their food.

Half an hour later, he was preparing dinner when two young women and a man, all about the same age, walked through the door. "Hi, I'm Mike Teter, the operator on the 5-meter tonight. Are you the observers I'll be working with?"

A tall, muscular woman wearing a plaid shirt, with sleeves rolled up past the elbows, and tan pants took a step forward and shook Mike's hand. "I'm Maya Williams."

A slightly shorter woman with wavy, blond hair, wearing shorts, a tie-dyed T-shirt, and hiking boots waved. "I'm Claire Yarbro."

The young man with long, unkempt hair and a camera case slung around his shoulders stepped forward. "Evan Burkholder. We all work on Gene Carter's team at Princeton." He wore jeans and a T-shirt with a picture of Neil DeGrasse Tyson. He removed a backpack and placed it in the corner.

Mike nodded. He'd worked with Gene Carter on observing runs years ago. The man was a brilliant theorist, but didn't understand how telescopes actually worked nor did he have an intuitive sense of the night sky. Carter often complained when an operator told him an object had already set or not yet risen, meaning the telescope simply couldn't point at it. When he first worked at the observatory, Mike had been surprised how many astronomers could read off a set of coordinates without having any idea where in the sky they actually were. Mike hoped Carter's students had other professors who had given them a better background in telescopes and the sky. "So, have you been out hiking?"

"Yeah," said Maya. "We got in yesterday afternoon. We heard there're some great trails around the mountain."

"A lot of history in this area," said Claire. "Didn't Billy the Kid ride through here?"

"He was a little farther north," said Mike. "Up around Lincoln County."

Evan grabbed a set of glasses from the cabinet, while Maya pulled a pitcher of juice out of the refrigerator. "The Apaches have been in this area for a long time, haven't they? I heard they believe this is something like the Garden of Eden."

Jerome appeared at his office door, apparently having overheard the conversation. "That's close. The story is that the first humans came to this world through these mountains."

"That's so cool," said Evan.

Bethany stepped into the kitchen and joined Mike at the table. Mike had already set a plate for her.

"See anything interesting on your hike?" asked Bethany, tucking into her chicken salad.

"We were hoping to see some wildlife," said Claire. "Didn't see much, just a doe and a fawn. That was cool, but I'd hoped we'd see something more, like an elk or even a mountain lion."

"The mountain lions keep to themselves," said Jerome, "and you're more likely to see elk after dark. There are some raccoons around here, but they turn up around sunset."

"We did find a couple of caves to explore," interjected Evan. He pulled a flashlight out of his hip pocket as he sat down and poured a glass of juice.

Jerome's brow creased as he reached around and turned off his office light. "You didn't take anything from any of the caves, did you? Those are sacred Apache sites. The elders get testy if people are even in there."

The three students looked at one another. Mike wondered if they were hiding something, or just couldn't decide who should speak first. Finally, Maya spoke up, but her words were measured. "We did find some neat petroglyphs and a few potsherds . . . but we didn't take anything."

Evan patted his camera. "Leave only footprints, take only pictures," he said, a little too cheerfully.

Jerome narrowed his gaze, but didn't say anything more to them. "I'm all done for the day. Call if you need anything," Jerome said to Mike as he locked his office door.

"How's your grandfather doing?" asked Bethany as Jerome turned to leave.

Jerome stopped just before the outside door, turned back to them and shrugged. "He says he feels better, but every now and then he twinges, like he's feeling some pain. Whenever I ask about it, he denies it, but the aspirin supply at home keeps going down, like he's still dealing with frequent headaches. I'm not quite sure what to do." He folded his arms. "Kendra's a little afraid to leave him alone with Derek and I can't say I blame her."

"Your grandfather wouldn't harm Derek or anything, would he?" asked Mike.

"Nothing like that." Jerome waved his hand. "But what happens if Derek gets in trouble and my grandfather is incapacitated?"

Mike and Bethany exchanged concerned glances.

"Kendra said the MRI didn't turn up anything." Mike took a sip of his water. "Do you think they goofed up?"

"I don't know what to think at this point." Jerome shook his head, resigned. "Just figure we'll keep an eye on him as best we can. Can't get him to slow down. Kendra is staying home this week to help take the load off Mateo. I hope it works. Of course, my grandfather is the type that never takes it easy. If he's not watching Derek, he'll be over helping at the youth center, or at the tribal council offices."

"He sounds like quite a guy," remarked Claire with a smile.

"He is that. He knows a lot about the old ways. More than anyone around here. So if you guys have any questions about the hiking trails let me know. I wouldn't want you to get lost or hurt." Jerome stared at each of the students, with a sharp look in his eyes. Mike noticed the three young people squirm and exchange glances before nodding.

"Keep me posted on how things go this week. If you're

comfortable operating the telescopes on your own, we'll shift the schedule around, get Stan onto days full time."

"Sounds good." Mike refilled his plate with chicken salad.

Jerome waved as he left. The three graduate students excused themselves to shower before the night of observing began.

Just as Mike thought he and Bethany would have a little time alone, Stan Jones stepped into the kitchen. "Hey, guys! How's it going?"

The two waved at Stan, who grabbed a TV dinner from the freezer, and popped it into the microwave. He poured a cup of coffee and sat down bleary-eyed while the meal heated up. Soon, the beeper sounded and Stan gingerly grabbed the hot container with two fingers and danced across the floor, dropping it on the table. He pulled back the plastic and looked at the food dubiously.

"You should cook your food from scratch," said Mike. "It tastes better and it's better for you."

Stan sighed and patted his belly. "But then, how would I keep my trim, manly physique?" He dug into his meal and finished it a few minutes later. Standing, he tossed the plastic service tray into the trash. "Besides, cleanup's a cinch. I don't have to wash dishes like you do."

"Great," said Bethany, "then that gives you extra time to get the telescope ready for calibrations."

Stan gave an exaggerated sigh. "I guess it does at that. What part of the wide cosmos are we exploring tonight, Professor Dwyer?"

Bethany explained that she'd been granted time for her on-going survey of distant galaxies. "Point the telescope, take a long exposure and move on. Should be a simple night."

"Simple is how I like 'em." Stan stood and grabbed his cup of coffee. "See you over there in a few minutes."

After Mike and Bethany finished up, they went back to their room and gathered their things. They strolled outside holding hands. The clouds had thickened, looking dark and ominous.

"Still think we'll be able to open?" asked Bethany, glancing at the shadows cast by the clouds.

"I'm guessing these will dissipate soon after sunset. I think we'll get a lot of data."

"I hope you're right," said Bethany. Mike accompanied her to the 2.5-meter telescope. He wanted to be with her as long as possible. He still couldn't shake the feeling that something bad was going to happen. When they got to the entrance, he gazed at her face, wondering if their son or daughter would inherit their mother's beautiful hazel eyes.

"Why are you looking at me like that?" Bethany asked him, as she touched his face with her free hand.

"Like what?"

"Like you're trying to memorize my face."

"I just like looking at you. You're my beautiful wife," he said around the sudden lump in his throat.

"She wrapped her arms around his neck and kissed him." It was a slow, lingering kiss. He wished it could go on forever.

She pulled away and whispered in his ear. "I love you."

"I love you too, babe." He whispered back. "Never forget that." He gave her a brief tight hug.

"Take care, sweetheart. Call me if you need anything. Okay?"

"I will, I promise."

Watching her as she waved and went inside, he hoped everything would go smoothly over the coming hours. He jogged back to the observatory truck parked outside the dorm building and drove up the narrow, winding road to the 5-meter. As he parked by the building, he looked out over the site. The sun was low enough that it cast an eerie, orange light across the landscape. The mountain's shadow stretched across the valley floor. Mike shuddered. For a fleeting moment, he had a feeling someone was watching him. Was there someone out there? Or was it his mind playing tricks on him again?

CHAPTER 17

"Ye stars! which are the poetry of heaven," wrote Lord Byron.

Maya, Claire, and Evan were gathering data on stars that were believed to host planets. The picture on the computer screen was a long gray stripe produced by a spectrograph mounted to the 5-meter. Maya pointed out black lines cutting across the stripe—the star's unique chemical fingerprint—and teased out meaning as though understanding a poem.

A new image appeared on the screen and Claire wrinkled her nose. "I can't tell. Did the lines move?"

"We'll have to reduce the data before we can tell." Evan sounded haughty to Mike, as though the answer should be obvious. Movement in the lines from one image to the next meant a planet tugged on the star, but most observers couldn't tell that just from looking at the screen. The movements were so subtle, they could only tell after analyzing the data carefully at the university.

Mike manned the telescope as the students concentrated on their research. As their observations progressed, clouds began rolling in, obscuring the stars over the site. Some astronomy experiments required the light from sources in the sky to be completely unobstructed, but this work could be done through a few clouds, as long as the dark spectral lines were visible. Bethany, however, would be having a much more difficult time getting the images she needed.

Maya, Claire, and Evan discussed the data that rolled in. Mike grabbed his copy of Tony Hillerman's *A Thief of Time*. A good mystery would help pass the time. The observers would stay on the current target for a while. Around 9:30, the phone rang, startling him. He put the book aside and picked up the phone.

"Hey Mike, have you looked at the clouds, they're getting kind of thick out there." He recognized Stan's voice.

Mike looked at the all-sky camera's display. Sure enough, the cloud cover had increased. What's more, the guide star that enabled the telescope to fine tune its tracking was fading in and out. "I see that. You think the clouds are threatening?"

A groan sounded from the students, overhearing the conversation and realizing they might have to close the telescope to protect the equipment.

"I think so," said Stan. "Why don't you check it out? I'll do the same."

Mike hung up and grabbed one of the walkie-talkies that sat on a nearby shelf so he could discuss the situation with Stan while away from the phone. "Looks like I need to go check out the sky," he told the students.

"It would be great if we could finish this spectrum. We only have about thirty minutes left on it," pressed Maya.

"I know," said Mike, "but if it looks like we may get rain, I'm going to have to ask you to finish early. I know it hurts your science, but if the telescope gets damaged, that keeps others from using it."

Maya looked as if she was going to argue but seemed to think better of it and nodded. No doubt Gene Carter had emphasized the value of telescope time. The National Science Foundation and the universities paid five million dollars a year to keep the 5-meter telescope operating. That was money no one in the astronomical community wanted to see wasted. Mike stepped into the red-lit elevator, leaving the students to their data.

As he reached the bottom floor, the wind howled. The garage door next to the main entrance banged and rattled alarmingly. The wind speed itself hadn't been that high, but it came from just the right direction to make a lot of noise.

Outside, Mike made his way around the enclosure's base and gazed up at the sky. Despite the cloud cover, he could still see the stars fairly clearly. Without warning, a flash of lightning appeared to the south, revealing the overcast to have the thick, billowing structure of rain clouds. He thumbed the talk button on the radio. "Mike to Stan, those clouds look pretty mean."

"I agree." Stan's voice buzzed over the radio. "Time to close up."

Just as Mike turned around to go back inside, a sharp crack sounded, followed by another flash of light, illuminating the dome. Nothing to be done. They'd have to shut down for a while. He hoped Bethany was okay. If only he'd been assigned to work with her and not Stan, maybe he wouldn't be feeling so anxious right now. He hurried in and rode the elevator back to the control room.

"Okay, we gotta close up. We've got a storm moving in fast," said Mike.

The three students groaned in unison. "Can't we go just a few more minutes?" asked Evan.

Mike shook his head. "Nope, abort the exposure now. I don't think we have much time." As he spoke, the control room lights flickered briefly. "Lightning is getting close."

The light flicker made Mike's case better than any verbal argument. Once Maya aborted the exposure, she nodded to Mike, who stowed the telescope, closed the mirror covers, and started the dome shutter closing. He stood to close the louvers on the sides of the dome.

"Mind if I come with you?" asked Maya.

"Not at all," said Mike. He ambled through a pair of doors that kept the control room's heat from escaping into the dome. Dark as it was, the louvers didn't offer much of a view across the mountaintop, but they could still see flashes of lightning in the distance.

"I guess you were right," said Maya. "Looks like we closed just in time. Professor Carter said we should watch out for telescope operators. He said they like to close up early just so they can have free time."

"Yeah, well, that's a common misconception," he said with a smirk. "The truth is just the opposite. It's actually easier for us when we're working and things are going smoothly. I can kick back and enjoy a good book during the long exposures. Now, I've got to keep a close eye on the weather, just in case we get a chance to open again." He activated the control, which closed the louvers before walking across the dome to close the other set.

Once they were closed, the wind caught the louvers and a

low moan sounded, causing the hair on the back of Mike's neck to stand on end.

"What was that?" Maya aimed the flashlight at her face, no doubt to alert Mike to where she was. The light reflected off her glasses. For a moment, they looked like a pair of demonic, glowing eyes.

"Just the wind on the louvers." Mike fought to keep a stammer out of his voice.

Another keening wail shot through the dome. The dome shutter had nearly closed and the brakes had engaged, stopping the multi-ton structure.

Stan's voice crackled from the walkie-talkie. "I just felt a few raindrops. Did you get closed up there?"

"Dome just shut. Sounds like we got it just in time." Mike shot a glance at Maya, but doubted she could see his concerned expression in the darkened dome. He switched on his flashlight and returned to the control room. Maya followed close behind.

"How long do you think we'll be closed?" asked Claire.

Mike shrugged. "This storm wasn't in the forecast, so it's a little hard to say. It kind of looks like a normal summer monsoon system though. They usually rain themselves out and we're back on the sky by midnight."

"It's a little early for a monsoon, isn't it?" asked Evan, pulling his long hair back into a ponytail. "I thought those really got going around mid-July. This is only mid-June."

"Weather's been strange in recent years," said Mike. "Some say it's climate change. Others say it's just normal variation. All I know is that we'll stay closed until the rain stops."

"Well, I think I'm going to take advantage of this break and go visit the restroom," said Claire, following safety protocol by telling them where she was going.

Mike handed her another walkie-talkie from the shelf. "You should take one of these."

"For the bathroom?" She arched an eyebrow at him.

Maya laughed. "Trust me, those corridors get kind of confusing in the dark. You'll be glad you have it if you get lost."

"Do you have a flashlight?" asked Mike.

She held it up, then clipped the walkie-talkie to her belt. As she left, Mike checked the all-sky camera and the wind readings.

He decided he had about thirty minutes before the storm had any chance of letting up enough to be worth checking on again.

As things quieted down, and he checked once more to make sure all the gear was fine, Mike's mind drifted back to that night . . . The huge, ominous monster appearing out of nowhere, looking as though it had stepped out of a sci-fi movie . . . The coyote rising from the dead, warning him of terrible things to come . . . The blood seeping from Wallerstein's severed head . . .

He closed his eyes and fought to push his dark thoughts aside. After a moment, and a few deep, calming breaths, he poured himself a cup of coffee. He needed to get his mind onto other things, so he opened his Tony Hillerman novel and picked up where he'd left off. He managed to get to the end of chapter seven before the sound of thunder crashed through the building and the lights went out. The glow of the computer monitors, kept alive by a bank of backup batteries, bathed the room in a ghostly light.

Mike waited a moment, expecting either line power to come back or the generator to kick on, restoring the lights.

"Are we safe up here?" asked Evan.

"Building's designed to shunt lightning to the ground. We're safe," said Mike. "Probably safer in here than we would be down at the office."

"Does it seem like Claire's been gone for a long time?" Maya's brow furrowed.

Mike turned around and checked the time on the computer monitor. Fifteen minutes since he closed the dome. Perhaps a little long for a quick tinkle, but not beyond the scope of a routine bathroom visit, especially if she took the stairs. "She has her flashlight," said Mike. "She should be okay."

Five more minutes ticked by, and still no power. Mike didn't think the batteries would last much longer than an hour. He keyed the radio. "Stan, has your power gone out?"

Silence.

Could the lack of power have knocked out the repeater down in the office building? Strange. It should also have a battery backup.

"Yeah, we're dead over here, too," Stan responded at last.

"Is your phone working? I can't get a dial tone."

Mike hadn't thought to check. Living in New Mexico, where thunderstorms were common in the summertime, he'd heard about people being killed because of lightning traveling down phone lines. He avoided the phone during serious storms. Nevertheless, he picked up the handset. Sure enough, there was no dial tone.

"My phone's dead, too," he said. "Say, you want me to go check on the generator? It should have kicked on by now."

"Nah, I'll go over and check it out. You're up twelve stories, man," said Stan. "It's raining pretty solidly now. If a relay blew, you'd need my help anyway. No sense in both of us getting wet."

"Thanks, man. I owe you one."

"You got that right."

"Is Bethany okay?"

"She's fine man. She's munching on some healthy nature bar shit."

"Good, tell her to relax, we'll get this sorted out."

"Will do."

"I'm starting to worry about Claire," interjected Maya. "She left almost twenty minutes ago. Shouldn't she be back by now?"

Mike looked at the time. Maya was right. The corridors were dark and confusing enough with the lights on. If her flashlight batteries died, or the bulb burned out, she'd have no hope of finding her way back. "All right, let's go take a look."

"Do we all need to go?" asked Maya.

"Probably a good idea if you and I go," said Mike. "I know the corridors better than you, but it would be kind of awkward for me to check in the bathroom."

"I'll hang out here," affirmed Evan.

With that, Mike and Maya left the control room. Mike looked at the elevator and turned to Maya. "Give me a hand." Pocketing the flashlight, he slipped his fingers into the seam where the two halves of the door came together in the middle. Maya saw what he was doing and pushed her fingers in below Mike's. They pulled in opposite directions, opening the door. Mike examined the cab with the flashlight. Wherever Claire was, she had taken the stairs.

With Maya close behind, Mike descended two flights, and followed the darkened corridor to an alcove of unmarked doors and pointed at one. Maya knocked. "Claire, are you in there?" When no one answered, she entered. A moment later she reappeared. "No sign of her."

"Suppose she went down to the dormitory floor? The bathrooms there are a little nicer and heated," suggested Mike.

"She knows about them. We explored the building yesterday." With that, Mike and Maya continued down two more flights of stairs. Reaching the women's room, Maya knocked. Receiving no answer, she went inside. "Still no sign," said Maya when she reappeared.

Mike's heart kicked into high gear as he thought of Dr. Burroughs's grad student, crushed in the dome trucks. With the power out, it was unlikely Claire had encountered anything so terrifying, but what if she was lost and the power suddenly kicked on?

"Time to step up this search."

CHAPTER 18

"Why don't you try calling her?"

Mike sighed his frustration that he hadn't thought of that.

"She has to answer," said Maya.

He thumbed the transmit button. "Mike calling Claire. Is everything all right?" He let go of the button and listened. Silence. "Mike calling Claire." There was still no reply. The wind howled through the building, setting ventilators banging and squeaking. "It could be her battery is dead or she forgot to turn it on."

Maya shook her head. "You pulled it directly from the charger, and I saw her turn it on."

Mike frowned. He flipped to the walkie-talkie's other channel. "Mike calling Claire." There was still no response. After one more attempt, he flipped it back to the main channel.

Frowning, Maya pulled her cell phone out of her pocket. "Damn, the battery's dead. I just charged it this morning."

"Probably drained looking for a signal. They don't work worth a damn up here. That's why we use the radios," said Mike. "Do you think Claire has her phone with her?"

"I don't know. She might have left it in her bag in the control room."

Mike nodded. "Let's check to make sure she didn't get lost around the base of the telescope."

They climbed the darkened stairway. Instead of continuing down the hallway to the control room stairs, Mike passed through a storage room and entered the dome. Maya scanned the vast, empty space with her flashlight. A tiny spot of light appeared on the very top of the dome, several floors above and a high-pitched screeching rent the air. Shadowy creatures swooped at them from every direction.

Maya screamed.

"Bats!"

They covered their heads and ran to the wall as the bats flew back up to the top of the dome's interior.

"What the hell?"

"Did I mention that we have bats in our belfry?" quipped Mike to lighten the mood.

Maya shook her head with a *don't go there* look in her eyes.

"Sorry." He stared up to the top of the dome. He'd never seen the bats fly all the way down like that. Animals were said to be able to sense danger. Had something about the storm spooked them? "We should keep going."

Immediately to Mike's right was the alcove that led into the dome trucks. He tried the door, but found it locked. When Burroughs's graduate student had been killed, the door had no lock. Just to check, Mike tried the general master key—the same one assigned to the observers. It didn't work.

"Claire?" called Maya. Her voice seemed tiny and hollow in the large, dark space. Mike had long ago noticed the weird acoustics of the dome. In some places, you could whisper to the wall and someone on the other side could hear you speak. In other places, your voice just seemed to vanish, no matter how loud you shouted. "She's not here," said Maya in a worried tone.

"If she were just idly curious, where do you think she might have gone?"

Maya shrugged. "The dome would be one place. I suppose she might have gone outside to take a look at the storm."

Mike led the way back into the hallway and stopped at the door to the console room staircase. "Why don't you go back upstairs? There's one more radio. I can call you guys if I need you. I'll check downstairs."

"I'd like to go with you," said Maya.

"I'd rather you stay with Evan. If I don't find her, I'm going to see if I can help Stan with the generator." He scanned the darkened hallway. "I think that would do more to help our search than anything. Also, if you're up there, you can call me on the radio if she does return."

Maya opened her mouth as if to argue, but seemed to

reconsider, and nodded. "All right. I'll give you a call when I get to the control room just to make sure that radio's working."

"Good plan."

Maya disappeared through the door and Mike trudged through the darkened hallway to the main stairwell. He shone his light down the five floors—ten flights of stairs in all. Going down was easy. He didn't look forward to the climb back up, though. He was glad he was in good physical shape. He hoped Stan would get the generator going soon.

As he descended in the dark, his hearing became heightened. His breathing seemed louder. Even his clothes made a raspy, rustling sound as he moved. He poked his head through each door as he continued on, and called out for Claire. Each time he did so, his voice echoed, bouncing off the walls. It felt as if he were completely and utterly alone. As though every other living thing had vanished. As though he were the last person on Earth.

Mike reached the ground floor and all was quiet. He took a deep breath, relieved that the rattling had stopped.

A sudden blast of wind hammered the garage door. Mike whipped his flashlight around. Rain seeped under the gap at the bottom. A gust of cool air sent a shiver down his arms.

Heart pounding, Mike walked up to the nearby door that had a safety glass window. He turned the handle and pushed, but it wouldn't give. The wind was blowing so hard, it seemed as though it was locked from the outside. Torrents of water hammered the window. Unfortunately, the nearby garage door required power to open.

Mike realized he hadn't heard from Maya. He called her on the walkie-talkie.

"I tried calling, but didn't get a response." Static crackled through Maya's words.

Mike spat a curse, before he thumbed the switch. "I bet the storm's messing with the repeater."

"Any sign of—" Maya's voice broke off suddenly.

"She doesn't seem to be down here." Mike didn't want to say that she would be in serious trouble if she'd wandered outside before the storm had gotten bad. If she had, he hoped she'd found shelter.

". . . let you . . . if she . . . here . . ."

"Can you repeat?" asked Mike.

Thunder boomed and lightning flashed, illuminating the room, and making the storage tanks and pipes look like a row of robots, standing at attention.

"I'll let you know if she turns up." This time Maya came through loud and clear.

"I'm going to go down and check the power relays." Mike opened a door off the hallway, to a set of stairs that descended into the building's basement. The building's foundation swallowed up many of the sounds Mike heard from above, making him feel as if he were walking through a vacuum. He reached a room with water pipes and electrical conduits. His flashlight beam landed on a dead mouse. The small rodent had curled up around itself. Flattened and desiccated with decay, it no longer smelled of death.

Mike continued around a corner to a rounded corrugated metal tunnel. The pipes and conduits followed the tunnel down through a door, where he found the building's main power relays along with the air conditioner units. They were mounted on a ledge that stood out on the edge of the mountain. This allowed them to be connected to both generator and line power. Water was easily pumped up to this point from the site's well.

The corridor reminded Mike of the ship in *Alien* or the Jeffries Tubes in *Star Trek*. Alone in the dark as he was, the first image particularly unnerved him. He crept to the door at the end of the corridor and opened it, worried for a split second that he'd find some otherworldly creature on the other side. He continued down a few more steps until he illuminated a bank of power relays with his flashlight. All the contactors were in the correct position.

He moved over to a nearby window and peered outside. Although most of it reflected back, he saw the rain was still coming down hard.

Metal clattered against concrete. Mike whirled, pointing his light towards a fallen pipe. A pair of glowing green eyes peered back at him, accompanied by a deep growl.

Mike took a step back, his heart thudding. Until he saw the mask of black fur surrounding the intruder's eyes. The raccoon's striped tail bristled as he grabbed a foil pouch in his jaws. With a snort, he scurried around a water tank. Doubtless, he'd found his way in through an air vent.

Where would a raccoon find a foil pouch down here?

Mike examined the animal's hiding place. Cans of beans, stew, and vegetables were stacked up in the corner, along with bags of potato chips, and boxes of Pop-Tarts. The raccoon had knocked down the cans when Mike startled him. He'd evidently torn into boxes and bags and had been enjoying a good meal, as there were crumbs everywhere.

Why is there food here in the first place?

No one accessed the area unless there was an emergency, and if not for the raccoon, he might not have looked around the corner.

"Boo!"

Mike dropped his flashlight and jumped back three paces. As the light hit the floor, it went out.

Stan Jones turned on his flashlight and shone it up under his chin, casting eerie shadows. "Beware creatures lurking in dark places," he droned in an ominous voice.

"What the hell are you doing down here?" asked Mike. "I thought you were checking the generator."

Water dripped from Stan's red hair and his clothes clung to his body like wet rags. He stooped to pick up Mike's flashlight and handed it to him. "I was. Line power is out. I tried to fire up the generator, but no go. It's full of gas. Everything looks good, but it just won't start up. I have no idea what's wrong. I came down here to see if there was some load problem that might be drawing the generator down. I tried to call you on the radio, but didn't get through. I think the storm's messing with the repeater."

"Yeah, it's been dicey for us too. Why didn't I see you when I came in?"

"I was around the corner, checking the junction where the wires enter the building. I didn't want to startle you."

Mike rolled his eyes. "You did a damn fine job of that."

Stan turned his flashlight on the stockpile of food. "What's all this doing here? You been getting ready for Armageddon?"

"Not me," said Mike. "One of the other operators?"

"I can't imagine Kendra or Gwen keeping anything down in this dank space. Lots of animals get trapped in here and die."

Mike nodded. "I know."

"Maybe Jorge." Stan shrugged, referring to one of the operators who worked during Mike's days off. "He doesn't seem too picky about what he eats."

Mike waved the speculation aside. "So, if you're here, does that mean you left Bethany alone at the 2.5-meter?"

"Didn't think it would do her any good to be out in the storm," said Stan.

Mike conceded that point. Nevertheless, he was worried about her. He unclipped the walkie-talkie from his belt. "Mike to Bethany, are you there?"

"This. . . . Bethany. You're breaking. . . barely hear . . ."

"Everything okay over there?"

"Yeah, fine . . . think Stan just came back . . . heard the door downstairs."

Mike and Stan exchanged glances. "Stan's with me here," said Mike. "Must just be the storm."

"I only caught part of that. Stan's . . . you?"

"Yeah, he's right here."

There was no reply. Mike thumbed the walkie-talkie again. "Mike to Bethany, do you hear me?" When she didn't respond, he tried, "Mike to Maya, come in."

The only sound was the wind and the rain.

"Damn! This is so frustrating," said Mike, clipping the radio back onto his belt.

"I'm sure she's fine," said Stan. "Besides, I'm not sure if we can even get out of the building the way the storm's blown up."

"Yeah, I know, I checked the main door earlier." Mike pointed his flashlight toward a window. "What's more, we have a missing student over here. She probably just went off exploring, but we need to find out what happened to her. I could use your help searching the building."

Stan's happy-go-lucky attitude vanished. "Sure thing, just tell me what you need me to do." He might be a goofball with some odd quirks, but Mike realized this was the Stan Jones that Jerome Torres trusted.

Everything will turn out fine . . . It's just a storm. That's all.
So why couldn't he shake this sense of impending doom?

CHAPTER 19

Claire was lost.

She'd been washing her hands in the restroom when the lights had gone out. Fortunately, she'd heeded the safety briefing and had a flashlight with her. The restroom was nestled in an alcove with three other doors. When she'd entered, a small light in the alcove illuminated the doors. Now it was quite dark in the cramped space. The power outage had disoriented her. She needed to focus, otherwise she'd be stuck there until the electricity came back on.

The batteries in her flashlight were weak and the beam only lit the way a few feet in front of her. She opened the door across the alcove and discovered a bench spectrograph lab. She loved antique science equipment. A large, silver-topped black table that looked something like an air hockey game dominated the room. Behind it shelves lined the wall, containing lenses and spectrograph gratings. She smiled at the faint rainbows reflected from the gratings in the weak light of her flashlight beam.

She backed out of the room and turned. To the right was another door. Despite her need to focus, she had to admit a nagging curiosity about what lay beyond every door in the labyrinthine building. But, with the power out and the wind howling, she would have to shut down her geek-o-meter and find her way back as soon as possible before the others started worrying. She opened the door and discovered a landing to a set of stairs descending into pitch darkness. Vertigo made her light-headed and she backed out.

For some reason, the building's designers had decided to construct two separate sets of stairs that were split, instead of one that went from bottom to top. She vowed to look at the building diagram when she reached the control room to see if she could figure out the purpose for the design. Whatever the reason, it was a damn nuisance. The stairs from the control room were behind her, on the other end of the long corridor she now occupied. She worked her way down the dark hall, trying to remember the distance to the other staircase.

After a few feet, she came to a door with a red light bulb overhead. She opened the door and a potent, chemical odor assaulted her. *I wonder if that's what embalming fluid smells like.*

She shook her head at her morbid thought. The room held a pair of sinks, a silver box, that looked a little like an old-fashioned oven, and plenty of countertop space. Dusty, brown bottles filled with liquid stood silent vigil on the shelves below. Apparently, this had served as a darkroom but had been abandoned in the age of digital detectors.

She closed the darkroom door and continued down the hall. The next door she came to was locked. Walking a few more feet, her light winked out. She shook it a couple of times, but it refused to light up. She thought briefly about the radio at her belt. She could call for help, but she hated being perceived as helpless, at least not without giving it a little more effort. She unscrewed the back of the flashlight, then screwed it back on, hit it a couple more times and it finally came back on.

A few more steps and she reached a door at the end of the hall. She opened it and found herself in another alcove containing multiple doors. The one ahead was locked. The one to the left opened into a large, vast space. Curious, she forged ahead and discovered she'd entered a storage room for instrumentation. There were digital cameras that looked like gold cans, spectrographs that took several different shapes from octagonal to cylindrical, depending on the resolution they delivered.

Eerie shadows danced on the angular, silver walls as she flashed her beam around. "Hello, is anyone in here?"

She paused a moment and listened. The only sounds were her own breathing and a hinge squeaking somewhere as it moved back and forth from the wind no doubt. A *thwack* and a *bang* in the darkness to her right startled her. "Hello?" Her flashlight went off again, plunging her into pitch-blackness.

Her breathing quickened and she flicked the switch again. Once more the dim light returned. She swallowed convulsively as she as realized she was well and truly lost. She picked a direction and walked forward, eventually coming to a set of double doors. Pushing them open she found herself staring at a great, tapering gray column. She shone her flashlight along its length and discovered the column was one of four that constituted the telescope's base. She breathed a sigh of relief. If she'd found the telescope, the control room couldn't be too far away. Across the room, was another door. She decided to push ahead and strode under the telescope, toward her objective.

Halfway across, her feet slipped out from underneath her and she dropped with a thud. Stunned, more than seriously hurt, she felt around with her left hand. The floor was coated in a thin film of oil. Groaning, she turned her flashlight back up toward the telescope's base and saw the oil reservoirs that supported the telescope's weight, allowing a small one-horsepower motor to point it precisely.

Claire eased herself to her feet. Out of habit, she dusted herself off, but swore when she realized she'd just coated her clothes in oil. Consoling herself with a reminder that she was dressed in grubby hiking clothes, she proceeded toward the door, which was her original destination. Finding herself in a spectrograph room, she was even more confused. Was it the same room as before or another one? She suddenly understood how a mouse in a maze must feel.

She eased her way around the spectrograph bench, which dominated the center of the room, and through the door at the far end. She came out in the familiar alcove, facing the restroom door. She stood there for a minute, deciding what to do next. She could stay put and radio for help, or she could try to find her way back one more time. Dark and spooky as the building was, she was actually quite fascinated by everything she'd seen. She realized there was a third option, but she should contact the control room and let them know she was okay.

She took the radio off her belt and thumbed the switch. "Uh . . . this is Claire. I'm fine. Just found myself in the bathroom when the power went off. I have my flashlight. Going to find someplace safe to settle in till the lights come back on." She stood there for a moment, and realized she'd need to release the button if she wanted to hear a response. When none came, she tried one more time. "This is Claire. I'm heading for the lounge." She released the button. Was the thing even working? She looked at it. A display indicator on the front said, "Channel One." She figured it must be tuned correctly. She pushed the button again and a little green light appeared on top.

She shrugged, figuring the power outage must have done something to the walkie-talkies. She went around the corner into the stairway. She'd seen the lounge when she toured the building the day before, and figured it would be a comfortable, safe place to wait until the lights came on. The stairway down would be comparatively easy to navigate if the flashlight went out again. She grasped the handrail tightly lest her vertigo return as she made her way down to the next floor.

It didn't look familiar, so she continued downstairs, checking each door as she went. She didn't recognize anything from the tour and began to fear she'd made a bad decision. At last, she came to the ground floor. The garage door in front of her rattled alarmingly. Wind and rain pressed against the main entrance. Stepping outside would be a poor choice. She would explore the ground floor instead. Maybe someone had come down to check the power. Maybe she could find some fresh batteries. If not, she'd head back upstairs and try for the control room again.

Turning left, she walked through the machine shop. It smelled of oil, and metal shavings littered the floor. Someone must have been working on a piece of instrumentation in the recent past. She smiled when her flashlight beam fell on a sign that read, "Heihachi's Zone." Presumably Heihachi was the name of the machinist.

On the other side of the workshop was a large handling floor. To her left was a ladder. Turning her light upward, she saw that it passed several doors.

A little farther ahead, she spied a door in the telescope pier. That surprised her; she would have thought the pier was solid. Opening the door, she found something that looked a bit like a mausoleum. Sure enough, she spotted a plaque with the name

Burroughs. She recognized it now. The place where astronomer Robert Burroughs was interred.

A rustling of cloth drew her attention to the side. A bald man with a white, handlebar mustache in a tweed suit stood there. She raised her hand to her chest, momentarily startled. "Sorry, I didn't hear you." The man reminded her of one of her professors at Princeton. Nothing about him seemed especially out of place or alarming in an observatory . . . until she realized that she could see him perfectly in the dark.

CHAPTER 20

A light beam hit Mike in the face.

"Claire, is that you?" The question came from Maya Williams.

"No, it's me—Mike."

Maya lowered the flashlight and Mike blinked back the spots before his eyes. A soft glow still suffused the control room from the computers, their screens dancing in a swirl of colors from their screensavers. Mike couldn't imagine they had much more time before the backup batteries were drained completely. He stepped fully into the control room and introduced Stan Jones to Maya and Evan.

"Have you seen any sign of her at all?" asked Maya.

Mike shook his head. "I have no idea where she's gotten to, but this is a big building. I think it would be a good idea for us to organize a search from top to bottom.

"I tried calling her," said Evan, "but my phone won't get a signal. Do you think it's the storm?"

"Even if it were clear, you wouldn't get a signal up here," said Stan. "Closest cell tower is over in Toledo."

"What about the power?" pressed Evan. "It would be a whole lot easier to search the building if we could see where we're going."

"I agree." Mike turned to Stan. "Any ideas?"

He shrugged. "All the lines seem fine. I can't find any load drawing the generator down. As far as I can tell, the power should be working. The problem is, it's not." He dropped onto a couch and scratched his jaw. "The only thing I can think of is to inspect the generator again. Maybe there's a fuel line clog or something."

Mike walked over to the operator's console and dropped

into his chair. "I don't think that's going to happen until the storm lets up." A rumble of thunder, muted by the thick walls, punctuated Mike's words. He turned to study a chart of the building mounted on the door to the dome. "There are seven levels in this building—eight if you count the basement—and four of us. I think the best thing to do is split up and see if we can find out where Claire got to. She may have stumbled in the dark, dropped her radio down a stairwell, and can't call for help."

"Not like the radios have been much help," grumbled Stan. "The way they keep cutting out."

Mike nodded. "I think we should split up, each of us takes two levels and searches as thoroughly as we can. If any of us finds Claire and she's fine, everyone can return to the control room. If she needs help, stay with her and radio the rest of us. Either way, keep in constant communication until someone responds."

Evan raised his hand. "I thought there were twelve stories up to the console room. What happened to the other five levels?"

"There's more space between some of the floors than most buildings," said Mike. "It's not like an office building where they need to use all the available space."

"Should we keep looking until we find her? What if none of us manage to locate her?" asked Maya.

"Let's all meet back here in one hour. If we haven't found her by then we'll regroup and try again," suggested Mike. "It's a good check-in point. If anyone doesn't return, we'll know where they should be."

Maya and Evan looked at each other and nodded, seeming to agree with the plan. Mike studied the building's floor plan, deciding the best way for them to split up. Some levels were more dangerous than others and some had more locked doors than others. Claire wouldn't have been able to get into one of the locked rooms, but if a door had been left ajar and closed behind her, she could be locked in. Just as he formed a plan, the phone rang.

"What the hell?" Stan sat up on the couch. "I thought the landlines were out."

Mike looked at it doubtfully. The thunder and lightning

outside made him hesitant to grab the receiver. The phone rang again—the characteristic double-ring of an outside line. Maybe it was Jerome calling to check up on them, although Mike thought he'd know better than to call during an electrical storm. On the third ring, Mike finally answered.

"Is Evan Burkholder there?" asked a deep, resonant voice on the other side. Mike's shoulders tightened.

"May I ask who's calling?"

"Certainly. My name is Vassago. Solomon Vassago."

Mike nodded. "All right, one moment, but please keep it short, there's a pretty bad storm here and it's not safe to talk on the phone." He held the phone out to Evan. "It's for you. A Mr. Vassago."

Evan and Maya exchanged glances before he took the phone. Stan stood and beckoned Mike over. "You're serious? Vassago, as in Solomon Vassago?"

Mike shrugged. "You know him?"

Stan shook his head. "Not personally, but he's a big shot lawyer from back East. Bought the old Montwood house in Toledo. Wonder what connection he has to these guys?" He spoke in a hushed tone and inclined his head toward the graduate students.

Mike turned his head and listened.

"Yeah, we found it," said Evan. "Yes . . . Yeah, it was hot, like someone just had it in the fire." Another pause. "No, I had some gloves in my pack." He listened intently. "Tomorrow afternoon? Sure." After a moment, he hung up.

"So what was that all about?" asked Stan. "Vassago an attorney for Princeton or something?"

"No, nothing like that," said Evan. "He's just an eccentric collector of some kind."

Maya shot him a warning glance.

"Collector?" asked Mike. "What kind of collector?"

Evan looked at Maya and swallowed.

"Nothing in particular," she said. "Just a rock hound looking for some specimens."

Stan narrowed his gaze. "How the heck did a big shot attorney get hooked up with some grad students if he's not connected to the university?"

"He called us," Evan blurted out. "Asked if we'd have time to do some hiking while we were up here."

"What? He can't collect his own rocks?" Stan shook his head and returned to his perch on the couch.

"He is kind of an older guy," said Evan.

Maya shot Evan another look. He nodded nervously and sat down.

"These rocks," began Mike. "They wouldn't be in any of the caves up here, would they?"

Again, Maya and Evan exchanged glances, but both remained silent.

Mike sighed and returned to the operator's chair. "Look, the Apaches are pretty sensitive about people poking around in the caves up here. The observatory has had an uneasy relationship with the tribe over the years. It only really smoothed out a few years ago when NMSU hired Jerome to be the site manager. Even though we're not on reservation land, the tribe considers Carson Peak sacred. If they discover astronomers have been poking around in the caves, it could really make trouble for us."

Stan nodded agreement. "What's more, if you took rocks, fossils or artifacts from BLM land you could be facing a really hefty fine. Vassago would have to be a pretty damned good attorney to get you off the hook."

"So, did you, or did you not, take something from one of the caves?" pressed Mike.

Evan shuffled back and forth. "Just a coin of some kind. I'm not even sure it's Apache. The cave had all kinds of footprints, like people had been in and out recently."

"Great!" Stan threw up his hands. "It's probably a ceremonial cave. There were probably footprints because the Indians go up there and hold rituals."

"He's right," said Mike. "When the storm lets up, you should put that coin back."

Maya snorted. "You don't know what you're asking."

"I'm asking you for the good of the observatory." Mike sat back and folded his arms. "Even if it just seems like some silly coin to you, it probably means a lot to the people who left it there. If that doesn't convince you, listen to what Stan says about the fines."

Maya stood and stalked across the room. "Do you have any idea how much it costs to go to college these days? How much debt we build up? After college is grad school, maybe a couple of post doc positions, and if we're lucky maybe an assistant professorship at a small college. Do you know how long it takes to pay that all back?"

Mike's brow furrowed. He'd been lucky, and hadn't accumulated much debt, but they were still paying Bethany's student loans. "Yes, of course I do," he said. "But what does that have to do—"

Evan interrupted. "Vassago offered to pay off our student loans if we found this coin."

Stan whistled long and low. "That's a lot of money for a coin."

Mike blew out a breath, took off his glasses and rubbed his nose. Finally, he slipped the glasses back on. "Yeah, I can see why you don't want to put it back, but look at it this way. You could probably walk into a museum in Santa Fe, steal a Georgia O'Keefe painting and sell it for enough to make back a good chunk of your student loans, but it would still be stealing."

Evan nodded. "I see what you mean." He looked up. "Maya?"

She stood rigid with her back to the others. Her hands shot up. "Fine! I'll think about it." She whirled around. "But while we're sitting here talking about Indian gewgaws, Claire still hasn't shown up. She could be hurt somewhere."

Mike sighed. "You're right about that." He turned to the desk. "Let me just call Bethany and check that she's all right, and then we can make a search plan." He picked up the phone. There was no dial tone. He tried dialing anyway, just in case. The line was still dead. He looked at the bulletin board and found Jerome's home number. He tried that, just to check if the outside lines worked. That one also failed. Finally he hung up. He looked at Stan, his brow furrowed. "Line's dead again."

"Could be an intermittent problem, or maybe the phone company's working on it."

Mike nodded, but remained unconvinced. They needed to find Claire, but he also had to reach the 2.5-meter to make sure Bethany was all right.

Bethany sat alone in the control room of the 2.5-meter telescope, bathed in the soft glow from the monitors. She shivered and scrounged in her bag for her sweater. It might be New Mexico in the summertime, but she was on a mountaintop during a thunderstorm. The little heat source gestating inside her usually kept her warm, but this wasn't a usual situation.

The metal sheeting at the bottom of the dome—the so-called dome skirt—rattled and banged with an ever-changing cadence as the wind whipped by the building. The door downstairs thumped several times followed by an alarming rattle and thump, like cabinets opening and closing.

Stan must not have closed it properly when he left.

If the wind had opened the door, it could fling open cabinets as it blew through the building. Optical components and delicate equipment could be damaged. Just as she stood to grab a flashlight, she heard something like a shout.

It has to be either Mike or Stan.

She walked out of the control room and down the hall to the top of the stairs. Standing there, she heard a pair of voices, neither of them familiar.

"I checked the cabinets in there. Nothing but a bunch of science junk," said one male voice.

"It's all oily back in that room," said another voice. "You'd think scientists would keep the place cleaner." There was a pause. "Let's check upstairs."

Bethany's heart thumped in her chest. These weren't people she knew, nor did they sound like people just lost in the storm seeking shelter. They were looking for something specific. She flicked off the flashlight and on silent feet, backed away from the top of the stairs.

CHAPTER 21

"Do you think something bad happened to Claire?"
Maya turned her anxious gaze to the three men.

Stan's gaze darted from Mike to Evan. "Well, there was the one guy cut in half by the dome's wheels," he said.

"That was a long time ago." Mike frowned at Stan. "Before we established our safety protocol. Besides, the power's been off, so no chance of that happening."

"There are some pretty good drop-offs." Stan shrugged. "She might have tripped over a rail in the dark."

Even in the faint light cast by the flashlights, Mike saw the blood drain from Evan's face. "I'm sure she's all right," he said. "At worst, I suspect she's got a broken leg or something and can't walk back."

"There are those high voltage power racks on the pump floor," said Stan. "Even without power, the capacitors up there could hold quite a charge . . ."

"Stan!" Mike flashed his light in his fellow operator's face. "You're not helping. Let's focus on finding Claire."

Evan and Maya nodded in unison. Maya set out through the doors that led into the dome's upper level while the others proceeded downstairs.

"Building's like a maze," muttered Evan. "We could walk right by her and never know."

Mike patted Evan on the shoulder. "That's why we're doing a systematic search."

"And, if we don't find her?" Evan's voice sounded wobbly.

"We'll have to assume she got outside before the storm hit," Mike replied. "We'll cross that bridge when the time comes."

"Okay." With that, Evan trudged down the stairs to search the ground floor.

151

"Do you think the kid will be all right?" Stan's voice held a note of concern that Mike wished he'd shown a few minutes earlier.

"I'm sure he'll be fine." Mike reached for the door handle.

"Say, Mike, what if Claire doesn't want to be found?"

Mike blinked. "What do you mean?"

"What if she's deliberately hiding out somewhere? It would be easy to do in this building."

Mike conceded the last point. "Why would she want to hide?"

Stan shrugged. "Just how well do we know any of these visiting astronomers? You and I have met a few who were real pieces of work. These kids already stole something from the cave to sell to that big shot lawyer."

"Yes, that worries me too," Mike said, recalling Jerome's warnings about the Apache artifacts.

"Yeah, and some of them are so obsessed with their work, they're virtual psychopaths. Remember that guy who threw a computer monitor at an operator who wanted to close the dome."

Mike swallowed hard, recalling the legendary story. "I remember . . . Look, we can't do anything about it now. Let's finish the search before we start concocting scenarios."

"Sure, sure. Just watch your back." With that, Stan continued down the staircase.

Mike opened the door labeled "Mezzanine." Inside were racks of computers that commanded telescope functions and controlled cameras and spectrographs. Other machines collected data and sent it down to servers at New Mexico State University for archiving.

Mike walked behind the racks and swept his flashlight around, but he couldn't find any evidence that Claire had been here. Stan's warped mind must have been getting to him, because he even checked the large air conditioner vent, thinking it was a place someone could deliberately hide.

He continued to the next level, hoping one of them would find Claire soon. He arrived in the long dark hallway that led to the restroom. Even knowing his way around, he had to think about which direction to go. He turned and stopped at the first door, which led to an old darkroom. A quick search with his flashlight revealed no signs of Claire, he continued down the hall and unlocked a door that allowed access to pipes and ventilator shafts running through the building.

When he arrived at the restroom, he knocked on the door. Getting no answer, he opened it and aimed the light inside. Convinced Claire wasn't there, he turned around and entered the bench spectrograph room. He walked all around the bench, just to be sure, before moving on to the base of the telescope. As he walked under it, his feet slipped and he swung his arms to regain his balance. Keeping himself steady, he shone his flashlight downward.

He expected to see a smooth sheen of oil. Instead, he made out a zigzag of scuff marks. Clearly, someone else before him had lost his or her footing. He tugged on his pant legs and knelt. It looked as if someone had taken a fall. If so, they had picked themselves up and walked away.

Mike stood. He became aware of another light shining down from above. He stepped away from the telescope's base, avoiding the railing that blocked the hatchway in the floor. "Is that you, Maya?" he called.

"It's me," she said. "Find anything?"

Mike shook his head. "Just a hint that someone slipped in some oil down here, but for all I know that could have happened anytime in the last couple of days. Maybe one of the day crew . . ."

Maya nodded. "I don't see any sign of her up here. I'm going to check the dorm room level."

"Sure thing." Mike scanned the vast space with his flashlight once more. He even checked the net underneath the telescope, which was used to catch tools or small parts that might fall. Seeing nothing unusual, he looked over to the alcove with the door leading to the dome trucks. He strode across and checked the door. He breathed a sigh of relief, finding it locked as he remembered, but knew he should look inside anyway. As he reached into his pockets for the keys, the hairs on the back of his neck tingled.

He turned, gasping at the sight of the swirling, glowing dust motes.

He scanned the length of the telescope. Was the light coming from Maya's flashlight? Although he saw no sign, he remembered Stan and his glow-in-the-dark mask. Mike stepped forward, his hand out. He wouldn't put it past Stan to wander around in the dark, playing a joke when they needed to be searching.

As his hand pushed through the swirling dust motes, he felt a cold prickling, as though someone had dribbled liquid nitrogen on his skin. He yanked his hand back and held it to himself.

The dust motes formed into a face. At first, the mouth was merely a slash, but it turned into lips and a mustache. Dark holes became kindly eyes. The mouth moved, as though trying to say something.

Mike was rooted to the spot, knees trembling. His gut churned as his mind swirled between fear of this new apparition and something like relief that he now knew he'd never been hallucinating. He willed himself to step closer, trying to hear.

A whisper of air blew by, a soft sibilance, and he just made out the word "Professor."

"Professor Burroughs?" Mike's eyebrows knitted. "Is-is that you Professor?"

The face nodded and the mouth formed five syllables. Mike couldn't quite hear. He shook his head.

He had no idea how this was happening. But it seemed as though the Professor was trying to help him. "Professor Burroughs . . . We're looking for Claire Yarbro, she's a graduate student."

A breath of air passed by his ear. Mike could have sworn he heard the word, "safe."

"Claire is safe?" The apparition gave a gentle nod. Mike breathed a sigh of relief. Compelling as the apparition was, he needed to resume the search. He started to turn away, but the cold sensation struck his shoulder, like a cold hand. He turned back to the figure. Burroughs was moving his mouth again. Mike pushed the bridge of his glasses up and tried to read the lips. He thought he could make out "Professor Dwyer."

"Professor Dwyer?" Mike's mouth went dry. "Bethany?"

Again, the apparition nodded.

"What about Bethany?"

"Trouble." The word was distinct in Mike's mind, more like he thought it than heard it. He blinked and the figure vanished.

Bethany slipped back into the control room at the 2.5-meter telescope. She searched for something she could use as a weapon. Steps resounded on the stairs down the hall, outside the control room. She looked behind her. A glass door led into the computer room, which adjoined the control room. Just on the other side was a long push broom. After unscrewing the handle from the broom, she pressed herself against the wall behind the door.

A cable tray over her head allowed sound to come in from the control room where a door whispered open. Feet tromped through the room. "Hey, look what we got here. A bag."

Bethany cursed herself for leaving her bag out in plain sight.

"You suppose someone's here?" came a second voice.

Silence.

They were probably gesturing to each other now. A nod? A shrug? Bethany resisted the temptation to peep around the corner and see what the men were doing, knowing her flashlight beam would give her away. She heard a rustling of fabric and an ominous metallic clicking. Switchblades? Gun safeties? She hoped the sound of her breathing wasn't audible to the men on the other side.

The door leading to the telescope opened. "Shit man, check this out."

"You find the blow?"

"Nah, but this is fuckin' cool. It's like somethin' out of some sci-fi movie."

Their voices died down and the door closed. They must have gone to look at the telescope. How was she going to get out of here to call for help? One of them was looking for "blow." Why would men come to an observatory looking for cocaine? Sure, she knew some astronomers who had experimented with drugs here and there. A few were even foolish enough to bring them along for observing—get high with the altitude.

Astronomers granted time at an observatory like Carson Peak
were often brilliant, but they were also human and prone to
human vices.

A bang and a crash sounded from the dome, followed by
"Shit!" Bethany's pulse kicked up furiously as she tried to guess
what they might have crashed into. In addition to the precision
instruments were canisters of compressed gas. Knocked
over with valves jammed open, those could become deadly
projectiles, perfectly capable of bursting through the drywall
that separated the computer room from the dome.

The door to the dome opened again. "I tell you, it ain't
here. It's probably in that bigger building, or maybe the office
building."

"Yeah, but they were locked. We're just lucky someone
didn't close the door all the way on this place."

*Stan! When I get out of here, I'm going to wring your neck for
leaving that door open.*

There was a scrape of plastic against wood, followed by
a clatter and a tinkle. She imagined a computer monitor had
been shoved aside and her messenger bag dumped out. "Check
this. Keys!"

"You suppose one of those opens the other buildings?"

"Worth a try," said the first voice.

Please leave. Please leave. Please leave.

"But I want to finish checking this place out first."

CHAPTER 22

Bethany held her breath.

The transparent computer room door opened and someone scanned around with a flashlight. Bethany huddled in a recessed space behind the door, knowing she wasn't visible unless the person turned to look. The man who stood there wore a sweatshirt with the hood down around his neck. His hair was cropped close in a buzz cut. She gripped the broom handle tighter, ready to bring it crashing down on his head if she had to, but she knew there was another guy lurking around. Did they have guns? She suspected they did.

The man shook his head as he stepped back from the door. "Damn, it's a room full of computers. Why the fuck do those scientist nerds need all these computers anyway, and why are they on when all the other power is out?"

"Battery backup," said the other guy. "They must be able to play some awesome games."

A mouse shuffled against a tabletop. "Da'fuck is all this? Just a bunch of words and buttons and shit." The mouse clicked twice more. "You gotta be shittin' me. Solitaire? Minesweeper? That's the best they can do with all this hardware?"

"Doesn't matter," said the other one. "Let's go check outside, see if the storm's let up. Try these keys on the other buildings."

"You got it, bro."

Footsteps tromped toward the control room door.

"Mike calling Bethany."

She jumped as the radio on her belt suddenly burst into life.

"Hey, did you hear something?" came a voice from the control room door.

"Mike calling Bethany. Come in please."

Bethany reached down and turned the radio off. The click

157

of the switch sounded very loud to her ears, even though she knew it was whisper soft.

"Yeah, someone was calling on a radio."

"Where'd it come from?"

Bethany imagined eyes sweeping over the counters in the control room. "This is Mike calling Bethany, can you hear me?" This time the voice came from the other room. It was one of the extra radios lying next to the computer.

"Looks like some kinda walkie-talkie," said one of the men. "So there *is* someone else on the mountain."

"Where do you think they are?"

Skin *thwacked* against skin. "The other buildings, asswipe," said the other one.

"Then why's there a radio on in here? And this bag?"

The silence returned. A moment later the computer room door opened again. The same man entered, letting the door close behind him. As he turned around and faced her, she whacked him in the face with the broom handle. He fell back against the wall, stunned, and shook his head. She pulled the broom handle back, whirled it around and jabbed at his crotch. Missing, she hit his thigh.

"Goddamn it, that hurt!" he shouted.

Laughter filtered in from the other room. She stood in front of the clear glass door. The other man aimed a gun at her. He shook his head and beckoned for her to come out. The man she'd attacked drew a knife and rushed at her. She jumped back out of the blade's range, but he reached out and grabbed her wrist and yanked hard. She whimpered in pain.

"Ricardo, bring her out here," said the other man.

The man called Ricardo held the knife up. It trembled with the man's suppressed rage. "You heard him. Get out there."

Bethany felt a sob build up in the back of her throat, but willed it down. She would not cry in front of these men. She stepped around the man with the knife and opened the door.

"So, we find someone here after all," said the man with the gun.

"Who are you? What do you want?" Bethany's words sounded braver than she felt.

The man with the gun grinned. Like the other man, he had

close-cropped hair. A thin mustache sprouted from his upper lip. A tattoo of a skeleton in a dress adorned his forearm. "I ain't nobody." Hyper-aware in her terror, Bethany suppressed a hysterical giggle at the double negative. "I'm just lookin' for some stuff that was stolen from me an' my brother."

She turned her head. Sure enough, she could see a family resemblance between the two men. The other—the gunman called him Ricardo—was clean-shaven, taller and thinner than the tattooed guy, with a face cratered by acne scars. "This is an observatory. We're astronomers, not thieves."

"Yeah? Well, someone up here's a thief." The gunman stepped close. He brought the pistol up under her chin. The metal was cold and hard against her skin. As she swallowed, she felt the barrel press into her throat. "We followed the trail up here to the mountaintop, then the storm started."

Bethany found it difficult to think with the gun pressed against her neck. "If you shoot me or stab me, all you'll have is a body on the floor, and no one who can help you. Could you please put the gun and the knife away?"

The gunman narrowed his gaze. He stepped back, but kept his gun aimed at her. He gave a brief nod and Ricardo took a step back. She breathed a little easier with the extra space. "What do you think was stolen?" she asked.

"Seventy-five kilos of prime . . ."

The gunman made a slashing move across his throat with the gun. "It's none of your business, *chica*."

"I can't help you if I don't know what you're looking for."

"Why would you want to help us?" The gunman said, pointing his chin at her.

"I want to get out of this alive if I can."

The gunman pursed his lips and shrugged. "Makes sense to me, but I ain't makin' no guarantees, especially if I find out you stole our stuff."

Bethany tried to force her brain to work through a haze of fear. "Seventy-five kilos of what? Marijuana? Cocaine? That's a lot. It would be hard to get that much of anything into a building around here without being seen."

"Now you see," said the gunman, "this is why I think you're in on it."

She shook her head. "I just got here today. I haven't seen seventy-five kilos of anything in one place. How do you know someone didn't just take whatever you're looking for and already left?"

"We followed tracks up the old Forest Service road," said Ricardo from behind her. "They came up here and disappeared."

Bethany let out a sigh. She tried to think how she could get these men to go away, buy herself some time, and warn the others. "Let me call the other telescope on the radio. My . . . friend was calling earlier. He'll be worried. I can ask him if he's seen anything."

"Why would he tell you anything?" snarled Ricardo.

"Why would he lie?" countered Bethany.

"What's to stop him from calling the cops on us while we're here?" said the tattooed guy.

"The phone lines are down and there's no cell service. The power is down. So he can't call anyone." She tried to use a reassuring tone so they would trust her.

The gunman considered her words for a moment. Finally he nodded to the radio. "All right, but you say one wrong word, you're dead. You got that, *chica*?"

Bethany swallowed and nodded. She swayed her hip a little to show that she wore a radio on her belt. Slowly she reached down, grabbed it, and turned it on. "Bethany to Mike, are you there?"

There was silence for several heartbeats. She feared the radio repeater had died again.

"This is Mike. Thank God. Are you all right?"

"I'm fine," she lied, though grateful for the clear channel and relieved to hear his voice, even if he wasn't close enough to help her. "Have you heard about anyone going down the old Forest Service road in the last couple of days?"

The gunman tightened his grip on the pistol. Was he paranoid about her being so direct? Did he fear she was sending some kind of coded signal?

"As a matter of fact, these grad students went down there. Said they found something . . ." If Mike said something else, it was cut off.

The gunman exchanged a glance with his brother.

"Can you repeat that? You cut out again."

"They promised to put it back," said Mike.

The gunman shook his head. "Tell me another bedtime story," he whispered.

"I've gotta run," called Mike. "One of the students is missing."

"Missing?"

"Yeah, disappeared when the lights went out," said Mike. "I love you."

Beads of sweat emerged on Bethany's forehead. She hadn't wanted to admit a close relationship to the man on the other end of the walkie-talkie, afraid it would give the gangsters some kind of leverage. "I love you, too," she said, reluctantly. She hoped her reluctance wasn't audible or hurtful. If it was, he didn't broadcast any indication.

"Now ain't that sweet," said the tattooed gunman. "I think you better show us where 'they' are."

Bethany swallowed hard, fighting back tears.

"Let's go downstairs." The gunman held out his hand, and Bethany shuddered as she edged past him. There was too little space in the control room. She led the way and opened the exit door.

Rain came down in torrents; a gust of wind splashed water through the door, like a wave rolling over a ship at sea. From the corner of her eye, Bethany noticed the gunman holstering his pistol. Apparently, he didn't want it to get wet. She breathed a sigh of relief; he must not think her much of a threat at this point. That meant she might live, but she still worried about Mike.

A flash of lightning revealed the 5-meter enclosure's white dome. "They're over there, in that building." If the gunmen left, she could call Mike on the radio, warn him that they were coming. Maybe between him, Stan, and the students, they could set up some kind of ambush.

"All right, let's go." The gunman put his hand on her back, ready to shove her outside.

"You don't need me to go with you."

"You're our insurance," said Ricardo.

Another flash of lightning and Bethany's next words froze in her throat.

Something was coming their way. But it had nothing to do with the storm. It was huge and hunched, reminding Bethany of the velociraptors from the movie *Jurassic Park*. Moving on stilt-like legs it looked wild and shaggy, as though the wind and rain had ruffled its fur or feathers. She gasped as she realized this was the creature Mike had seen the night Wallerstein died.

Oh my God, it's real!

"Holy shit! What the fuck is that?" Ricardo croaked.

The creature whipped its head around. Dark as the wind-swept rainy night was, its eyes were even darker, as though they absorbed everything they gazed upon. She remembered Mike's stories of the apparition he'd seen two years ago. If this was indeed the same creature, he hadn't conveyed the full horror of coming face-to-face with it. Lightning flashed again. The creature began sprinting toward them, releasing a wailing sound somewhere between a hawk's screech and a mountain lion's roar. Her heart pounding in her ears, Bethany watched in terror as the beast swooped down on them.

The men pulled her back into the building, slamming the door behind them. Bethany backed away from them as the two gunmen leaned against the door to keep it shut. A second later, a hammering force reverberated against the metal door, bowing it inward. "Can we lock this thing?"

Bethany slipped by him and threw a deadbolt.

With a screech, the creature crashed into the door again. Ricardo looked wide-eyed at his partner, his body drenched from the storm and sweat. "What are we gonna do?" he asked? The knife hung limp from his fingers.

Bethany realized the two gangsters were as scared as kittens. Even though they were criminals, they were human, and whatever was out there was far more dangerous than these two. Whatever happened, they had to fight for their lives together.

CHAPTER 23

This was such a waste of time.

Evan had searched all through the machine shop on the ground floor. He even checked the cabinets and shelves, thinking someone could be hiding there. All he found were cans of oil, old machine tools, rags, and assorted pieces of metal stock ready for machining. He continued on through the next door. He was concerned about Claire but completely annoyed with the situation. All of this trouble was interfering with his work.

The observations they'd hoped to collect would likely contribute to all of their graduate theses. Maya was the senior student, so she would benefit most. Evan was next in line, and Claire had never been observing before. She had accompanied them to learn how to observe, and now she had gotten herself lost. Evan had met Claire at the beginning of the previous school year and he wondered whether or not she was PhD material. She often sat in the graduate student lounge, reading a novel rather than doing her homework. Either she was quick at her homework, or she put it off until the last minute.

Evan passed through a door and the ceiling disappeared into the darkness above. Crates stacked twenty feet high or more stood to his right. Shining his flashlight upward revealed a distant, ribbed ceiling with a hatch in the middle. That must be how instrumentation was lifted up to the observing floor, or the primary mirror lifted down. He could imagine what it would be like for the technicians lowering a two-foot thick, precisely machined hunk of glass down all that distance. What if the crane cable snapped? Of course anyone underneath the mirror would be splattered instantly. What's more, the mirror itself cost a small fortune and the observatory would have to shut down while a new one was made. He was surrounded by all of this advanced technology and yet if even one thing broke down, the entire operation came to a screeching halt. As it had now.

He frowned and examined the room with his flashlight. Ahead of him stood an enormous metal structure that looked like a great bell, sitting over a base that reminded Evan of a pie-plate. He guessed it was a vacuum chamber, possibly used to coat the giant mirrors with aluminum. Turning his flashlight beam, he spotted a door in the telescope pier. He took a step toward it and tripped over a railroad-like track in the floor.

He went down on his knee with a crack and a groan. Rolling over onto his rear end, he rubbed his knee, cursing his clumsiness. Earlier in the day, he'd climbed down into the back of that strange cave with the thick atmosphere and found the mysterious talisman. The rich, odd-ball lawyer, Solomon Vassago, had given him the exact directions. Vassago had creeped Evan out, with his weirdo eyes and his need to possess the artifact. He was like some dude out of one of those old Dracula movies.

Whatever. He was paying them a fortune and that made all this shit worth it. The nerve of that operator guy, Mike. If all that old stuff in the caves was so important to the Apaches, why didn't they keep it in a museum to protect it? The talisman probably wasn't even Apache. It was probably Aztec or something. If so, the Apaches wouldn't miss it. He'd make a show of going down to the cave tomorrow to get Mike off his back, but he had no intention of actually returning it. "Yeah, when Hell freezes over." Evan snickered and pulled himself to his feet with only a minor twinge in his knee.

Gene Carter had told them that most telescope operators were failed astronomers who couldn't cut it in grad school. That would probably be Claire's fate. Why did universities even bother with them anyway? He was certain he could learn how to operate one in half an hour or so.

He grabbed the flashlight and continued into the pier where he found a white marble, domed structure with Greek columns and a heavy door—the tomb of Robert Burroughs. Now there was an astronomer! He took observations until the day he died. Evan circled the tomb until he reached the back.

A ladder disappeared through a hatch above, which he estimated to be lower than the ceiling in the previous room. He wondered if the techs even thought about searching the pier. When he finished checking the ground floor and the one above, he'd come back and try the ladder.

"Claire!" he called out, just in case she could hear.

His voice echoed so loudly in the narrow, round chamber that he had to clamp his hands down over his ears. He wondered which was worse, the loud echo or the silence of his own thoughts. He made his way to the vacuum chamber and did a double take. Did he just see something move on the other side? He stepped closer. A hydraulic rod supported the bell-shaped top about three feet above the plate-like bottom. Evan pointed his flashlight beam across the way. There was a door on the other side and some tanks where someone could hide. As he scanned his beam across the area, he saw someone beckoning him to that side.

He tried to ease his way around one side of the vacuum chamber, but found it too close to the wall. The control panel blocked the other side. Evan climbed onto the pie-plate like structure, so he could crawl across. As he did he heard a *chug-chug-chugging* sound.

Several thoughts went through his mind at once. Had the power come back on? Had the storm settled down? If so, should he get back to the control room in case observing started up again? But would Mike let them observe with Claire still missing?

In the next instant, all thoughts flew from his mind as he realized the top of the vacuum chamber was coming down fast. He dove for the far side, but the dome closed over him before he could make it. Luckily, it wasn't a small space, there was plenty of room for him to stand inside the closed structure. Four small windows afforded a view outside, but he couldn't see much . . .

"What the hell?"

Someone stood at the controls. Evan banged on the window. "Hey, you! Let me out!"

The figure looked up at him with bright, orange eyes, glowing like hot coals.

Evan blinked and looked again, but whoever it was had vanished.

The walkie-talkie! He unhooked the device from his belt loop. "This is Evan. Did the power come back on?"

"Evan?" Stan Jones had finished his check of the pump floor and was making his way down to the basement. "Can you repeat? I didn't catch all of that."

"I said . . . power come on?"

Stan reached the next landing. There was a light switch on the wall beside the door. He flicked it on and off again.

"Nope," he called into the radio. "No lights. What's going on?"

"The hydraulic motor for the vacuum . . ." Evan's words crackled into static. ". . . trapped inside."

Stan's brow furrowed. "I didn't quite copy that. You said you're trapped inside a vacuum chamber? You mean the aluminizing chamber?"

"Yeah, could you come get me out?"

Stan released a guffaw. He shook his head wondering how someone could be stupid enough to get himself trapped in an aluminizing chamber. Then again, the power was out, so how could the chamber have moved on its own? Maybe the brakes released and it just dropped? He shrugged. Getting him out without power might be a challenge.

Stan continued on to the ground floor, cut through the machine shop into the mirror handling area. Sure enough, the aluminizing chamber was shut tight. A flashlight beam poured from inside. Stan approached and shone his light through another porthole. Evan turned toward him, a sour look on his face.

Stan pressed the button to lift the chamber's top. Nothing happened, which didn't surprise him, but a good tech always tried the simplest thing first.

Footsteps pounded from behind and the machine shop door flew open. Stan whirled to discover Maya. "Did I hear that Evan's trapped down here?"

Stan pointed up to the chamber. "Yeah, I'm guessing the brakes released. There's no power to the console." He scanned the adjoining shelves for a crowbar, something to lift the bell enough for Evan to get out.

Mike's voice came through the radio. "Is Evan trapped in the aluminizing chamber?"

Maya answered. "He is."

"How'd he get in there?"

"I was trying to get to the other side. There's a door over there. I thought I saw someone," Evan replied.

"Claire, maybe?" asked Maya.

Stan keyed his transmitter so Evan could hear. "That just connects up to the entry area, makes a full circle of the bottom level. You could have reached her by going around the long way."

"Would have been nice if someone had told me that," grumbled Evan.

Mike's next transmission revealed his irritation. "We showed you the building plans." After a moment he spoke again. "Can I help?"

Stan keyed the transmitter. "Yeah, see if you can find a crowbar or two. I think we're going to have to lift the top."

"Can you . . . I only caught . . . of that."

Stan swore under his breath. "Bring two crowbars."

"Crowbars, gotcha," said Mike.

Just then, Stan saw the red light flicker on the console. "What the fuck? I just checked that. There isn't any power."

A rumble reverberated around them followed by a rhythmic chugging.

"What's that noise?" asked Maya.

Stan ran to the console. The air pressure in the chamber was dropping.

"No, no, no!"

Jerome Torres stood by the window watching sheets of rain pouring down. The power had been off for more than two hours. Kendra had set up candles around the house. Their soft, flickering glow gave a mystical feeling to the old miner's house he called home.

It was cool for a summer evening and Kendra had started a fire in the woodstove. She assembled a homemade stew of odds and ends from the fridge she didn't want to spoil.

Mateo sat in the recliner telling Derek a story.

"One day, Coyote and his friend, Bobcat, heard that the white men were making whiskey. They snuck into camp and stole the whiskey. When they got a short distance away, Coyote couldn't help himself, he began to drink it. 'Bobcat,' said Coyote, 'I must howl at the moon, I can't help myself.'

"'Don't you dare,' admonished Bobcat. 'The white men will know you've stolen their whiskey and they'll put you in jail.'

"'I'll just howl a little,' said Coyote." Mateo held up his finger and thumb, just a short distance apart and winked at his grandson. Derek burst into giggles.

Jerome couldn't help thinking about Roscoe Perkins and his inability to stop himself from drinking, which led him to do stupid things. Was Mateo telling this story for Derek's sake or for his?

"Coyote howled. At first it was just a little howl, like he said." Mateo let out a tiny sound, like a mouse imitating a coyote. "But a moment later, Coyote couldn't help himself and he let out a loud yip and yowl." Mateo lifted his head, "Yip, yip, yeoww!"

Derek joined him in the howl and both the old man and young child laughed together.

"Sure enough, the white men came along, arrested Coyote, and threw him right in jail."

Kendra shook her head. Jerome winked at her. He knew that his wife approved of Mateo telling Derek traditional stories, but he also knew she sometimes wondered whether all of them were appropriate for young boys.

"What happened to Coyote?" asked Derek, eyes wide.

Mateo frowned, sat back, and rubbed his chin in deep thought. "Well, after Coyote sobered up, he made a plan. You see, he saw the white men outside training a horse, but no matter what they did, those white men couldn't get that horse to behave. Coyote called out to them. You see, he had horse magic and he knew what to do. He made a deal with them to let him out of jail if he could train the horse . . ." Mateo paused, his brow knitted.

"What happened next, grandpa?" Derek moved closer. "You can't leave the story there."

"What's wrong, Grandfather?" asked Jerome in concern.

After a moment, Mateo shook his head. "Nothing, just a strange feeling . . . What do you call it? *Deja vu.*"

CHAPTER 24

Mike saw three flashlight beams.

One came from a trembling Maya, the light continuously bouncing between the control console and the dome's window. Another sporadically gleamed from inside. He couldn't imagine what Evan was feeling at this point. Frustrated? Worried? Scared? Probably that times ten. Stan aimed the third at the console and swore as he punched buttons.

Mike tripped on the rails as he ran forward, almost dropping the crowbars onto his feet. He righted himself just as Maya hopped down from her perch. He handed her a crowbar and they struggled to open the chamber, but neither could break the seal. In frustration, Maya slammed her crowbar against the chamber.

"Damn it, what . . . was that for?" called Evan.

Maya unclipped her radio from her belt. "Sorry. How are you doing?"

"It's . . . stuffy. Hard to . . . breathe."

Although there were pauses, Mike didn't think the radio had cut out that time. He looked over to Stan who shook his head.

"I can't get the vacuum pump to shut down." Stan took a step back and put his hands on his hips.

"You can't give up," called Maya. "Do something!"

"I am," he shot back. "I'm thinking, okay?"

Mike had no idea how this could have happened in a power failure. But given the fact that he'd seen the ghost of Professor Burroughs, he sensed it had something to do with his premonitions. He also knew without a doubt that Evan didn't have much time left.

Stan slapped his forehead, then pointed. "I'm going to see

170

if I can pull the vacuum pump's plug. See what you can do." With that, he ran for the machine shop door.

Mike toggled the main power switch. Nothing.

Maya let out a sound halfway between a gasp and a sob. "He's in trouble!"

Mike clambered up onto the lip of the chamber and shone his light in through the porthole. Evan had collapsed onto his knees, holding his throat, gasping for breath. A moment later, he toppled over sideways, eyes wide open and staring.

A rattling sounded from the door on the other side of the chamber as Stan fumbled with the keys. Once he burst through, he pulled on the power cord with both hands, but it wouldn't budge. "Throw me one of those crowbars!"

Mike hopped down from the aluminizing chamber, grabbed a crowbar and threw it through the narrow gap on the side. It clattered against the concrete wall forcing Stan to scramble after it. He shoved the sharp end of the crowbar into the power cord, unleashing a shower of sparks and throwing him backward into the entryway.

"Stan!" called Mike.

"I'm okay," sputtered Stan from the other room.

Mike glanced at the console. The pressure continued to drop.

"Oh my God," whispered Maya.

Mike peered in the window. Evan wasn't moving. His eyes had rolled back in his head. The skin on his face and hands was swelling up, as though he'd suffered a bad allergic reaction. The vacuum pump had sucked all the air out of the chamber and the gasses and fluids in Evan's body were expanding.

Maya leapt down from her perch and together they tried the crowbar again, grunting in their efforts. Nothing. It wouldn't budge. Maya screamed and leapt on the chamber, pounding the glass with her fist. Mike scrubbed his hands over his face, feeling her frustration. He aimed his flashlight into the window again and what he saw would haunt him for the rest of his life. Evan's skin began to shrivel and wrinkle, like he was aging into an old man on fast forward. In a matter seconds, he turned into a mummy no different than Tutankhamen.

"No, no, no!" Stan's voice bordered on hysteria on the other side of the chamber. He hopped off the aluminizing chamber's lip and grabbed the crowbar.

Mike hopped off as well. "No, Stan, don't!"

Stan looked wildly from the pump to the aluminizing chamber. He climbed up on the chamber again and swung at the glass of the porthole. The crowbar bounced off. He took another swing, which also bounced off.

"Stan, he's already gone!" yelled Mike.

"He can't be . . ." This was from Maya who stared in through the porthole, sobbing, shaking her head. "He can't be dead. How can he be dead?"

Stan swung at the glass of the porthole again. This time, too late, the glass cracked. Unable to get to Stan directly, Mike ran from the room and circled the building's perimeter. He burst into the room from the other side, and watched as Stan shattered the glass. The momentum carried Stan's arm through the porthole.

Stan screamed.

Blood seeped around the porthole, where Stan's arm was embedded in shards of thick glass. Without warning, the power shut off on its own.

With the pump quiet, the only sounds came from the rattling of the large garage door, punctuated by Maya's broken sobs. Mike scrambled up next to Stan and pushed on his arm, completely breaking the seal. Stan gasped as his arm was driven farther into the broken glass, but Mike was now able to help him ease his arm out from the chamber.

The two dropped down to the floor. Mike searched for a first aid kit and then dressed Stan's wounds as best he could, given the darkness. He almost laughed at the thought of that first aid refresher course Jerome had set up for him his first week back.

"How do you feel?" asked Mike.

Stan's skin had lost all its color and his eyes were wide. "How the hell do you think I feel?" Stan gave a dismal shake of his head. "Why didn't I think of smashing the glass sooner?"

Mike sniffed, barely holding back his own tears. "Thick as the glass was, I didn't think it would smash at all . . . It was good thinking."

"Too damn late," said Stan. "We've gotta find Claire." He shook his head. "We've gotta find her before it's too late."

"How did this even happen?" asked Mike.

"I don't have a fuckin' clue."

Mike looked around. "Something's different."

"What?" asked Stan.

"It's quiet."

The wind had stopped. It was eerily calm. All they could hear was the sound of Maya's sniffling.

Just as Mike thought the worst was over, a shrieking roar erupted from outside.

Stan's head jerked up. "What was that?"

Mike stilled, trying to listen over the hammering of his own heart. "I don't know . . ."

"Do you think it's the louvers?"

Mike locked eyes with Stan. He could see the fear in his eyes and knew it mirrored his own.

The sound was different from the continuous rattle they'd heard for the past hour. It was unearthly . . .

The shrieking was punctuated by a thunderous slam against the garage door . . . and then nothing.

A moment later, the wind resumed its howling.

Kendra served dinner while Jerome continued his vigil at the window. "I hate to think what this storm is doing to the observatory. I hope everyone is okay with the power out."

"I'm sure they're fine," said Kendra. "Probably better than us. After all, they have generators."

Jerome nodded and smiled. "Still, I imagine there will be a lot of branches to clear in the morning. Not looking forward to that."

Mateo emerged from the bathroom.

"Did you take the ibuprofen?" asked Kendra.

"Yes, I'm feeling better. Thank you, Granddaughter." Mateo smiled reassuringly. He turned his attention to Derek. "Now, where were we?"

"Coyote was in jail and he saw the silly white man's horse," the boy replied. Mateo sat beside his great-grandson and continued his story.

Jerome and Kendra exchanged glances as Kendra filled four bowls of stew. She passed one to Jerome to hand to Derek. Jerome knew Kendra was pleased for Derek to identify with his Mescalero Apache heritage, but he also knew she didn't want Derek to think of his Anglo half as "other" or "alien" in any way. Kendra wanted Derek to think of himself as a human being first. Jerome understood all of that but he also understood the legacy of centuries of oppression.

Mateo nodded. "Yes, Coyote had a plan."

Jerome smiled as he remembered the story. There were good lessons in this story that had nothing to do with race. He ruffled his son's hair and winked at his wife, letting her know it was okay.

"Coyote called out to the white men and told them if they gave him money to spend when he was released, he could train the horse."

"Did they give him the money, Grandpa?" Derek's eyes grew wide as he took a big bite of stew.

"They did," said Mateo. "They let Coyote out and he climbed in the saddle and calmed the horse with his mind. He tapped the horse's flanks with his feet as though he were trying to get the horse to move. The horse just stood there, and Coyote said, 'This horse won't go with this horrible old saddle. Bring a nice pretty saddle.' The white men did as they were told. This time, when Coyote climbed in the saddle, he commanded the horse to go with his mind and the horse shot right out of town before anyone could stop him."

Derek listened with rapt attention. He ate without looking, scooping up even the vegetables in the stew. Jerome thought Kendra would appreciate knowing that trick.

"The white men chased after Coyote. Meanwhile, Coyote took the money he was given and strung it up in a tree. When the white men caught up with him, Coyote pointed to the tree and said, 'I found a tree that grows money. If you give me more money, I will sell you this tree.' Coyote saw it was mid-day and kicked the tree. All the money fell down and he collected it up. The white men even helped him. Coyote said, 'You must harvest the tree at noon each day. It will not produce more money before then.' The white men gave Coyote more money and he rode off, while they waited for the tree to grow a new crop."

Derek laughed at the story. "Does Coyote only fool white men?"

Mateo looked up at Kendra and Jerome and smiled knowingly. "No, Grandson. Coyote has been fooling Apaches far longer than he has fooled white men."

Jerome snorted. "Next thing you'll tell us is that Coyote taught the Apaches to build the first casinos."

"I wouldn't be surprised if he did," said Mateo.

After Derek drank his milk, he wiped his mouth on his sleeve. "You know, Coyote wouldn't have gotten in trouble in the first place if he hadn't tried to steal the white men's whiskey."

Mateo smiled broadly. "That may be the most important lesson you could learn from this story. No one really needs the white man's whiskey. Coyote may be a trickster, but he is often fooled himself."

Kendra looked at Mateo's full bowl. "Derek did a great job on his dinner, but you've hardly touched yours. Is it okay?"

Mateo scooped up a chunk of meat and brought it to his mouth. He chewed and swallowed it down. "Excellent," he said. He dipped his spoon back into the bowl for another bite. As he did, his gaze went blank and the spoon clattered on the table. His teeth clamped together, He grabbed the side of his head, as though he was having a seizure.

"What's wrong with Grandpa?" Derek jumped from his seat. Kendra pulled him back.

Jerome knelt and took his grandfather in his arms. "Come, we need to get you to the hospital."

Mateo violently shook his head from side to side. "I'm not the one in trouble," he shouted. "We need to go to the observatory. *Bindáayee'ighání* is loose."

"*Bindáayee'ighání*? He Who Kills With his Eyes?"

"Yes. He's loose and the damage this storm will cause is minor compared to what he'll do. Once he's finished there, he'll move on. He won't stop until all humans are destroyed."

"You can't be serious."

Mateo looked up, his gaze deadly serious. "I have never been more serious about anything in my life."

CHAPTER 25

Stan's arm hurt, but it was nothing compared to his spirit.

He and Mike trudged around the building's perimeter to rejoin Maya. She sat on a concrete lip at the base of the telescope pier, her face red and blotchy from crying.

"What is happening? Maya's voice choked on emotion. "Is there any hope of finding Claire alive at this point?"

Stan looked away, afraid he would burst into tears if he met Maya's gaze. That wouldn't help right now.

The wind continued to roar outside. Mike ran his fingers through his hair. "There's no reason give up on Claire yet." He glanced in the direction of the chamber where Evan lay dead and shriveled. "This was a terrible freak accident. But what are the odds of two accidents?"

"Yeah, real freaky," said Stan. He couldn't figure out how power had been supplied to the aluminizing chamber's vacuum pump, but not anything else in the building. "I'd like to take a few minutes and check the building schematics. It might give me a clue why this happened."

Maya heaved a sigh. "Figuring out why this happened is not important right now. We need to find Claire!"

Mike held up his hands. "I agree, but I think Stan has a point. Somehow the chamber got power when nothing else did. If he can figure out how that could have happened, it might give us a clue as to how to get the power back on, which would help our search."

Stan took a deep breath. "Finding Claire is our first priority, but unless we know what happened, there's always a risk of another accident."

"What about Evan?" Maya glanced at the aluminizing chamber. "We can't just leave him in there."

"I don't think we have any choice." Stan's voice cracked and he struggled to control it. "Until we get power back on, there's no way to lift that lid."

"Let's list the places we've checked so far and figure out what's left," suggested Mike.

They discussed the places they'd searched. They still needed to follow up in the basement, the second floor storage area, and the dorm room floor.

"I never got into the dome wheel access area. I was heading there when . . . when the cry for help came over the radio," said Mike.

Stan nodded. "I'll head over there after I check the plans. That area should be locked though."

"I found a few doors that should have been locked, but weren't," Mike went on. "I wouldn't rule anything out."

"What about the pier?" asked Stan. "There's a ladder that runs up to some intermediate service levels."

"Why don't I start with the ladder climb?" Mike looked at the door that led into the pier and the crypt. "We've been to the basement since Claire vanished. Up the pier seems a little more likely for someone who's lost and is looking for a straight shot back up to the control room."

Mike disappeared through the door into the pier while Stan and Maya climbed the main stairway. They passed the equipment floor and continued up to the dorm room floor. They both entered at the same time, but Stan pushed ahead of her to the charts, relieved to leave her behind. Her silence proved more damning than any words she could have shot at him.

Truth be told, he couldn't tell if she blamed him for Evan's death or not. It didn't matter anyway, because he blamed himself. Evan would still be alive if he'd thought of breaking the window sooner. He only thought of it when she pounded on the glass with her fist. Breaking the window would have allowed a constant supply of air in until he'd figured out how to stop the pump. Then again, what if his arm had been sucked in and blocked the hole as it did? Would he have survived?

For the life of him, he couldn't figure out how the vacuum chamber had functioned with no power. The building's battery backups had surely failed by now, and even if they hadn't, the chamber shouldn't have been wired into the same circuit. Even if a high-voltage capacitor in the system could have held some charge, it should have dissipated in seconds. Were there batteries or a generator he didn't know about? If so, he could at least get the power back on.

Stan found the plans hanging in the recreation room near the racks of astronomical charts. It took him a few minutes to locate the ones for the aluminizing chamber and the first floor. He perused them and confirmed what he knew to be logically true. The power line flowed into the main power junction in the basement. He grabbed the basement plans and examined them. Sure enough they connected into the main junction racks, same as the lights, elevator power, telescope power and everything else. Everything was as he remembered. He knew without a doubt that there was no way the aluminizing chamber could get power when everything else was dead.

And yet, it did.

"This makes no fucking sense."

He paged through the plans until he came to one labeled, *Electrical Revisions*. Just as he reached for that chart, he heard a loud crash.

Maya ran into the room. "Did you hear that?"

"Sounded like it came from downstairs."

Maya turned back toward the stairwell.

"This way's quicker." Stan rushed to the door that looked out along the telescope pier. He scanned the mirror and instrument handling area with his flashlight beam. A gaping hole now stood in the garage door.

"What the fuck?" Stan shook his head, as he continued to search the area. Piles of crates cast eerie shadows on the walls, preventing him from seeing into the corners. Rainwater drizzled in over the floor.

"What could have caused that?" asked Maya.

Stan raked his fingers through his hair in agitation. "When the wind gets real strong, it can blow rocks and branches around. I'm guessing we got hit real hard. Something was banging into the door earlier."

"If it was a branch or a rock, where is it?" asked Maya.

Stan found it hard to think with the grad student's constant flow of questions. Not to mention, he was all too aware of her body pressing close to him. She was tall and muscular, attractive in an athletic sort of way. His higher brain knew he shouldn't be fantasizing at a time like this, especially with one dead student and another one unaccounted for, but he was distracted nonetheless. "It must have rolled into the shadows," croaked Stan. "Maybe it wasn't a rock, maybe there was a microburst or something and it just ripped a hole into the door."

"The edges of that hole face inward. Wouldn't a microburst just rip the whole garage door out?"

The question held just enough of an edge that it snapped Stan from his fantasy. "Whatever it was, there's not much we can do about it until the storm lets up. Claire is still our first priority."

"Agreed." The word came out as a sigh. Maya left to resume her search and Stan returned to the racks holding the schematics, both frustrated and relieved to be away from her.

He checked the revisions and saw no more clues to the power switching on mysteriously. The only thing he could come up with was that the power had been applied to one line temporarily. They had been so focused on getting Evan out that they hadn't tested all the possible lines. After Evan was killed, the power had gone out again. He shuddered, remembering the shriveled body. That would explain the power part, but not necessarily why the vacuum chamber started up on its own. Unless Evan had fiddled with the controls before he'd climbed over. None of it seemed plausible. He'd have to figure the rest of it out after they'd found Claire. He was determined to find out what had happened, so that it could never happen again.

He saw Maya as he passed through the old kitchen. "I'm on my way upstairs to check the dome trucks."

"All right. I'm almost finished on this floor. I'll go down to the storage area once I'm done," she said.

Stan trudged up the stairs to the main floor at the base of the telescope. As he proceeded down the long dark hallway to the bench spectrograph room, he heard a huffing, like an asthmatic. He turned his flashlight and scanned the area. "Hello," he said. His voice sounded hollow in the dark, empty space. "Anyone there?"

No reply. Stan continued down the hallway. From time to time, he caught a *tip-tap-tipping*, like claws on concrete. He stopped and turned around, flashing his beam down the hall in the direction where he'd come.

Even this far away from the hole in the garage door, the wind through the building had dropped in pitch, taking on a mournful tone. The ventilators still squeaked, but their frequency had changed slightly. He found it difficult to place exactly, but somehow the walls seemed closer and he had to remind himself to breathe.

He entered the bench spectrograph room. Out of habit, he reached for the light switch. As he should have expected, nothing happened. He continued through to the door, which led out into the base of the telescope. He took the long way around the perimeter of the building, avoiding the oil that had a tendency to build up under the telescope.

He grabbed his keys as he reached the door that led to the dome wheels. Once in, everything appeared normal at first glance. His light illuminated one of the wheels. The walls were grimy from the oil used to maintain the wheel assemblies.

Stan was tempted to leave, but he knew a person could go farther back. He continued into the room and climbed down into a service pit under the wheel tracks. He followed that for a few feet, and climbed out into another service area. His eyes widened as his flashlight beam revealed items that shouldn't be there.

An army cot and a stack of food similar to the one down in the basement. Someone had set up a microwave and a small, portable TV. Goose bumps prickled along Stan's arms. On the stand next to the TV were a couple of pistols. Whoever set this up must be in the building somewhere. *Did they have more weapons? Were they behind the power outage? Could they be behind Evan's death? Was it some kind of sabotage or terrorist act? But why Carson Peak?* Too many questions crowded his brain and he had no answers.

He continued with the search but after a few moments he stopped when his flashlight beam caught a flash of white. At first he thought it was a stack of bricks. He took a step closer and discovered they *were* bricks of a sort, just not the type used in construction. These were bricks of cocaine, wrapped in plastic. "Well fuck me."

Stan grabbed the radio from his belt. "Stan to Mike." There was no response. He tried again.

"Fine time for the radio to stop working again."

He caught a movement out of the corner of his eye. He turned fully to look, but no one was there. *That's odd.* For a moment he thought he saw a figure beckoning him. Could it be Claire? Was she too scared to call out? Or was it the guy who'd stashed the cocaine?

He clipped the radio to his belt and climbed back into the pit, walked along it and climbed out, leaving his flashlight on the floor. As he stood, a shadow filled the doorway and he heard asthmatic breathing. Stan held up his hands. "I'm guessing you're the guy who's camping in here." Dark as it was, Stan couldn't tell if the figure was aiming a gun at him or not.

As Stan's eyes adjusted, he realized the figure was all wrong for a human. The legs were too thin and the head too large. A pair of black eyes, darker than shadows, bored into him.

He bent down, grabbed the flashlight, and pointed it at the figure. It spread a pair of reptilian arms, adorned in grizzled, rain-soaked feathers. Its beak-like mouth opened in a horrible piercing cry. Stan turned to jump back into the service pit when sharp talons pierced his back. He screamed in agony, as the creature's claws punctured internal organs. He dropped his flashlight and toppled over. He had the oddest thought as he lay there, dying: *Now I'll never know if Maya would go on a date with a guy like me . . .*

The beam from the flashlight glowed into his eyes. It was the last thing he saw.

CHAPTER 26

The door closed with a resounding ka-chunk.

Mike entered the 5-meter telescope's pier, where Professor Burroughs was interred. Between Evan's death and Claire going MIA, it definitely seemed like one big tomb. The marble crypt glistened as though it were wet. Mike checked the floor just in case, but saw no sign that rain had encroached this far.

He thought about his encounter with the professor's ghost and his cryptic warning. But, since Bethany seemed fine when he'd checked in on her, he decided to stay focused on finding Claire. Once they found Claire, he would head over to the 2.5-meter where Bethany was, no matter how hard it was raining.

He stepped around the crypt to the service ladder behind it. Shining the light up the ladder, he contemplated climbing it while holding onto the flashlight. His only options were to hold it in his mouth or in one hand. Neither seemed doable, and he'd more than likely drop the flashlight or stumble and fall. Instead, he turned it off and shoved it in his pocket. "Better safe than sorry."

He waited a few moments for his eyes to adjust to the darkness before grabbing onto the rung closest to him. His eyes never adjusted, so he stepped onto a lower rung, and began to climb. *Slow and steady. Just feel your way up.* He couldn't see how far up he was, nor how far down he could fall, which was just as well. His relief was short-lived however, as he began to feel a prickle along his spine. He paused for a moment and it went away. As he started to climb once more, he felt it again. He couldn't shake the eerie feeling. As though someone was standing right behind him. *Can ghosts hover in empty air?* He honestly didn't know.

As he climbed, he became aware of a floor around him. He reached up to the side and felt its solid presence. He went up a few more rungs, and stepped over with his left foot. Just as he was sure he stood on something solid, he heard a crash from below. He gasped, his head spinning with vertigo from the sudden noise. For a moment, he feared bolts had given way when he placed his weight on the floor and he'd end up crashing down on top of Robert Burroughs's tomb.

He took a few calming breaths and let go of the ladder.

He grabbed the flashlight from his back pocket and scanned his surroundings. The floor was empty. A short, three-rung ladder led from the opposite side to a door. The ladder he just ascended continued upward. Thinking about the crashing sound, he went to the short ladder and out the door onto the pump floor. He walked past the breaker room, through an old storage room and unlocked a door that overlooked the aluminizing chamber.

At first, he didn't see anything amiss, but then he spotted the gaping hole in the garage door. He searched around with his flashlight, but from his height, the beam didn't reveal enough to tell what had caused the damage.

He returned to the pier, crossed to the long ladder, and climbed up to the next floor. There he found a hatch. As he pushed it open, something tried to grab his arm. He yelped and yanked his arm back.

"What the fuck!"

He cautiously raised the hatch and aimed his flashlight but there was no one there. Just a piece of machinery nearby. He must have brushed against it, but he could have sworn he felt fingers.

"Get ahold of yourself, Mike."

The overwhelming stress of the past few hours must be taking its toll on his imagination. He blew out a breath and examined the space with his flashlight beam. He saw an oily, cramped, steel cave, dominated by a hydraulic cylinder and squat, sturdy motors. He was in a crawlspace immediately below the telescope that allowed the daytime maintenance crew to service the equipment lift. There was no sign of Claire and no exit. He climbed back down and returned to the pump floor.

A burst of static erupted from the radio. For just a moment, Mike thought he heard Stan's voice. "Stan, is that you? Were you calling me?"

No response.

Mike realized it had been some time since he'd heard from Bethany. He keyed the microphone. "Mike to Bethany. Come in." Not getting an answer, he tried again. "This is Mike calling Bethany, can you hear me?"

"She can hear you."

A chill went down Mike's spine at the sound of the unfamiliar voice. "Who is this?" His voice was slow and deliberate, almost a hiss.

"My name isn't important. Only two things concern me. First, we have lost something very valuable. Second there is some kind of . . ."

"Fuck!" Mike screamed in frustration as the radio cut out again. He took a deep breath and hit the transmit button. "Who are you? Where is my wife?"

No reply.

Mike cursed again. After a moment of indecision, he ran to the stairwell and sprinted down the stairs as fast as he could. Even in the dark, he was getting to know them so well, that he could navigate them quickly. He reached the bottom and bolted for the main door. As he pushed it open, a gust of wind rose up and blew it shut in his face, toppling him backward onto the concrete floor. Stunned for a moment, he held his head, trying to regain his bearings. He'd heard a thump when he'd fallen. It must have been the radio. He dug out his flashlight from his pocket and rolled over. His head was swimming and his back ached from the fall. He eased himself up to a sitting position and searched the area with his flashlight.

His eyes landed on the radio.

"*Shit!*"

The battery had popped out of its slot.

"Oh, God, please don't be broken . . ."

He crawled over to the radio and carefully slipped the battery back in. He sighed in relief when the green power light came back on. "Mike to Bethany. Can you hear me?" When there was still no response, he called again.

He groaned in frustration and pain. The impact from his fall had given him a raging headache. Needing to clear it so he could think, he went to the medicine cabinet hanging on the wall next to the useless elevator. He grabbed two aspirin and swallowed them down his parched throat.

Because they'd agreed to return to the control room, he decided it was the best place to go. He had to get to Bethany, but he needed help. What's more, he hoped the phones had come back to life. They'd be more reliable than the radios and he could get more help. As he set out for the stairwell, his flashlight beam caught a glimmer on the floor.

It was a puddle. Rain from when he pushed the door open? He turned toward the machine shop and spied a trail of puddles. He didn't have time to puzzle it out right now. He would return later, after he contacted Bethany.

As Mike made the long ascent to the control room, his head gradually began to feel better. Once he arrived, he discovered the battery backups had run down. Had it only been a few hours since he was last here? It seemed like days. Disheartened to find no one in the prearranged meeting place, Mike dropped into the operator's chair.

Insulated from the rest of the building, the control room was eerily silent. He unclipped the radio from his belt and keyed the microphone. "This is Mike to the 2.5-meter telescope. Can you hear me?"

"You cut off. Look man, there's a fucking monster on the loose."

"A monster?" A chill swept up Mike's spine. "What the hell do you mean by 'monster'?"

"I've never seen anything like it," said the voice on the other end. "It was like a dinosaur with feathers."

Mike's heart kicked into high gear. *The vision!* What had Jerome called it? *He Who Kills With His Eyes?*

"Where's Bethany?" Mike's voice sounded desperate even to himself.

"Tell me where the cocaine is first."

"Cocaine?" Mike shook his head. "What are you even talking about? What cocaine?"

"Look, *amigo*, let me make it plain for you. Someone brought cocaine up here to this mountain. That cocaine belongs to me and my brother. If I don't see it within the hour, I'm going to feed this lady here to that fucking monster out there . . . I'm pretty sure you don't want that to happen. Do you?"

"We've been searching this building for the last two hours. No one has found any cocaine here. If they had, I would know. It's not here."

"Maybe I'll shoot your girlfriend first, then get away while the monster feeds on her cooling corpse."

Mike's knuckles grew white as he squeezed the radio. He struggled to gain control of his temper.

"The hour starts now," said the voice on the radio.

Mike glanced at his watch. It was half past midnight. It suddenly occurred to him how clear that transmission on the radio was. Maybe the storm was finally letting up. Perhaps he could get over to the other telescope now.

"It sounds like you need help."

Mike jumped at the sound of the gravelly voice. He lifted his flashlight and aimed it at the door.

"Roscoe Perkins?" The man looked older than he remembered, and haggard. His clothes were rumpled, as though he'd been sleeping in them. Even from across the room Mike could smell his body odor. Clearly, Perkins was roughing it. "How long have you been back there?"

"Just got here. I've been listening to your chat with the lovely gentleman across the mountain. I thought it was time to make my presence known."

"Do you know what's happened to Claire Yarbro?" asked Mike.

Perkins shrugged. "Haven't got a clue. Haven't really been looking. From the bits and pieces I've been hearing on the radio, I'm guessing she's lost out in the storm."

"You're just a bundle of sunshine, aren't you?"

"Do you want my help or not?"

Mike gritted his teeth. He didn't believe a word out of Perkins' mouth. He'd probably been aware of everything that had been going on tonight and had purposely stayed hidden. Hell, maybe Perkins was responsible for Evan's death. If anyone had the technical ability, it would be him . . . But why? Was it some crazy revenge plot for being fired? Somehow, that felt too cinematic to be true.

He didn't have time to speculate. The drug dealer said he'd kill Bethany. So at this point, he didn't care if the Devil himself showed up to help. They could also use Maya and Stan, but he couldn't chance contacting them on the radio and alerting the drug dealers about their plan. Nope, he was stuck with the Boy Scout from Hell. He glanced at his watch. Time was running out.

"All right, let's get going."

CHAPTER 27

Something about that guy creeped her out.
Maya breathed a sigh of relief when Stan left to check the telescope's base. She continued on her search, hoping that she would find Claire alive and well.

She completed her check of the lounge area with its antique green leather chairs that canted at strange angles and rocked on their own when the wind hit the building and moaned. It was spooky. And here she was alone, with Evan dead, and Claire still missing. How could a night that had started out so amazing have ended up like this? She snorted. Hell, the longer he was gone, the more she began to miss Stan. She must be going crazy! With a shudder, she continued down to the second floor storage room.

As she approached the second floor landing, she saw a golden glow from the door's small window. She was afraid to hope it might be Claire's flashlight. No one else should be in the building. She trotted down the last few steps and burst through the door.

"Who the hell are you?" she asked, with her hand to her chest.

The man's mouth moved, but she heard nothing. The first thing she noticed was his old-fashioned tweed suit. He looked like a college professor from days gone by with his matching vest, bow tie, and pocket watch chain strung across his belly. On an ordinary night, it might not even surprise Maya to meet such a man at the observatory. He could easily be an older faculty member from New Mexico State University up for a visit.

As she moved in closer to try to hear better, she realized the man was glowing, as though illuminated from some outside light source. What's more, she could actually see *through* him.

She was frozen to the spot, uncertain whether to confront this strange man, retreat, or ignore him and continue the search for Claire. "Are you lost? Can I help you?" she asked him.

The man's brow furrowed as though he also had a difficult time hearing. Finally, he turned and took a few steps. He looked over his shoulder, as though checking to see if Maya followed. She swallowed and fell in step behind the stranger. He led her past some old signs, a pair of reel-to-reel computer drives, and around a storage shelf.

Huddled in a ball and crying was Claire Yarbro.

"Claire! Thank goodness you're all right."

Claire looked up and sniffed. "Maya, is that really you?"

Maya dropped down to the floor and sat next to her friend. "We've been so worried, looking all over the building for you. Why didn't you return to the control room?"

Claire shook her head. "I'm not really sure what happened. The power went out and I got turned around a bit and I just started looking around to find my way back, and then I got well and truly lost. I found my way to the telescope pier and came across Professor Burroughs's crypt and there was this man . . ."

"Yeah, he's right here." Maya looked up. "He *was* right here." She jumped to her feet and walked around the racks, but the old man had vanished.

"He does that." Claire snorted a half-laugh. "When I was an undergrad, I took a course in the paranormal and the scientific method. We learned that there was no reliable evidence for the existence of ghosts." She snickered again. "Who would have thought one of the best laboratories to study ghosts would be in a prestigious astronomical observatory?"

Maya's brow furrowed. "Claire, what do you mean?"

"That man *is* Professor Burroughs, or his ghost, rather. Good thing you found him. There's another ghost around here and he isn't nice."

"You're kidding." Maya sat down beside Claire again and shuddered as a thought crossed her mind. "Evan's dead."

"I know," whispered Claire. "I was up here when the chamber came on. I heard you guys shouting. I-I was so scared.

After you left, I went down and looked. I saw his body. What a horrible way to go."

"Claire." Maya leaned forward and placed her hand on her friend's forearm. "What if this Professor Burroughs look-alike, whoever he is, is responsible for Evan's death?"

Claire shook her head. "No. There's another ghost. He tried to make me fall. I think he lured Evan into the chamber and turned it on." Claire took a deep breath and let it out slowly. "There's something else . . . Did you hear that horrible crash?"

"The one where the garage door was broken? It was a rock or something."

"It wasn't a rock." Claire's breath came in short, sharp gasps. "It's a creature of some kind. It moves like those velociraptors from *Jurassic Park*, only faster."

"What?" Maya's eyes widened. You mean there's some kind of monster loose in the building?"

"Remember when Evan went down in the pit, we heard that strange noise that sounded like some combination of a mountain lion, an eagle, and an angry horse?"

"Yeah." Maya shuddered again. "Evan didn't see anything."

"The creature made that same sound after it burst through the door."

Without warning, Maya's radio came to life. Mike called his wife, but a stranger responded. Maya trembled and reached for Claire's hand. The two students looked at each other in shock. What was going on? It sounded like a man at the 2.5-meter telescope was holding Bethany hostage. Things were going nuts.

The radio went quiet and Maya tried to focus on what Claire had said. "Are you saying we released this evil?"

Claire took a deep breath and let it out slowly. "I don't know what to think anymore." She closed her eyes. "Back in the paranormal class I took, I read about people who believe there are ways that evil spirits can enter our realm. I didn't believe it then. But now . . ." Claire's eyes flew open, shocking Maya with their intensity. "I think that when we took that coin from the cave, we released something dark. I don't know if we freed th-that creature or if it's trying to get the coin back or what." She looked up, past Maya. "I suspect that the energy feeds the ghost of Professor Burroughs and the other spirit I've seen."

Maya laughed in spite of herself. "Maybe you should change your major to paranormal studies as opposed to astronomy . . . So are you saying that the ghost of Professor Burroughs is fed by some kind of evil energy? If that's true, why couldn't he be responsible for Evan's death?"

Claire reached out and squeezed Maya's shoulders as though to make her understand. "No, it's more like the energy is enabling him to manifest. He's not evil, but he's trying to keep us safe from the evil. He's trying to help us."

"But there *is* an evil spirit, you say?" Maya asked the question despite her doubts. She thought it was important to keep Claire talking, so she wouldn't burst into tears again.

Claire sighed and leaned back. "You've heard about Jim Murray, right? Dr. Burroughs's graduate student?"

Maya nodded but the radio came to life again, interrupting them. This time, the stranger said something about a monster on the loose. Was Claire right? Was there really some of kind of evil creature out there? He also talked about stolen cocaine— as though things weren't weird or scary enough. The stranger said he'd kill Bethany in an hour if Mike didn't tell him where the drugs were.

Maya stood up and began pacing. "It seems there really is a murderer on this mountain. Whoever that was talking to Mike must be responsible for Evan's death."

Claire shook her head. "Jim was responsible for Evan's death."

"Jim?" Maya blinked.

"Jim Murray . . . Dr. Burroughs's graduate student." Claire seemed irritated that Maya had lost track of the previous conversation. "They say spirits have unresolved issues. I think Jim is angry about his death. He strikes out at everyone and everything around him. Dr. Burroughs blamed himself for Jim's death. I think helping us is his way to atone for that."

Maya looked down at the floor. "Look, there's a lot of weird shit going on here tonight . . . I feel like this is all my fault." Maya's voice cracked and she took a deep breath.

"What do you mean?" asked Claire in a worried voice.

"When we went on that hike, yesterday . . . Do you know why Evan and I wanted to explore that cave? We went in to find something . . . some kind of amulet that a big-shot collector wants. For money. Lots of money. All I could think about was the money . . . Getting out of debt you know?" Tears started streaming down Maya's face. "I-I shouldn't have done that. I'm sorry Claire. If it wasn't for me, Evan wouldn't be dead and we wouldn't be here right now."

Claire reached out and hugged her friend. "You had no way of knowing any of this would happen. None of us did. We just need to stay safe."

Maya shook her head and swiped at her eyes and nose. "Look. Some kind of strange creature is in the building. Drug dealers are taking hostages. A creepy old guy is running around pretending to be a ghost." Maya released her own near-hysterical laugh. "Evan's dead for God's sake! Between you and me, I think it's time to get the hell out of here."

"I dunno." Claire shook her head. "Professor Burroughs led me here. I think he's trying to keep me safe, keep us safe."

Maya held up her hands. "All right, one last question. Why didn't you call anyone on the radio?"

Claire laughed again. "I tried. God knows I tried, but every single time, the radio cut out, as though something was keeping me from broadcasting."

Maya squeezed her friend's hand. A loud thumping drew their attention to the stairwell. Maya held up her finger to her mouth to be quiet.

The stairwell door crashed open and a keening howl resounded through the room. Without thinking, Maya pointed her flashlight at the stairs and her mouth dropped open at what she saw.

It was huge. Grotesque. And it was peering at her with eyes that absorbed light from her flashlight. It was something out of this world. The kind of monster special effects wizards dreamed up at LucasArts. Between its eyes was a beak, glistening with the same red gore that covered its front. There were chunks of . . . something, vaguely flesh colored. Maya tried not to think about it. If she did, she would vomit.

The creature made no move in her direction. Instead,

it just held her in its gaze. Mesmerized . . . And then she blinked and realized Claire had pulled her back among the shelves and turned off her flashlight. They stood silent, listening. The creature's breathing sounded raspy, like old wood rubbing against dry leather. If it moved, its steps were perfectly silent.

Maya took a step toward the nearest storage shelf and listened. She took another step. Still nothing. Finally, she was close enough that she could peer through the stacks of discarded electronics.

The creature's movements were not dissimilar to hers. It took a step, stopped and listened, then took another step. With each step, it bobbed up and down on its legs, like a gigantic rooster walking around a farmyard.

Suddenly the creature turned and looked right at her.

She knew she hadn't made a sound. She stood as still and silent as she could. Perhaps it didn't see very well in the dark. Perhaps it relied entirely on sound.

It rushed forward. Again, Claire pulled her out of harm's way as the creature slammed itself into the shelf, knocking it over, right where Maya had been.

Claire dragged her behind a set of storage cabinets. The creature rushed after them and flung the cabinets through the air with one swipe of its massive wing-like arms.

As fast as they could go, Claire and Maya weaved in and out of old the electronics racks and discarded furniture in the vast room. The creature followed, nimbly knocking things aside, and easily leaping over anything in its path.

They finally reached the railing that guarded against a two-story drop off. Nowhere else to go, they crouched down, trying to hide, but knowing it was futile. The vacuum chamber that served as Evan's tomb stood silent vigil below. Maya turned and faced the creature. She considered their options as it fixed her with its gaze. She looked at Claire.

"It can't get both of us at once. I'll go to the left and you go to the right. Maybe we can confuse it," said Maya.

Claire shook her head. "I've got a better plan. There's a ladder a few feet to my right. If we're calm and quiet, maybe we can make it to that and get down to the ground floor."

"That'll just bunch us up," said Maya. "Are you with me or not?"

"I don't know," said Claire.

Without waiting for Claire to make up her mind, Maya rushed forward and darted to the left.

"No Maya! Stop!"

Maya leapt as far as she could, but tripped, hitting the concrete with a sickening thud. She blacked out for a moment and when she opened her eyes, she found herself staring into the deepest void she'd ever seen . . .

CHAPTER 28

The stench was overpowering.

Mike followed Roscoe down the stairs. The former technician's salt-and-pepper hair was long and matted, his jaw covered in a scraggly beard. His wrinkled, stained flannel shirt hung on his skinny frame. His black jeans were streaked with dirt, and something else Mike didn't want to identify. Mike tried to avoid breathing when he passed near Roscoe as they descended the stairs. He reeked of whiskey, stale cigarettes, and sweat.

"So, what exactly are you doing here?" asked Mike.

"Laying low," said Roscoe. "Apaches took my car and they locked me out of my house. I needed a place to stay."

Mike's brow furrowed. "I thought Jerome fired you. Didn't he take your keys?"

"Yup." Roscoe snickered. "I had a spare set made a long time ago. That way if I lost a key, I wouldn't have to report it."

"So where, exactly, have you been staying? We've turned this building upside down looking for a graduate student who disappeared . . ." Mike snapped his fingers. "That was your food down in the basement wasn't it?"

Roscoe tapped the side of his forehead. "A little slow, but the boy's starting to put it together."

They left the stairwell and turned into the instrumentation storage area. "But there was no sign of a cot or anything. Where have you been sleeping?"

"I needed someplace no one was likely to go," he said. "I've been hiding out in the dome truck service area."

Mike stopped in his tracks. "That's a pretty nasty place to make a home. Kind of dangerous, too, if the dome should start up."

"Back in the alcove's safe enough. Just need to know what to watch for when coming and going." Roscoe turned around and faced Mike in the dark. "The relays click, and it takes time for the motors to ramp up. As long as you pay attention, and don't cross when things are moving or about to, you'll do fine." His teeth gleamed in the reflected light from Mike's flashlight beam. "You've been through this whole building, and aside from one stash of food, you haven't found any evidence of my existence, have you?"

"But why here at the observatory?" Mike narrowed his eyes. "Even if the storm hadn't happened, something could have gone wrong and you'd have been found."

"Being found by observatory staff wasn't my concern," said Roscoe. "I'm hiding from the people who left a nice, expensive present for Uncle Roscoe down on the old Forest Service road."

"Expensive . . ." Mike frowned. Finally his head snapped up and he met Roscoe's eyes. "You have the cocaine those cartel men are after."

"Five hundred points for the goody-two shoes."

"You greedy, fucking asshole!" Mike spat out. "It's your goddamned fault that Bethany's in danger!"

He dropped the flashlight and lunged at Roscoe. The electronic tech's alcohol-softened reflexes were too slow and Mike shoved him into the pointed corner of a spectrograph. Roscoe yelled and rolled away as Mike threw a punch that landed on the metal surface. Roscoe crawled between two more instruments. Mike grabbed his flashlight.

As he did, Roscoe tackled him from the side and sent him sprawling. "Look you idiot, I offered to help you get rid of those guys who have Bethany. I'm on your side!"

"You're on nobody's side but your own!" Mike heaved his body around and pinned Roscoe underneath him. A thought suddenly occurred to him. Only one person knew the building's systems better than Stan Jones. "What do you know about Evan Burkholder's death in the vacuum chamber? Were you messing around trying to get power on? Is that how come the chamber started up on its own?"

"I don't even know what the fuck you're talking about!"

Roscoe freed an arm and clapped the side of Mike's head with his open hand.

The sudden pop on Mike's ear made him fall back. The electronics technician slithered away and disappeared among the instruments.

"I don't know why the power went off," called Roscoe from his hiding place, "but I couldn't give a rat's ass whether it came on or not. The only good thing about the power being on as far as I'm concerned is that means you morons are up in the control room and not looking for me."

"So, why were you even out of your hiding place?"

"Man's gotta take a leak sometimes."

"Then why did you appear when you did?"

"I heard the chatter on the radio . . . Look, I've known Bethany for a while, too. I'm not a complete bastard. I really thought I could help."

Mike brought himself to his feet, grabbed his flashlight again, and swung it around. Not seeing any sign of Roscoe getting ready to pounce on him, he turned off the light and fell back into the shadows. "How exactly do you think you can help? Are you willing to give up the cocaine?"

Roscoe was silent for a long time. When he spoke, he chose his words carefully. "If I thought it would do any good, then yeah, sure. But these guys are serious drug dealers, boy. Bethany can now tell people what they look like. I know about the cocaine. Now you know about it, too." Roscoe paused for a moment. "They won't let us get out of here alive, son."

The word "son" rankled Mike. His own father had been a man of impeccable integrity, not a self-serving jerk. "All right, what have you got that will help?"

"The one thing cartel men understand. Guns."

Mike blew out a shaky breath. He knew he shouldn't be surprised. He remembered that Roscoe liked to hunt, but he still felt as if he were on a fast-plummeting elevator. How had the night gone from routine observations to this colossal mess? One student dead. Another one missing. Bethany in danger from deadly drug dealers. And God knows what else was lurking around.

Mike didn't want Roscoe's help. He wanted help from

someone like Jerome, or better yet, he wanted to call 911, but the phone was out. What choice did he have? He could try to clobber Roscoe, call the gangsters and offer to turn over the cocaine. He knew where it was now, but he feared Roscoe was right. Even if he turned it over, the drug dealers would probably kill them anyway.

"All right," said Mike at last. "Let's make a plan."

"Promise not to tackle me if I come out?" called Roscoe.

"I promise," said Mike.

"Turn on your light, so I can find mine."

Mike switched on his flashlight. A moment later, Roscoe emerged from behind a tarp-covered imager. He bent over and picked up his own light. Without another word, he walked toward the double doors that led out into the dome. Mike followed close behind.

The smell hit Mike before anything else.

As a kid, Mike used to take a short cut home from school behind a meat market. The metallic tang of blood had never left his memory. The odor that assaulted his nose was similar, but overlaid with raw sewage.

He'd been out in the dome earlier in the night. There had been no such smell.

"Jesus Fucking Christ." Profane as the words were, Roscoe whispered them, almost like a prayer.

Mike stepped around the corner and saw the carnage in Roscoe's flashlight beam. Bile rose in his throat and he fought not to vomit.

The door to the dome wheel access lay open. On the floor, just inside were the remains of a body. The spinal cord had been ripped out through the back and tossed aside, ribs hanging obscenely to the side. Something had rummaged through the internal organs from the back. The body's head lay to the side. Empty, bloody eye sockets stared out from under a shock of red hair, as though pleading for help that had never arrived.

Mike didn't want to admit what his mind was telling him . . .

Stan Jones.

Without further conscious thought, Mike dropped to his knees and threw up. He crawled away from the vomit and tried not to look into the alcove.

"Who the hell did this?" asked Roscoe.

"Ask your cartel friends," Mike spit out. His gut clenched anew at worry for Bethany while a sob of despair at the loss of his friend threatened to break loose. Stan might have been an odd duck, but he was a good man.

Roscoe eased around the carnage and climbed into the service pit. "Goddamn it to hell!" His voice echoed through the dome.

Mike stood and leaned heavily against the telescope mount. He rested his cheek against the cool metal and prayed for this nightmare to end.

Roscoe appeared beside him a few minutes later. "I think you're right. The cartel men must have been over here. The cocaine's gone." He shook his head. "The only thing I don't get is that my guns were right where I left them. Why would they take the cocaine, but leave the guns?"

Mike swallowed, tasting his own bile. He would give anything for a sip of water. He wished he'd never agreed to take this job. This fucking observatory was cursed. He should have realized it his first week back, when he started seeing strange things on his rounds. But even if he'd said no to the job, Bethany would still be on this mountain and in danger. And he would be in no position to help her. He stood upright and willed himself to take another look at the body.

"Is it even possible for a human to do that to another human? That looks like some big animal got him," said Mike.

Roscoe shrugged. "Who knows? Some of those cartel guys like to keep exotic pets. Maybe they have a mountain lion or something."

"Hand me one of those guns," said Mike. "If they've hurt Bethany . . ."

"Have you ever used one of these?" Roscoe patted the two guns in his waistband.

"My dad taught me to shoot . . . but that was a long time ago."

Roscoe pulled out one of the guns and pointed to the safety. "This one's probably the easier of the two to use. If you keep it in your waistband, keep the safety on. It's got a real gentle trigger."

Mike nodded and took the gun. "We should find Maya, get her someplace safe," he said.

They strode toward the far end of the telescope enclosure. As they did, Mike's light fell on a set of three-pronged dark patches, like tracks from a giant bird. The trail led to the bench spectrograph room. It took Mike's overloaded brain a moment to realize these were the tracks of whatever had killed Stan. Tracks made from Stan's blood.

He aimed his flashlight at the bench spectrograph's door, which had been ripped off its hinges. It lay on the telescope floor in a crumpled heap of metal.

"Whatever did that was no ordinary animal," said Roscoe.

They stepped inside, finding equipment and instruments strewn about. Shattered glass littered the floor throwing up little rainbows in Mike's flashlight beam. The door at the other end of the room was also torn off its hinges.

Mike tried to think what kind of animal could have done this. Whatever it was, he couldn't imagine it was some wild pet that belonged to a human. An image flashed to his mind. The creature he saw on his last night at the 2.5-meter—a feathered monstrosity with great talons that could shred a man with its beak.

"This is Claire! Damn it! Can anyone hear me?"

Mike blinked. He grabbed the radio from his belt. "Claire, this is Mike. You're coming through loud and clear. Where the hell are you?"

"Second floor. Hurry! A giant bird has Maya!"

Mike's eyes flew to Roscoe's.

"We're on our way," said Mike.

"Hurry! Oh my God . . ." The radio cut off.

Mike and Roscoe pushed their way through the ruins of the bench spectrograph room, past two more shredded doors, and down the stairs.

CHAPTER 29

This night was just too fucked up.

A set of voices sounded over the radio. The first was a woman Carlos hadn't heard before. "This is Claire! Damn it! Can anyone hear me?" At first, he grinned. A new voice might mean new information. The woman shouted about some kind of bird attacking someone. Was it the monster they'd seen out in the rain? She cut off after the next call.

They listened for a few more minutes, but nothing more came through. Carlos paced and Ricardo played game after game of Minesweeper. The woman astronomer just sat in the corner, hugging her stomach. Her eyes showed more defiance than fear. It was time to change that.

Carlos drew his pistol and aimed it right between the woman's eyes. "What's going on over there?"

"You heard them," snapped the woman. "There's some kind of monster attacking them. If I had to guess, it was the same thing we saw outside."

"And just what the hell was that thing? Some fucked up science experiment you're growing up here in this lab?"

The woman rolled her eyes. "This is an observatory, not a genetics lab." She snorted. "For all I know, that was the real Sasquatch."

"Sask-what?" asked Carlos.

"Bigfoot," chimed in Ricardo, his eyes never leaving the computer monitor.

"No one asked you," growled Carlos. The situation had spiraled out of control. The woman showed no fear. His brother was playing stupid-ass games. Carlos jammed the pistol in his waistband and dropped into a chair, knowing he couldn't just sit around on his ass, but not sure what else to do.

He looked down at the Santa Muerte tattoo on his forearm. Better to live short and well than live long and poor. He remembered his *abuelo*—his grandfather—living in one of the *colonias* just outside Juarez. The house—hell, it was something between a wood crate and a shack—seemed as though it would blow away in a stiff wind. Rat turds had littered the corners.

His *abuelo* had lain on a dirty, moth-eaten wool blanket. His moist, red-rimmed eyes stared upward at the ceiling. His chest rose and fell in jagged gasps as he breathed. Carlos, only a little boy at the time, sat by his bedside. "Juan? Help me, Juan." Juan was the name of Carlos's father.

"*Papá* isn't here," said Carlos. "Just me."

"Juan?" His *abuelo* blinked, uncomprehending. The smell of piss and shit permeated the decrepit little room. The old man had soiled himself, but he had no more clean clothes. He couldn't do anything for him anyway. He was dying . . .

Carlos feared that fate more than anything. He feared dying in poverty, in a shack that couldn't keep the rain out, not recognizing those he loved. Losing control of his bodily functions.

He feared that more than anything else . . .

He remembered a few years later when Tío Nesto brought him to his house, also in Juarez. His eyes widened at the sight of the guard tower outside. Inside the front hall, a crystal chandelier hung over a polished marble floor decorated with the finest rug Carlos had ever seen. Tío Nesto told him it was from the Orient. That first visit, the maid fed him tamales and atole in an opulent dining room. The plate was rimmed in gold and the fork he used was gold as well. "This could all be yours one day," said Tío Nesto. Carlos would do anything to make that a reality. All he had to do for his uncle was take a packet of marijuana across the border to El Paso.

Carlos had to crawl through a concrete pipe filled with fetid water and raw sewage. Rats scurried past him. When he wanted to turn back, he remembered his *abeulo*, dying in a pile of his own shit. And he had his little brother to think about. His family. Still he pushed on and completed the mission his uncle had set. Tío Nesto paid him one-hundred dollars for that job. It was more money than he'd ever seen in his life.

A year later, Carlos stood in a warehouse next to Tío Nesto as he questioned a man who'd "lost" a shipment of meth. The desperate man was full of excuses. Tío Nesto stood there like a king, regal and composed, not saying a word, while his minion dug himself deeper and deeper. Finally, he shook his head. The look on his face was a little sad. He passed his pistol to Carlos. "Would you do the honors, *mijo*?"

Carlos swallowed down the lump his throat. His hand shook a little as he took the gun. Tears flowed down the man's face and Carlos grew disgusted. What kind of man cries when he's about to die a quick, easy death? He walked up to the man and put the barrel of the gun against his temple. He pulled the trigger.

A wellspring of emotions rose up in Carlos with that first kill. He'd killed many more men after that day. Always quick and lethal. Completely unlike the long, drawn out suffering of his grandfather. If he was gonna die, he'd want it to be quick. Not painful. Definitely not like his *abuelo*.

He glanced at his little brother who was still playing computer games. Ricardo didn't have that instinct. Which is why he always volunteered to do the kills. Carlos had worked hard to move them both up in their uncle's organization. He wasn't about to let some asshole scientists and an overstuffed bird stand in his way.

Mike's heart thrummed in his ears as he launched himself down the stairs. His ragged breathing echoed off the walls. He grabbed the railing to whirl himself down to the next landing. Roscoe's footfalls thudded behind him, at a steady, but slower pace. As Mike reached the fifth landing, he missed and stumbled. Roscoe tumbled into him with a curse, which propelled him down the next flight of stairs at an alarming rate.

As he ran, Mike feared what he would find below. His nightmare vision from two years ago kept flashing in his brain. Had it been an omen? Was Wallerstein's car crash connected, too? Confronting a nightmare that haunted his dreams for over two years would not be easy. Nothing about tonight had been easy so far. Why start now?

Mike burst through the door of the second floor, shining the light around, trying to discover what had happened. It took him a moment to realize the keening wail he heard was not the wind through the louvers above but an actual, god-awful scream. Roscoe shot out of the stairwell, dashing past him. Mike picked up his pace but almost fell as he slid onto a sticky wet patch on the floor that resembled a puddle of spilled soda in a movie theatre. Stopping, he crouched down to examine it and realized it was blood. He stood and kept going.

Claire leaned over the railing overlooking the floor below, the radio discarded at her feet. Both rails had been ripped apart with jagged edges. It was as though someone had driven a car off the storage-room floor and crashed it onto the floor below.

Mike looked over the edge. It was like something out of a nature TV show, with a vulture peering into a bloody carcass, deciding which piece of meat to grab next.

"Holy Shit!" Roscoe stood frozen beside him, his mouth open in shock.

Mike's nightmare had become real.

Oblivious to the flashlight beams shining from above, the creature bobbed low and grabbed a glistening piece of fresh meat. Tilting its head back, it swallowed it whole.

A cold chill skittered up his spine at the sight of the creature's eyes. Eyes that could reach in, grab your soul, and strangle it. He knew what it was. Jerome's grandfather had foretold this. Fortunately, those eyes did not look up. If this really had been a bird, or even a prehistoric creature, the eyes might have held contentment at the capture of fresh prey. These eyes held nothing but death.

Mike focused his attention on the bloody remains the creature fed upon. Black hair splayed out around the victim's head like an obscene halo. It was Maya Williams.

If there had been any food left in his stomach, he might have vomited anew. Instead, he stood there frozen, watching the creature feed. It didn't even seem to care about Claire's screaming, which had grown hoarse and broken with sobs. Indecision wracked Mike. Comfort Claire and get her to safety or make a plan to deal with the creature?

"Hey, you fucking bird! Up here!" Apparently, Roscoe fought no indecision. His pistol was out.

When the creature looked up, it presented Roscoe a clear view of its chest and he fired off five rounds in quick succession. At least two hit the beast dead-on. It staggered back from Maya's corpse as two downy poofs burst from its feathered chest.

The creature followed the direction of the gunfire with its eyes. Roscoe stood transfixed. The gun spun limp on his finger and the flashlight clattered to the floor. He took one step toward the break in the railing. Another.

Mike grabbed the pistol in his own waistband, took aim and tried to fire. The trigger wouldn't move. He remembered the safety. Awkwardly, he found the little button next to the trigger, released it, and aimed again. He tried to remember what his father had taught him. Steadying his breathing, he squeezed the trigger. It seemed to take an inordinately long time before the gun fired, the recoil sending a sharp pain up his wrist and elbow. *Shit.* He missed. Concrete dust flew up next to the creature.

Mike aimed and fired once more. Again, he missed. Its gaze darted from one of them to the other. The expression on its reptilian-avian face was still unreadable, but it no longer seemed dispassionate. Did it feel anger? Fear?

It cocked its head as though listening to something, and then let out a keening screech that drowned out Claire's hoarse sobs. The sound felt like a file scraping against Mike's skull. He dropped the pistol in spite of himself and clutched his ears. When the wailing stopped, Mike found himself on his knees. He grabbed his flashlight and searched the floor below. The creature was gone.

Roscoe stood at the railing, blinking in a trance-like state. Mike grabbed his shoulder and shook him. "Come on, it's getting away," he yelled, shocking himself out of his own half-daze.

He stopped to pick up the gun and ran for the stairwell, vaguely aware of Roscoe shaking himself, grabbing his flashlight and pistol before following. This flight down the stairwell ended too quickly. Mike really didn't want to face what he'd find at the bottom. He ran through the machine shop and into the room with the aluminizing chamber. He stopped cold, finding himself facing Maya's mangled corpse.

He clamped his hand over his mouth and nose, hit by the same fecal odor as before. His eyes landed on a piece of bowel, looking like a glistening, bloody sausage. He reminded himself that his beautiful wife and unborn child needed him. Bethany must be terrified. Was she hurt? Did the drug dealers hit her or worse? He needed to get to her.

Roscoe burst through the door behind him and skidded to a stop.

Three-taloned footprints led to the gaping hole in the garage door, which rattled in the wind, as though it too were trembling.

Mike eased his way around Maya's body and followed the tracks to the door. This side of the building faced a road, and just beyond was a rock wall. At the top was the actual summit of Carson Peak. The rain still came down in sheets, but the wind had let up. If they couldn't push the main door open, they could get out this way. They might even make it somewhere without being killed by the storm. The creature was another matter altogether.

"Where'd it go?" asked Roscoe.

"I'm not sure," said Mike. "Maybe you wounded it and it's gone off into the woods."

"I don't think so." The voice came from above. Mike looked up and saw Claire, leaning over the section of railing that remained. "It heard something. It may even have been something it liked. I think it went to check it out."

"What does a creature like that want?" asked Mike.

"Suffering and pain." Roscoe's face was blank. "It was in my mind. I could feel it." He pointed to Maya's body on the floor. "A creature like that doesn't really live on the food it consumes. It's feeding on our fear, our anger, our hatred . . . to build its own strength."

"So, you know that," said Mike, "but you don't know where it went?"

Roscoe snorted. "It didn't exactly invite me to look around its own brain while it probed mine. All I can guess is that it found a better source of nourishment than it found here."

Mike felt as though someone just dipped his heart in liquid nitrogen. He shivered and worked to summon his courage. He would need to go out after that thing, but the sight of Claire's shadow, overhanging the railing above told him they needed to make a plan.

He grasped Roscoe's arm. "Do you have any bigger guns than these?"

Roscoe nodded. "Yeah, I've got something stashed away on the pump floor."

"All right, you get those. I'll get Claire to safety. Then we'll go confront your friends at the 2.5-meter."

CHAPTER 30

She couldn't feel the baby move or kick.

She wasn't far enough along in her pregnancy for that. But her child was inside her—Mike's child. Connected by love and life. And she would do everything in her power to protect it, both from these gangsters and that abominable creature outside.

The storm rattled the dome skirt, creating a din in the control room. When the wind abated from time-to-time, the relentless *tip-tap-tipping* of the younger brother playing computer games echoed around the room.

Bethany looked up at the clock. Less than thirty minutes had passed since the gangster had delivered his ultimatum to Mike. The way she saw it, there were three possible outcomes to the present situation. The gangsters could shoot her. She would avoid that at all costs, if not for herself, then for the fragile life growing inside her. The gangsters could toss her out to fend for herself in the storm with that monster on the loose. She didn't like that idea much better, but at least it would give her a fighting chance for survival. If she could make it over to the other dome, she could join up with Mike and they could make a run for their car.

The final option was to see if she could diffuse the situation. Find a way to give the men what they wanted so they'd go on their way.

"So, what's your name?" she found herself asking.

The older brother looked up, a deep frown on his face. He'd been sitting in a chair brooding in silence for the past half-hour. Her heart beat rapidly as she considered whether she'd crossed some line. "What's it to you?" he asked.

Bethany shrugged. "I just thought it would make talking to each other easier than me saying 'hey you.'"

He leaned forward, his eyes taking on a hard edge. "You already know too much about us."

Bethany sighed. "I can already pick you out of a police lineup. What's wrong if I know your name? It doesn't even have to be your real name. A nickname would do."

The tapping behind her stopped. "His name is Carlos. I'm Ricardo."

"I'm Bethany." She hoped they would find it harder to kill a woman whose name they knew. Could she use her pregnancy as a bargaining chip to dissuade them? Or would they use it as extra leverage against Mike and the others?

"That's a pretty name." Ricardo leaned back in his chair and folded his arms. "So if you astronomers have such good computers, why don't you have better games?"

Bethany let herself laugh a little at that. "It's true all this costs a lot of money, but that doesn't leave much left over for games." She risked a glance at the younger brother. "I'm sorry I hit you with the broom handle," she offered.

He waved her apology aside. "Ain't no thing. You were just trying to defend yourself. I get that."

"Games are the one thing we don't have time for," growled Carlos. He glanced at the clock.

She swallowed, hoping he wouldn't decide to accelerate the timetable. "I'm not playing games and I don't think my friends at the other telescope are playing around either. I think they're really trying to deal with that creature we saw out in the rain." She latched onto an idea. She wasn't certain whether it was a good idea or not, but she didn't seem to have many choices. "You know, we might have a better chance of surviving this night if we all joined forces."

Carlos's head snapped around and met her gaze. "What do you mean?"

"I mean we join up with the people at the other telescope and hunt the creature. When we know it's dead, we'll search for your cocaine. The technicians know every nook and cranny in this place. If the cocaine is here, they'll find it for you."

"She might be onto something." Ricardo genuinely seemed to consider the idea.

"She might also be trying to set us up for a fall," Carlos snapped at his brother.

Bethany saw her slight hope begin to fade away. She thought desperately to find something that these men would understand. Her eyes fell on the contents of her messenger bag, spread out on the table next to the computer. Each of these men had guns in their waistbands. "You've searched my bag. I don't have a gun. Do you think any of us up here is armed?"

Carlos actually did consider that for a minute without simply shooting back a retort. Finally, he shook his head. "Just because you ain't armed don't mean the others aren't."

She swallowed a curse.

A sudden crash reverberated from downstairs. All three whipped their heads toward the control room door. Another crash followed along with the sound of creaking metal. Finally, there was a third crash and a fearsome shriek. The wind howled as though it blew directly into the building.

Carlos swallowed hard and gazed at his younger brother for a moment before standing. "I'll be right back."

"You're not going alone, are you?" Ricardo leaped to his feet. "We should check this out together."

"No!" He grabbed the younger man's shoulders. "Look, I'm gonna take care of this, like I always do. Okay Ricky?" Ricky swallowed audibly and opened his mouth to say something but Carlos cut him off. "When this is over we're gonna head to Vegas right bro?" Carlos suddenly grinned. "You and me are gonna be made men."

Ricardo wrung his hands, then dropped back into the chair. "Let's find someplace we can hide, maybe ambush that thing."

"I'm tired of all this shit! I'm gonna blow the crap out of that thing, then we're going over to the other building and get that shipment."

Another shriek sounded from downstairs, stronger this time, as though fueled by Carlos's anger. Was it the creature, or just the wind? Bethany wrapped her arms around her stomach. Things had just accelerated. Although she'd glimpsed a sense of humanity in these gangsters, there was no reasoning with whatever was downstairs. Her chest tightened as she thought about hiding places out by the telescope.

Carlos took the pistol from his waistband and snapped off the safety. "Ricky. Listen to me." Carlos pulled his brother into his arms and gave him a brief hug, slapping him on the back. "Whatever happens, you gotta get the coke to Tío Nesto's buyer."

He pushed his brother away. "Back in a few. I got a big bird to kill." He slipped out the door.

"He won't be foolish enough to actually confront that thing, will he?" asked Bethany, surprised at the depth of emotion she felt for one of the men who held her hostage.

"Confront it?" said Ricardo, his voice cracking. "Man, he's gonna send it to Hell."

Bethany's shoulders slumped and she rubbed her temples. She didn't know what would happen next, but she had a feeling, that the creature wouldn't go down without a fight. The question was, would it kill them all first?

A quick succession of thunderclaps echoed from below. But these had nothing to do with the raging storm. Carlos had fired off several rounds. An otherworldly shriek followed the shooting spree. It went on for quite some time before silence ensued. Bethany's gaze flew to Ricardo's. His eyes reflected the burgeoning hope in her own. And then a terrifying, horrific, torturous, scream shattered the silence. But this time, it was human.

Mike and Roscoe raced up the stairs. Mike stopped at the second floor and examined the damage more closely. The creature had made a mess, scattering shelves and equipment.

He found Claire, sitting with her back to the overlook. She cradled her legs in her arms, but no longer cried. Her face was wan. Mike sat next to her.

"We were worried about you." The words sounded banal even to Mike's ears.

"I know," said Claire. "I tried to call. I thought about returning to the control room several times, but each time, Professor Burroughs wanted me to stay right here."

Mike lifted an eyebrow at that. "Professor Burroughs? The dead guy in the crypt?"

"You think I'm crazy."

Mike snorted. "After what I've seen so far tonight, I have no right to accuse anyone of madness." He looked over at her. "I need to get going, but for what it's worth, I think I've seen the professor's ghost, too."

She nodded. "Should I wait here?"

Mike thought about it, all too aware of two dead bodies on the floor behind them. He shook his head. "You should go up to the control room. It's more comfortable up there, and I suspect safer. You'll be on phone duty. Keep trying to get through to 911." He stood and held out his hand.

"What do I tell them?" She grabbed his hand and rose to her feet.

"Stick to the important facts. Tell them we have some drug dealers up here and a possible hostage situation." He shrugged. "Wouldn't hurt to let them know we have a wild animal on the loose. That's close to the truth, and they'll be better prepared."

"Will you walk up to the control room with me?" Mike nodded and led the way to the stairwell. The building seemed eerily silent. Even the wind had stopped howling.

Reaching the control room, they looked around with their flashlights. "Okay, I need you to stay here," said Mike once convinced the room was safe. "Check the phones. If they start working, call 911, then Jerome Torres, the site manager. Don't do anything to draw attention to yourself."

"All right." She gave him a brave smile.

"When Roscoe and I get rid of that . . . I don't know . . . monster . . . one of us will come back for you." Mike turned to leave.

"Wait. What about those gangsters? Mike . . . your wife . . ."

Mike gritted his teeth. He needed to get going. "We'll try to talk to them. We'll work it out." He pointed to the desk. "There are spare batteries in the drawer."

"But . . ." Claire looked as though she would break down.

Mike reached out and took her arm. "Hey, look at me." When she met his gaze, he continued. "We'll be okay. We'll come back for you. Just keep an eye on those phones, okay?"

Claire nodded and put on a brave smile.

"See you soon." With that, Mike ducked back into the

stairwell. He trudged down the stairs, worried about leaving Claire alone. His thoughts returned to Bethany.

Please let her be okay.

He picked up his pace and found Roscoe standing on the landing outside the third floor, a glum look on his face. He held a semi-automatic rifle. "Where have you been?"

"Getting Claire settled. Hoping she'll be able to call in the cavalry."

"That doesn't even happen in the movies anymore, asshole."

"I know." Mike cracked a grim smile. "That's why I'm hoping it might just work in real life." He clapped Roscoe on the shoulder and they continued down the stairs.

CHAPTER 31

It was a dark and stormy night.

The words came unbidden to Mike's mind as he watched the rain through the hole the creature had made when it burst through the garage door. The rain still came down in torrents, splashing in through the broken wall and making large puddles on the floor. Not enough water to wash away Maya's blood. Would there ever be enough?

Although the storm blew a gale, the handling floor's garage door faced a rock wall—atop that wall was the actual summit of Carson Peak. The rocks sheltered Mike and Roscoe from the wind's full onslaught. A good half-mile separated the 5-meter enclosure from the 2.5-meter dome. Walking that distance in the driving rain, with lightning striking all around, would be recklessly dangerous. Even making their way around the building's perimeter to Mike's car would be a challenge.

Roscoe tucked his rifle into the folds of the long fire coat he'd grabbed from a cabinet near the entrance. Mike and Roscoe exchanged glances. It was now or never. They dashed out into the downpour. The roads at the observatory were normally hard-packed dirt, but they'd softened considerably in the relentless rain. The two men sloshed through the muck around the building, slipping several times, but helping each other press forward. Thunder roared as a bolt of lightning revealed the entire mountain ridge. Trees stood out in stark relief. Mike caught the tang of ozone as he continued forward.

Before they reached the truck, the wind hit them full force. Mike had never felt anything like it. They were on a mountaintop in the middle of the Chihuahuan Desert, but Mike could swear he'd been hit in the face by a tidal wave. Roscoe linked arms with him, and the two leaned into the wall of wind-blown water, virtually blind, working their way inch by inch to the truck.

When they finally reached it, Mike grabbed the door handle and started inching it open, then the wind shifted and nearly wrenched both the door from its hinge and Mike's arm from its socket. He wasn't sure how long he stood there, holding the door, fighting to keep it from blowing off in the gale, but the force of it finally let up just enough for him to pull himself into the driver's seat and yank the door closed. He sat there blinking at the blurry view through the windshield.

Roscoe pulled himself into the passenger seat. "All right, we made it this far. Let's go!"

Mike started to pull off his glasses to clean the water from them, but discovered they had disappeared. They must have blown off in the gale without him noticing. "Hold on," he said. "I've lost my glasses. Either I need to find them or you'll need to drive."

"They're probably miles away by now," grumbled Roscoe. "Let me over there."

Mike's first reaction was to obey, but he thought better of it. "I'm not much help to you if I can't see."

The wind had died down a bit so Mike leapt from the truck and shone his flashlight on the ground. All he saw was muck and mire. On an off chance, he looked under the truck and there, right by the driver's side wheel lay his glasses. *Finally, some good luck.* He grabbed them and clambered back into the truck. He untucked his shirt and did his best to clean them. Placing the dirt-smeared glasses back on his nose with a sigh, he reached up to the sun visor where he'd stashed the keys.

"So what the hell was that creature?" whispered Roscoe.

Mike inserted the key into the ignition, but didn't crank the engine. "That's a good question. The Apaches tell stories about monsters who lived in these mountains when the first humans arrived. This thing sure looks like a creature from one of their stories. What if their ancient legend was based in fact?"

Roscoe made a noise under his breath, sort of a deep rumble that seemed to consist of half-articulated swear words. "One time, I went hunting on the Navajo Reservation. I stopped at a gas station and the attendant told me to watch out because a skinwalker roamed nearby. That's a shaman who not only wears the skin of an animal, but transforms into that animal as well. I laughed it off. Didn't believe it. Later that night, I was driving down the road, when this coyote started running alongside the car." Roscoe paused, trembling. Mike didn't think it was entirely because of his cold, rain-soaked clothes. "I was going fifty-five fucking miles per hour! The damned thing looked right at me with its red eyes before running off into the woods. I nearly ran the car off the road."

Mike thought back to Wallerstein's crash. He remembered a flash of something out of the corner of his eye after he went down to investigate. Could that have been a skinwalker? "I don't think the Apaches have a skinwalker legend," he muttered aloud. Too many questions and not enough answers. He started the ignition.

"Doesn't matter whether this is a skinwalker. If it's a Native American spirit creature, it's bad news." Roscoe waved his hand through the air. "Maybe this was something created during the atom bomb tests of World War II. They didn't happen too far from here."

Mike considered Roscoe's fear at the idea of this being a spirit creature. "Earlier tonight, Evan admitted he'd found some kind of talisman in one of the caves. You wouldn't happen to know anything about that, would you?"

Roscoe faced forward, his teeth chattering.

"Where exactly did you find that cocaine, Roscoe?"

"None of your damned business."

"You're the one who asked what the creature was." Mike took a deep breath and let it out slowly. "If you know something I don't, maybe you should tell me."

Roscoe's lips tightened, but he didn't say anything.

"That thing we saw looked partly like a bird and partly like a dinosaur. The most rational explanation I can come up with is that it's some kind of primitive animal that humans haven't seen before."

"Okay, that's the rational explanation." Roscoe finally turned to look at him. "Hypothetically, if this was a Native American spirit creature, which one do you think it would be?"

Anxious to get going, Mike released the parking brake, but somehow he sensed Roscoe was what tied everything together—the gangsters, the creature, maybe even the storm. The more he kept Roscoe talking, the closer he'd get to the truth. He thought back to his discussions with Jerome. "I think this one would be the one called 'He Who Kills With His Eyes.'"

Roscoe snorted. "Whatever it is, I think it's time for me to kill it with my gun." He pulled the automatic rifle from his coat and laid it across the dashboard. "Do the Apaches give any indication whether or not this thing *can* be killed?"

Mike shrugged. "I gather it was killed by one of the first people, a warrior called 'Killer of Enemies.' I'm guessing he didn't have more than a bow and arrow, or maybe an atlatl spear."

Roscoe shook his head. "Doesn't seem very dead to me, but maybe this is one of its descendants." He scratched his jaw. "When I shot that son of a bitch, I saw feathers fly. It didn't seem to bother it much, but maybe we just need to use more force or maybe hit it in the same spot multiple times." He eyed the rifle on the dashboard. "Either way, this baby should come in handy. You still got the gun I gave you?"

Mike checked the waistband of his trousers and nodded when he felt the cold metal of the weapon. He took a deep breath and faced forward, stepping on the accelerator. The engine revved, but the truck refused to roll forward. Instead, it sank back a little in the mud.

"Son of a bitch!" swore Roscoe. Without saying more, he hopped out of the vehicle.

Mike looked in his rearview mirror and saw Roscoe wave forward. He returned his foot to the accelerator as Roscoe pushed on the back of the truck, rocking it gently. Eventually, its tire caught and it lurched forward. Mike put his foot on the brake, but allowed the vehicle to continue rolling forward.

A moment later, Roscoe, drenched and mud-splattered, yanked the door open and pulled himself back into the passenger seat. Mike gave the truck a little more gas and they slipped and slid their way down the narrow road from the 5-meter enclosure. Mike didn't feel any traction under the tires. The vehicle slid into the rock wall and caromed off a small safety railing. By the time, they reached the bottom of the hill, Mike was breathing heavily from the exertion of keeping the truck on the road.

He gave the truck a little gas and they fishtailed past the generator house and the office building. As they turned toward the 2.5-meter telescope, a fierce crack sounded and a branch crashed in front of the truck in a shower of pine needles. Mike stomped on the brakes. "It's like something's trying to keep us from reaching the 2.5-meter."

"I think the two of us can move it," Roscoe said.

In the dark, with the wind whipping around him and the cold rain pelting his face, Mike had a difficult time moving, much less looking around the surrounding woods. Still, it struck him that the forest loomed especially dark and foreboding. Even out on the road between the two telescopes, Mike could hear the louvers howling at the 5-meter. It sounded even more eerie from where they were.

Mike reached out and grabbed the tree branch, clenching his teeth from the scrape of the rough bark and needles on his skin. Roscoe took hold of the other end, and together they dragged the heavy branch to the side of the road and climbed back into the truck.

Learning his lesson from before, Mike avoided gunning the truck's engine and eased his foot on the gas pedal. They continued on, arriving a few minutes later. Dread filled the pit of Mike's stomach. Pelted by wind and rain, the 2.5-meter looked as it had that night two years ago.

Roscoe grabbed his rifle from the dashboard, tucked it into his long coat and hopped out. They sloshed through the mud to the entrance. The door had been wrenched from its hinges and discarded on the concrete floor inside. "You say the Apaches call this thing, 'He Who Kills With His Eyes'?" asked Roscoe.

"That's what Jerome called it," Mike replied as they stepped into the building.

A man stood next to the stairs, like a wax figure. Arms akimbo, gun on the floor beside him. His skin was pasty. His eyes were crunched shut. Mike stepped closer.

The man's eyes sprang open.

"Fucking shit!" Roscoe spat out.

Inch-by-inch, the man crumpled to the ground, like a puppet whose strings had just been cut. Roscoe knelt down beside the stranger and felt for a pulse. He shook his head.

Mike fought for words. "There's not a mark on him."

Roscoe tapped the side of his head. "He Who Kills With His Eyes. This must be one of the gangsters."

Mike nodded. The man wore a T-shirt and jeans. A tattoo of a skeleton adorned his left arm. Mike looked back at the gun left on the floor. He reached over and picked it up.

A sneer crossed Roscoe's face. "That's one less bastard for us to deal with."

From upstairs came a crash and the splintering of wood followed by a woman's scream.

CHAPTER 32

It was pitch black.

Claire sat trembling in the dark. Her flashlight was dead. She'd groped around the desk in the control room and found another set of batteries, but they only provided a meager glow, so she'd flicked it off to conserve what battery power was left. If she got out of this alive, she would make it a personal rule to always carry a working flashlight and fresh batteries with her.

As a graduate student in astronomy, she should have been used to darkness by now, but most of her work thus far had taken place at a computer, analyzing someone else's data. In fact, as survey telescopes became the norm in astronomy, it was becoming increasingly rare for astronomers to conduct their own experiments at a telescope.

In high school, she'd discovered the science fiction of Lois McMaster Bujold and Anne McCaffrey, and although she loved reading about distant galaxies, and larger than life characters from the future, her own talents were in the computer realm. She'd expected to major in computer science. But Astronomy 101 changed all that. She was hooked. The endless mysteries of the universe mesmerized her. Her first professor had been thrilled to learn about her computer aptitude He put her to work writing code to combine images and look for patterns in the data. Working at a computer, doing her part to understand the universe, she began to feel like one of the heroines in the novels she enjoyed so much.

But sitting alone in the dark, with no light, no weapon, and no way out, she didn't feel much like a heroine. The louvers out in the dome had stopped howling. Silence pervaded the room punctuated by the occasional hiss of the wind finding its way through a vent shaft. From time to time, a finger of air would touch her shoulder and she would look around to see if the ghost of Professor Burroughs had returned. Had he abandoned her? Even worse, would the ghost of Jim Murray come after her again as he had before? She shuddered, wrapping her arms protectively around her chest. Would he succeed, luring her to her death as he had with Evan?

Twenty-four hours ago, she would have laughed her head off if someone had told her she would be coming face-to-face with ghosts and mythical creatures. Although she'd enjoyed her paranormal studies class it had been taught from a skeptic's point of view, and she'd dismissed the idea of paranormal science as bunk.

Yet, she'd seen Professor Burroughs with her own eyes—a glowing figure in an old-fashioned tweed suit. She had no doubt Jim Murray's ghost was responsible for Evan's death. Presuming she made it through this night alive, would anyone even believe her? Perhaps she could come back with cameras and recording equipment.

Then what?

She'd be like one of those paranormal investigators on the Discovery Channel hanging out in haunted houses, trying to prove to the world that ghosts really do exist.

As she sat in the dark, Claire became aware of a rank, putrid odor, similar to what had emanated from Maya's mutilated corpse. She swallowed back bile. She'd witnessed Maya's horrific death and glimpsed Evan's mummified body. She knew Stan Jones had been in the building from the radio traffic she'd heard, but he hadn't been with Mike, or that other guy, Roscoe, when they showed up after Maya was killed. Was he dead too? But who had killed him, the creature or Jim Murray?

Claire hugged herself. What became of a person when they died? It was a question she'd never seriously asked herself before. Her parents and grandparents were alive and well. Until tonight, she'd never really faced death. Her parents had taken her to church and they'd talked about Heaven and Hell, but those concepts seemed just as much a fairy tale to her as ghosts, vampires, and werewolves.

Did a person simply cease to exist after they died? She had no memories of life before birth and she supposed death was like that, too. Simple non-existence. The thought that she might stop being Claire Yarbro kind of spooked her. She supposed that was at the root of the entire ghost-hunting movement. Proving that we continue to exist beyond death.

A thump sounded from behind the door to Claire's left. Different from the ventilator rattling and wind moaning. It sounded like a door banging a couple floors below. Had Mike and Roscoe returned so soon? Switching on her flashlight, she went to the door, opened it and listened. "Mike?" she called. "Roscoe?" When no response came, she stepped back into the room and closed the door.

Claire's flashlight provided just enough dim light for her to find the phone. She picked up the receiver. Dead. She pressed 9-1-1, but all she heard was the cold click of the buttons. No dial tone. No reassuring operator at the other end. She hung up and switched off her flashlight to conserve power.

She thought she heard a rustling from the stairwell. The soft whisper of fabric. The thud and squish of wet shoes on stairs. She chanced to open the door a crack and listen more closely. Nothing, except the wind.

Claire shut the door and turned back to the control room. And then she froze. The room was no longer pitch black. Chairs, bookshelves, desks. Everything was visible. But where was the light source? She walked farther into the room and realized the glow was coming from the computer monitors. They'd come back to life! Had the power come back on?

She grabbed a mouse and wiggled it, but the computer didn't wake from its slumber. She guessed it needed a reboot, but she'd leave that job to someone else. The computers themselves were one floor below and she didn't know which machine went with which monitor. She could do more harm than good pushing random buttons.

She flipped the light switch. Her brow furrowed when it failed to come on. She suddenly remembered that the computers were on their own battery backups, but the lights weren't. Perhaps someone had installed new batteries? But why would they take the time to do that given the danger on the other end of the mountain? She checked her watch. Only about fifteen minutes had passed while she sat in the dark, ruminating on things that go bump in the night.

The door popped open and then fell closed again, as though given a slight push. A shiver skittered up her spine. She backed away from the door to the far end of the room.

"Is someone there?" Her throat was so dry it came out as a croak. A blast of cold air hit her, pushing her back and piercing her arms and thighs with a freezing stab of pain.

She gasped and ran to the room's second phone. She picked up the receiver to check again—dead like the other one. As her grip on the handset tightened, she saw something that would haunt her for the rest of her days.

Two words had formed on the computer monitor in front of her.

Get out!

Her eyes flew to the other monitors around her. All of them said the same thing.

Get out!

A coldness touched her cheek, like an icy finger. Turning, she saw two glowing orbs, like demonic eyes. She stood transfixed for a moment, but heard a crackling from the phone in her hand. She held the handset to her ear. A faint voice called out her name. *"Claire . . . Get out!"*

CHAPTER 33

It looked like a tornado had hit.

Mike swallowed when he glimpsed Bethany's empty messenger bag lying under one of the counters in the control room. Shattered glass glittered in the glare of his flashlight beam. Fragments of chairs and computer monitors lay strewn about the room as if a bomb had exploded.

"Shit." Roscoe whispered beside him.

They picked their way through the rubble and entered the telescope enclosure but froze at the sight before them.

The creature stood with its back to them. A tall, slim man with close-cropped hair, and a white tank top faced the monster. One hand grasped a .45-caliber pistol, the other held a flashlight. The creature inclined its head, but didn't approach the man. As Mike and Roscoe watched, the stranger's eyes grew increasingly vacant. His arm dropped to the side and the pistol clattered to the floor. A moment later, the flashlight dropped as well.

Mike swept the room with his gaze as the flashlight rolled away. Bethany huddled near the telescope's fork mount. She gasped when her eyes connected with Mike's. He put his finger to his mouth and waved her down, hoping that by staying put, she wouldn't attract the creature's attention.

Mike struggled with what to do. Clearly, the man caught in the creature's gaze was the other drug dealer. If he did nothing, the creature would likely take care of the asshole who'd threatened his wife.

But Mike couldn't do that. That would make him no better than the gangster. And what if the creature did gain strength with each killing and feeding? They certainly couldn't afford that.

Mike raised his pistol and aimed. Roscoe clamped his hand around Mike's arm and shook his head.

Roscoe was a bastard. Yeah, he'd stepped up to help, but it was his selfish actions that had endangered Bethany in the first place. Mike shook Roscoe's hand away and fired. The bullets struck the creature's back in a burst of feathers, skin, and blood. It lurched forward but didn't turn its head. Instead, it simply rolled its shoulders as though shaking off an annoying insect.

The gangster remained frozen in the beast's magnetic gaze. In a flash, the creature bobbed its head down, plucked the man's eyeball in its beak and pulled. An audible snap echoed around the dome as the man's optic nerve gave way, and a gurgle of blood gushed from his now empty socket. The creature lifted its head and gulped down the eyeball like an appetizer. It did the same to the other eye, and let out a loud screech as though delighted with itself.

The drug dealer's legs folded like an accordion, and he dropped to his knees. Blood oozed out of his now empty eye sockets. At that moment, Mike realized the gangster had been dead before their arrival. Frozen in death like his partner downstairs.

Mike gestured to Bethany, signaling her to go behind the telescope. She nodded, and disappeared.

The creature's talon sliced open its victim's abdomen. A moment later, his stomach, liver and intestines spilled out onto the floor. The creature grabbed the liver in its beak and tugged until a chunk came free.

As Bethany made her way over to Mike, her eyes were wide and her skin held a distinctly green cast. He backed into the control room with her, and wrapped his arms around her, squeezing her tightly. Roscoe followed close behind.

"What are we going to do?" Mike asked in a whisper. "Bullets, even at close range, don't seem to bother it."

"Ricardo emptied his pistol into it and it didn't do any good," said Bethany.

Mike lifted an eyebrow at his wife's use of the gangster's name, but he didn't say anything. This wasn't the time and it wasn't exactly useful intelligence anymore.

"There's one thing we haven't tried," rasped Roscoe. He

patted his semi-automatic rifle. "We've been going after it with small arms. Let's see what this baby can do." He strode toward the door. The wind slamming the dome skirt into the building provided a staccato drumbeat to Roscoe's march.

Mike leapt forward and caught his arm. "Let's take a minute and think about this. Maybe there's something else we can do. If we restarted the generator, we would have power . . . use the cranes, maybe even the telescope itself somehow."

Roscoe shook his head. "Yeah, and we'd be trapped in a tiny generator house with that thing hunting us. Even then, the plan presumes we could get the generator going again. I say we go after it now." He took a single step forward and studied the monster. The wind let up for a moment and the dome skirt stopped its staccato rhythm, only accentuating the sickening crunching, slurping noises as the creature fed.

"Why don't we just get out of here while that thing's distracted?" said Bethany.

The more Mike considered that course of action, the more he liked it. "We just need to pick up Claire at the 5-meter. She should be staying put in the control room."

Roscoe looked to the floor and let out a long, low breath that sounded like a balloon deflating. His expression was unreadable.

"What do you hope to gain by staying and fighting this thing, Roscoe?" asked Mike.

He was silent for a long moment. "Everything I had is gone," he said. "My job, my home, my car. I hoped the cocaine I'd found would let me find some dignity, but I don't even know where that went. For all I know that damned bird ate it!"

"Forget about the cocaine and let's go," urged Bethany.

Roscoe shook his head slowly. "If the cocaine has been destroyed, I have no hope of rebuilding a life once this is over anyway. If it's still here, I'll have to find it with this freakin' monster on my tail. How would I unload it and leave the country before getting caught? Every cop around will be on the lookout for me. Not to mention the boss of these two dead guys." He snorted.

Mike shook his head. "Right now, let's worry about surviving. We can worry about everything else later."

"*I am* thinking about survival." Roscoe's gaze met Mike's. "Yours and Bethany's."

"What do you mean?" asked Bethany.

"That creature isn't going to be occupied with that gang-banger's body much longer. I'll go in guns blazing. If I succeed, great. We all win. If I don't, you two kids will have the distraction you need to get the hell out of here."

Mike couldn't believe what Roscoe was saying. He was willing to sacrifice himself so that they could get away? The man had made some colossal mistakes but he didn't deserve to die.

He stepped in front of Roscoe, blocking his way. "I won't let you."

"Look, I let this happen. It's all on me. Get out of here now."

Bethany grabbed hold of Roscoe's hand and laid it on her abdomen.

He looked down at her belly, then up at her and Mike. "Look boy, I'm done anyway," he said in a gruff voice. "At least I'll take Big Bird on steroids down with me."

"Hold on a minute," said Bethany looking from one to the other with a gleam in her eye. "What happens if you mix water and liquid nitrogen?"

Mike blinked at her. "This isn't time for a chemistry experiment, we need to get going."

A grin spread across Roscoe's face. "You get a bomb, you asshole."

Mike gaped at Roscoe, pulling Bethany close as he suddenly understood. "Now I know why I love you so much." After planting a quick kiss on her lips, he ran over to the water cooler. He collected the half-empty bottle while Bethany went to the storage shelf behind and found a rubber stopper and duct tape. She handed them to Mike. He checked the fit and nodded.

"I'll need to get the nitrogen out on the dome floor. Once this is all together, it won't go off right away. It'll take a minute or two," said Mike.

Roscoe slapped him on the shoulder and nodded. "I gotcha covered." He turned and strode through the open door, already raising the rifle to his shoulder. "All right you son of a bitch, come and get me."

Mike turned around and shoved his keys into Bethany's hand.

"Get out of here and wait in the truck. As soon as you hear us coming down, start the engine."

Bethany shook her head. "I'm not leaving you here."

They both turned their heads at the sound of Roscoe firing his first shot. The creature wobbled back but remained standing. The shell ejected and Roscoe fired again. This time, the creature toppled to the ground.

Mike's eyes widened. Maybe the high-power rifle was just what they needed to buy them time. Moving as fast as he could, he carried the supplies for the nitrogen bomb out to the dome floor.

The creature twitched. Mike's breath caught. He aimed his flashlight beam in the creature's direction. No movement. It lay deathly still, lying on its back. He unclipped the nitrogen fill hose and dropped it in the water bottle.

"Jesus Christ!" Roscoe yelled.

Mike's eyes flew up.

The creature was pulling itself up, back rigid, like a silent-movie vampire.

"You motherfucking bird," Roscoe spat as he lifted the rifle back to his shoulder. The light mounted to the sight shone square on the creature's chest feathers. It riveted its gaze on the electrician, but Roscoe squeezed his eyes shut and turned his head away.

Mike opened the valve on the liquid nitrogen dewar. The sudden whoosh and cloud of fog coming from the water bottle caused the creature to whip its head around. Roscoe chanced to open his eyes. The creature moved toward Mike. Roscoe fired at it, forcing it back into the telescope mount.

Mike closed the nitrogen valve and stoppered the bottle, sealing it with duct tape. He picked it up and shook it as best he could. Inside, the nitrogen and water roiled and churned, filling the space at the top of the bottle with gas. Dropping it to the ground he rolled it toward the creature with his foot.

The creature now had a bald patch on its chest, weeping blood. Somehow, it looked all the more frightening as it shook off its injuries and stood upright again.

Roscoe took aim and began squeezing off round after round, keeping the creature pinned in place.

Mike gritted his teeth, willing the nitrogen bomb to go off before Roscoe ran out of ammunition.

Bethany rushed to him. "We should get out of here!"

At that moment, the bomb exploded, reverberating through the dome and filling it with nitrogen fog and the clatter of ice shrapnel and plastic shards pelting the telescope. Mike winced as a piece gashed his upper arm. His flashlight beam only penetrated the fog a few inches. He couldn't even see Bethany at his side.

Roscoe stopped firing, no longer having a target to aim at. The silence in the dome grew palpable and Mike hoped they may have lucked out. Between the bomb and Roscoe's barrage, maybe, just maybe the creature was finally dead.

The fog began to dissipate and Mike thought he saw something move.

"Roscoe?" he dared to whisper.

A horrible ear-splitting squawk filled the air. The ground rumbled, and Mike felt a trickle of something from his nose. He licked with his tongue and tasted blood.

The creature swooped out of the fog. Its talons clipped Mike's forehead, knocking him backward into the wall. He flashed back to his vision from two years before, only this time, it was no hallucination.

"Hit the dirt!" called Roscoe.

Mike and Bethany dropped to the floor as Roscoe began firing again, this time letting out a primal yell as he did.

The creature whirled around in the air over Mike and Bethany's heads and dove at Roscoe, grabbing him by the shoulders, blood gushing as talons tore into his flesh. Roscoe howled, dropping the rifle. The creature lifted him up and Roscoe clawed at its ankles trying to get it to drop him, but the beast held firm.

It continued flapping, speeding up, spiraling toward the dome above. Mike gritted his teeth, prepared for the crash. He expected the creature to crumple when it hit the dome and come plummeting back to the ground. Instead, it burst through the dome, still carrying Roscoe in its claws. Rain poured in through the hole, reviving Mike somewhat. He stumbled to his feet and turned to help Bethany up. They dashed through the control room, not stopping until they reached the truck outside.

CHAPTER 34

She flew down the stairs.

Claire's foot barely touched down on a step before she dropped to the next. She whirled around the landing before she realized it was pitch black. She slowed her pace, to keep herself from falling, and made it to the next floor below without a mishap. The problem presented itself when she reached the long hallway between the upper and lower stairways.

How many doors? How many doors?

She wracked her brain to remember the number she needed to pass to reach the main stairway. The stench of death and decay was everywhere. It made her eyes water.

She turned right and felt her way along the hallway. She came to an open door, too soon. She entered, just to get her bearings. Her hand fell onto a cold countertop. She followed it until her hand came to a bottle. She'd found the darkroom.

She retraced her steps back to the hall and came to another unlocked door. She turned the handle and screamed as her foot stepped off into nothingness. Her arms flailed wildly as she dropped into a service area just two feet below the floor, lined with sheet metal, insulation, and cables. Stunned, she lay there for a moment, before bursting into hysterical laughter. Evan and Maya were dead. As was Stan Jones. There was some kind of monstrous creature on the loose, and drug dealers with guns. Not to mention an evil ghost who wanted her demise. Would she even make it out of here alive? She needed to calm down and breathe. She eased to her feet and gasped as a sharp pain shot up from her ankle. *Oh, great! Now, I've got a sprained ankle, too.* She loved astronomy, but after tonight, she was never stepping foot in an observatory ever again. Clenching her teeth, she grabbed onto a cable attached to the wall and stepped up into the corridor once more.

Then the ground began to rumble.

An earthquake!

Trembling, she took a few halting steps, holding onto the wall. Just as quickly as it had begun, the rumbling stopped. Claire put her hand to her chest and tried to catch her breath. It sounded harsh and loud in the pitch-black corridor. The only other sounds were the louvers moaning their mournful wail from the storm, and the eerie creeks and groans of the structure around her. She fought another wave of panic. If she reached downstairs, where would she go? The storm was blowing fiercely. Mike and Roscoe had taken the truck. A distant boom and crash of thunder punctuated her thoughts.

Startled, she lurched and fell back against the wall, grimacing in pain from the impact on her twisted ankle. She sank down to the floor with her face in her hands. Whoever had told her to get out clearly didn't know what they were talking about. It seemed as though the building itself was against her.

The corridor quieted. She tried to think but the overpowering stench of rotting flesh wafted down the hall. Trembling, she noticed a faint orange glow. Go that direction or away from it? Was it Professor Burroughs showing her the way or Murray luring her to her death? She tried to stand, but her ankle spasmed and she dropped back against the wall. Tears sprang to her eyes. The air grew colder and her stomach knotted as the silence was broken by the *squish-thump* of distant shoes.

The footfalls around the corner stopped suddenly and the chill air warmed a little.

When she wiped her eyes and nose on her arm, she noticed her hands were illuminated by a soft golden light. She looked up. Standing in the corridor, clearer than she'd ever seen him was Professor Burroughs.

He held out a hand. Tentatively, she reached up and gasped when she felt it was solid. He helped her to her feet. "This is not a safe place to be, child," he said.

"I can understand you." She grasped his hand. "I can feel you."

"Dark energy has been released and it has strengthened

the force of Jim Murray," said the professor. "I can no longer contain him. I need to confront him and I cannot predict what will happen when I do."

Claire's eyebrows knitted. "Dark energy? You mean the stuff that's causing the expansion of the universe to accelerate?"

The professor flashed a sad and wistful smile. "That's merely a name for something not well understood. If only we had time, I could give you some clues as to its nature." He shook his head. "I fear the energy giving me strength is truly malevolent."

"Malevolent energies, good and evil. Do you mean to say there really is a God?"

The ghost of Professor Burroughs sighed. "I can't answer that."

"Can't or won't?"

He waved her question aside. "A side effect of this dark energy is that it feeds my spirit. At this moment, I am like a flame burning brightly. But my time is short."

The footfalls down the hall resumed. Two glowing eyes appeared, framed now by a skull. Flesh appeared on the skull and a body formed. Soon, she recognized an angry young man. Burroughs moved in front of Claire and took a step toward the evil ghost. "What are you doing? Why are you attacking these young people?"

"Perhaps I'm lonely after you abandoned me to my fate, Professor," sneered the other ghost in a voice that rasped like two pieces of sandpaper rubbing together.

"Your argument is with me, not with the living," barked the professor.

Jim Murray took a step closer to Burroughs. The professor's aura glowed brighter for a moment and then coalesced into a wave of energy that shot toward Murray, knocking him backward into the wall.

The ground rumbled again, shaking the building so hard the floor cracked.

Burroughs turned to Claire. "Our time grows short. We need to go."

He took her hand and led the way down the hall and through the door to the stairwell. He glowed brighter than ever, and Claire had no problem seeing the stairs. As they descended, she became aware that Jim Murray's ghost followed. She looked up and saw him two landings above. Wild orange hair grew visible, like autumn grass blown by a fierce wind and his body began to take form. A moment later, he released his own energy pulse. The floor listed to one side and Professor Burroughs faltered. She squeezed his hand and the ghost seemed to take strength from her. He urged her to follow.

They continued down the stairs until they finally came to the ground floor. She glanced at the door to the outside. "Will I be able to get out?"

He nodded. "The wind has shifted."

She swallowed hard. "What about the monster?"

"It has gone . . . for now. The energy of this place is nearly exhausted. It will search for fresh hunting grounds."

She turned to leave, but stopped. She looked back at Professor Burroughs. His light was beginning to fade, but a peaceful smile brightened his face. She stepped closer to him and kissed him on the cheek. "Thank you," she said.

"You're welcome, my dear." He smiled at her and he glowed so bright it seemed like daylight. "This is why I've lingered. You now know this universe is full of mysteries that go beyond those in your textbooks. There is still much work to be done, many lifetimes' worth. Even I don't fully understand the realm where I've remained. It is a real, physical place, and somehow tied to the very structure of the universe. You, and others like you, are the future. Stay on your path. Go now!"

The stairwell door burst open and Jim Murray stood there. Claire gasped. Had he become stronger than the professor? She didn't want to leave her ghost friend's side, but knew there was nothing she could do to help.

She turned around, pushed the door open and was almost at once blinded by a pair of headlights. She threw up her hand and blinked. A man leapt out of the truck and splashed through the mud toward her. It was Jerome Torres, the site manager.

A woman appeared next to him. "Kendra Torres." She reached out and shook Claire's hand. Kendra's eyes widened. She muttered something and ran to the building. She put her hand on one of the great, white exoskeletal girders that supported the dome above.

Claire swung around and saw what grabbed Kendra's attention. A one-inch wide crack had formed in the cylindrical girder. They both looked upward. The fissure ran as far up as they could see with Kendra's flashlight. She looked over at the adjoining girder and saw a similar crack.

Another rumble, but this time the ground did not shake. Claire realized it wasn't the ground at all, but the building.

Kendra looked at Jerome. "I think we better get the hell out of here."

"Where are the rest?" asked Jerome.

"Maya, Evan, and Stan are all dead." Claire choked back a sob. "Bethany was over at the 2.5-meter. Mike and Roscoe went to help her."

Jerome's brows shot up. "Roscoe—you mean Perkins?"

Claire shrugged. "I didn't catch his last name. Old guy with gray hair and stubble. Reeked of booze."

"That would be Roscoe Perkins," grumbled Jerome.

The building rumbled again.

"I don't think we have time for chit-chat," said Kendra. "Let's move."

All three ran for the truck. Kendra slid to the middle of the pickup's seat and Claire took the outside as Jerome started the vehicle and threw it in gear. He eased his foot down on the accelerator and drove away from the building. Although Claire sensed his urgency, she could tell he was being careful so they wouldn't get stuck in the slick mud. As they drove, the sky grew brighter.

Is this nightmare finally over?

Soon, they came to the bottom of the hill. Jerome passed the office building, and turned toward the other telescope. A pair of lights came toward them. Jerome slammed on the brakes, causing them to lurch forward in their seatbelts. He threw the truck into reverse and backed up toward the parking area. The other vehicle arrived a moment behind them.

Mike and Bethany climbed out of the observatory's pickup truck. Seeing who was there, Bethany ran forward and embraced them both. "Are we ever glad to see you?"

"What's been going on up here?" asked Jerome.

Mike shook his head. "This may not be the best place.

There's some kind of . . . creature on the loose."

"Creature?" Jerome shook his head. "What do you mean?"

"He Who Kills With His Eyes."

Jerome glanced at Kendra, but before he could say anything, a long, rolling rumble resounded from the direction of the 5-meter building. They all turned around. The sky had brightened just enough they could see clearly. The ground gave one tremendous heave as golden and orange auras crashed into each other. The cracks in the exoskeleton widened as they watched. The weakened girders crumpled under the weight of the dome above. It crashed down to the ground, the force of it shot through the entire area, knocking all of them off their feet.

As Claire rolled herself into a sitting position, she noticed the orange glow had vanished. The warm, golden light collapsed into a bright point, like a star. It drifted upward into the sky, then winked out. Claire couldn't explain it, but she became aware of Professor Burroughs's presence expanding around her, like the shell of a planetary nebula after a star has died. She was sad that she would never see him again, but was happy for him. She knew he'd destroyed Murray's evil. He would never kill again.

Mike scanned the skies back in the direction of the 2.5-meter. "We better get a move on. That creature's still on the loose."

Claire struggled to get up and winced at the sharp pain. She shook her head. "Professor Burroughs says the creature is gone. It's not around here anymore."

Jerome and Kendra helped Claire up. "Professor Burroughs told you?" asked Kendra.

Claire looked over to Mike for moral support. He and Bethany wrapped their arms around each other, as if they were holding each other upright.

"Whatever caused this creature to appear apparently gave Professor Burroughs the energy to manifest. He helped me get out of the building. I owe him my life."

"Is this what your grandfather was trying to warn us about?" Kendra asked Jerome.

He took a deep breath and blew it out slowly as he considered the question. "I think it goes beyond this." He shook his head. "This is bad. This is very, very bad."

"Why don't you two go on home?" Jerome suggested to Mike and Bethany.

Mike squeezed Bethany closer to his side as if he never wanted to let her go. "There's something else you need to know. Maya and Evan took some sort of talisman from one of the caves. Some guy named Vassago said he'd cover their college debt if they got it for him."

Jerome's eyes widened. "Where's the talisman now? Did they tell you?"

Mike shrugged and glanced back at the destroyed observatory. "Somewhere in that unholy mess, I'm guessing."

"We have to tell Mateo about this," Kendra said to Jerome.

Jerome nodded, his eyes filled with a deep sadness that Claire felt all the way to her heart. She hadn't known what Evan and Maya had sought in the cave. If only she'd known. If only they'd all known. Evan and Maya would be alive today, and maybe none of this would have happened.

"Roscoe is—or was—connected to all of this, too," Mike added. "Apparently this Vassago guy had originally hired *him* to get the talisman, but when Roscoe discovered a cache of cocaine in the cave, he didn't bother with the artifact, and instead, took the coke and hid it at the observatory. He was going to sell it and run off to an island somewhere. Two drug dealers figured it out and traced his footsteps from the cave to here. They took Bethany hostage at the 2.5-meter." Mike's voice broke. "Roscoe died saving us, man." Mike glanced around at the others. "He wasn't a bad guy. Just made a lot of mistakes."

"What about the drug dealers?" asked Jerome.

"They're dead too. The creature . . ." Bethany turned her head into Mike's chest. She was trembling and Mike gave her a squeeze.

"You guys need to get some rest . . . You can fill me in on the rest later." Jerome's brow furrowed with concern.

"What are we going to do about all this?" asked Claire.

Jerome studied the pile of rubble that only a few minutes ago was the 5-meter enclosure, then turned toward the 2.5-meter dome. Claire followed his gaze and saw the gaping hole in the roof. The rain had slowed to a drizzle, but the storm had already done its damage. The 5-meter was clearly destroyed.

She wondered if the 2.5-meter could be salvaged.

Finally Jerome shook his head. "There's nothing more for you to do . . . I'll call the authorities."

"Claire, come home with us, we'll take a look at that ankle. We can see about getting you home after you get some sleep," Kendra suggested.

"Thank you," Claire nodded, her eyes tearing up. "I appreciate it." With all the evil that had manifested tonight, she was also aware that good had prevailed. She would always remember Professor Burroughs and what he'd taught her. His wisdom would prove invaluable.

"Jerome, I'm sorry man—sorry about everything . . . If only we'd known two years ago what would come to pass." Mike scrubbed his hand down his face. "What else can I do to help?"

Jerome clasped Mike's hand. Like warriors of old, they were united as brothers. "You've been through hell and back Mike. It's my turn now." He turned back to gaze at what was once a great place of science, learning and exploration, now reduced to rubble.

"Grandfather and I need to set this right . . . It's what we have to do."

EPILOGUE

He was the luckiest man in the world.

Mike grinned as he looked into the eyes of his brand new baby daughter. He always thought newborns were supposed to have gray eyes. He'd have to ask the pediatrician about this, but her eyes were beautiful nonetheless. Behind a curtain, a nurse helped Bethany wash up, and change into a fresh gown.

After that fateful night at Carson Peak, Mike and Bethany had returned home and talked about the future. They discussed moving across the country and finding new careers, but Mike shook his head. "I'm tired of running away. Las Cruces is home. Let's see what we can do here."

Working at Carson Peak, Mike had been a university employee. He'd gone in and met with the observatory management and they'd helped him find a job in the physics department, running the stockroom and building lab demonstrations for the students. It proved to be busy and meaningful work. What's more, it allowed him to support Bethany and their new daughter while being home each night.

Over the past few months, Mike and Jerome had spent a lot of time in meetings, talking to insurance investigators and attorneys about the events of that night. Federal agents also interviewed Mike, seeking information about the missing cocaine and the dead cartel members. All Mike could tell them was that they'd fallen victim to the animal that had rampaged through the observatory. He was always careful to keep his descriptions vague. To let people fill in their own details. Most of them concluded that a mountain lion or a bear must have become frenzied by the storm and wreaked havoc.

A nurse tapped at the door. "You have some visitors, if you're ready."

"Already?" asked Bethany who'd settled back into the bed. "Word travels fast!"

"Well, I did call our friends when you went into labor last night . . ." Mike shrugged. The baby mewled and began squirming so Mike handed her over to Bethany. He turned to the nurse. "Tell them to come on in."

A few minutes later, the nurse led Jerome, Kendra, and Derek into the room. Excited, Derek ran up to the bedside and looked at the baby. Bethany held her up so the boy could see. "Wow, she has yellow eyes, like a cat!"

"I think they're more a golden color," said Kendra looking down at the baby.

"Have you picked a name?" asked Jerome.

"We're naming her Roberta," said Bethany.

"Roberta?" asked Kendra, "you mean after Robert Burroughs, the old professor?"

Mike quirked a smile. "He warned me about Bethany being in danger from the gangsters, and if you believe Claire, he helped her escape the building before it collapsed. If anyone was a hero that night, it was Burroughs."

"I think you were quite a hero that night, too." Bethany smiled at him. "You were my knight in shining armor who rode in when I needed you most."

Mike felt his cheeks flush and he had to turn away. He nodded to Jerome and led him out into the hall, with a brief excuse about sharing a cigar outside. Once they were in the hall, he turned to his friend. "So, any luck finding the talisman?"

Jerome snorted and shook his head. "We've been all over the site these last five months. No sign. It's like it just vanished. The creature, too." He heaved a deep sigh. "My grandfather says we haven't seen the last of them, though."

"What about that lawyer . . . Vassago? Anyone search his place?"

Jerome shrugged. "Police say they have no grounds." His frown deepened. "But he knows something. I went into the Ore House the other day for a burger and he was there. He just looked at me and grinned like he has some big-ass secret."

"If there's anything I can do . . ."

Jerome shook his head and slapped Mike on the back.

"There's nothing I can ask you to do. Take care of your wife and that baby of yours."

Before Mike could say anything more, Kendra and Derek emerged from the room. "The baby and Bethany are both pretty tired. We figured we should give them a chance to rest."

"Thanks for being here. You guys are great," said Mike.

"Our pleasure," said Kendra, "and congratulations." She gave Mike a hug. Jerome shook Mike's hand. "Call us if you need anything."

Mike nodded. "I will." He cast a meaningful look at Jerome. "You do the same, you hear me?"

Jerome flashed a non-committal smile, before ushering his family away.

Mike watched them go, praying Jerome and Mateo would be able to find the talisman and put it back. That fateful night two-and-a-half years ago, when he'd seen the apparitions, and witnessed Wallerstein's death, had made him believe he was weak and afraid. But he'd faced his fears head on to save Bethany, and he'd done everything he could to try to stop the mayhem at the observatory. He would no longer look back in fear. He would look forward to the future, with his family.

Solomon Vassago, comfortable in a tailored Armani suit, trotted down a spiral staircase into a subterranean chamber below the Montwood house. At the bottom, he faced a vault. On the door, snug in a recessed divot, sat the talisman found by Roscoe, recovered by Evan, and left forgotten in the observatory ruins. Next to it were two identical, but empty divots. A piercing shriek sounded from behind the vault door.

"Patience, Binda, patience." His name for the creature was shortened from its Apache name. "I have to return to New York on business, but when I return, we'll see about freeing your brothers."

The creature roared and something thudded into the door. Thick as the door was, Vassago knew the creature had thrown its whole weight into it.

"You've been trapped in another dimension for nearly

20,000 years. You can wait just a little longer." He started to leave, then turned. "You know humans have grown much stronger in the centuries you've been locked away. If they put their heads together they can defeat you alone. However, they will have a much harder time fighting you and your brothers. They'll need magic—magic I daresay they've forgotten."

The creature grew silent.

"Patience, Binda, and you shall have your revenge."

Vassago smiled and climbed the stairs. Binda and his brothers would have their revenge. And he would make it happen.

AFTERWORD

Over the past twenty-five years, I've had the fortune of working at a number of observatories around the United States. Currently, I operate telescopes at Kitt Peak National Observatory in Southern Arizona—essentially holding the same job as Mike Teter in the novel. I've also worked on telescopes at Apache Point in Southern New Mexico and served as a resident observer at the University of New Mexico's Capilla Peak Observatory. As an undergraduate student, I spent a lot of time during summers observing at Mount Laguna Observatory in California, not far from Mount Palomar. I was a graduate student at New Mexico Tech in Socorro and worked on an automated supernova search telescope on South Baldy Peak.

Although Carson Peak Observatory is entirely fictional, it's based on observatories where I have worked and visited. Probably the best example of a 5-meter telescope is at Mount Palomar Observatory, although most people still refer to it by its old-fashioned name—the 200-inch telescope. The skyscraper-like enclosure with its labyrinthine corridors was inspired by the 4-meter enclosure at Kitt Peak.

The story's 2.5-meter telescope with its advanced optical design and drive systems is an amalgam of the 2.4-meter telescope at Magdalena Ridge Observatory on South Baldy and the WIYN 3.5-meter telescope at Kitt Peak National Observatory.

Apache Point Observatory is a real, world-class facility in New Mexico's Sacramento Mountains. Like the fictional Carson Peak Observatory, it's operated by a consortium of universities and managed at New Mexico State University. Carson Peak's grounds take some inspiration from Apache Point, but they're also based on the grounds of Capilla Peak Observatory.

Over the years, astronomers have been interred in or near telescopes that they loved. James Lick is interred in the base of the 36-inch refractor at Northern California's historic Lick Observatory. Likewise, Percival Lowell, famous for popularizing the canals on Mars, is interred in a crypt just outside the 24-inch telescope at Lowell Observatory on Mars Hill in Flagstaff, Arizona. John and Phoebe Brashear's ashes are entombed below the Keeler Telescope at Pennsylvania's Allegheny Observatory.

For the record, I'll note that I'm a skeptic as far as the paranormal is concerned. That doesn't mean I dismiss the existence of ghosts. Rather, it simply means that I haven't seen any evidence that convinces me they exist. Over the years, I've had numerous instances when I felt like I was being watched, looked over my shoulder but found no one there. I've walked through a darkened corridor and felt as though I brushed near someone, even though I was completely alone. I thought I saw lights where none should exist. It's entirely possible these phenomena are purely psychological, or involve some trick of the light or air, but they do give me pause.

If there's one thing I've learned in all my years in astronomy, it's that the cosmos is an intricate, wondrous, and often dangerous place. Our understanding of it—and our place within it—is really just beginning.

ABOUT THE AUTHOR

David Lee Summers is the author of twelve novels along with numerous short stories and poems. His writing spans a wide range of the imaginative from science fiction to fantasy to horror. David's Space Pirates' Legacy science fiction series and his Scarlet Order Vampire series are both published by Hadrosaur Productions.

His short stories and poems have appeared in such magazines as *Realms of Fantasy* and *Cemetery Dance*. He's been twice nominated for the Science Fiction Poetry Association's Rhysling Award. In addition to writing, David edited the quarterly science fiction and fantasy magazine *Tales of the Talisman* for ten years and has edited four science fiction anthologies: *A Kepler's Dozen*, *Space Pirates*, *Space Horrors* and *Maximum Velocity: The Best of the Full-Throttle Space Tales*.

When not working with the written word, David operates telescopes at Kitt Peak National Observatory. Learn more about David at davidleesummers.com

Made in the USA
Columbia, SC
04 May 2023

15996251R00155